# LAST STOP TOKYO

# LAST STOP TOKYO

### James Buckler

**Doubleday**

LONDON · TORONTO · SYDNEY · AUCKLAND · JOHANNESBURG

TRANSWORLD PUBLISHERS
61–63 Uxbridge Road, London W5 5SA
www.penguin.co.uk

Transworld is part of the Penguin Random House group of companies
whose addresses can be found at global.penguinrandomhouse.com

Penguin
Random House
UK

First published in Great Britain in 2017 by Doubleday
an imprint of Transworld Publishers

A CIP catalogue record for this book
is available from the British Library.

ISBNs 9780857524966 (hb)
9780857524973 (tpb)

Typeset in 11.5/14.5pt Sabon by Falcon Oast Graphic Art Ltd.
Printed and bound by Clays Ltd, Bungay, Suffolk.

Penguin Random House is committed to a sustainable
future for our business, our readers and our planet. This book
is made from Forest Stewardship Council® certified paper.

1 3 5 7 9 10 8 6 4 2

*For Isabel*

# Prologue

ALEX TWISTED IN THE WINDOW SEAT, HIS BREATH FORMING circles on the glass. Some kind of storm would be appropriate, he thought. Lightning flashes and rolling thunder. Instead, all was calm. Night was falling, the darkness seeping towards Tokyo from the east, the clustered buildings vanishing into shadow. He could see a haze of smog lit up by the sodium glare from billboards in Shibuya and Shinjuku. The traffic moving in veins, headlights shimmering like stars reflected in a stream. The flight attendants passed along the centre aisle making final safety checks, their smiles fixed, the hydraulics of the under-carriage shuddering beneath their feet. Alex felt the stiffness in his limbs and tried to will away the creeping sense of fear. He knew there was no going back.

The plane banked left and started to descend, the ground rising up steadily to meet them. Alex tried to find his apartment building in the vast plain of grey and black structures passing shapelessly below. He knew his neighbourhood was to the north but there were no landmarks to orient himself, just the mass of rooftops and narrow streets. He looked further south for the school where he taught or the gallery where Naoko worked. The city was still unfamiliar. The rolling landscape skewed out of alignment the more he searched.

1

They touched down smoothly on the runway at Narita and taxied into an empty bay at the north terminal, everyone remaining obediently in their places until the seatbelt light was extinguished. Then the passengers rose together and began the scramble to retrieve baggage from the overhead lockers and jostle for position in the aisle. Alex remained seated. He was in no hurry.

When the aisle was almost empty, he stood and pulled the small leather holdall from the overhead bin and made his way to the open door. He thanked the attendant and stepped out on to the elevated exit ramp. The wind rattled against the thin metal walls. He'd been unsure in Bangkok whether to check his bag or carry it on board. He'd changed his mind back and forth during the taxi ride to the airport. Finally, he'd thought it would look suspicious to check in such a small bag so he'd kept it with him as he boarded.

He followed the passengers into the main terminal and along the starkly lit corridor towards the baggage reclaim. He'd decided in advance that it would be best to linger there, to stand alongside the carousel and appear as if he was waiting with all the others. To be first up at passport control was to invite attention. He needed the safety of the crowd. The businessmen returning from debauched weekends in Patpong, the western backpackers and gap-year students, the young Thai women heading for work in the hostess bars of Roppongi. He noticed an Indonesian family, the women all wearing neat black hijabs. It was best to avoid walking too close to them, he thought.

The luggage began to slide out on to the carousel, slowly at first and then in a flurry of suitcases and garment bags. As their owners retrieved them and stacked the baggage on to trolleys, Alex fell in among the crowd and followed the signs for the exit. He stepped on to the moving walkway feeding the passengers down a long corridor and waited. His eyes were focused on the middle distance, his expression neutral and unconcerned. The walkway was monitored by hidden cameras with unseen airport officials trying to pick out any signs of anxiety or unusual body language that might betray malign intent. Alex knew how to set his face so the Japanese were unable to read him. In the seven months he had lived in Tokyo he had faced enough situations where it had been critical to learn.

He looked clean and neat, wearing jeans with a pair of Converse and a button-down plaid shirt, freshly laundered at the hotel in Thailand. His short blond hair was combed back from a youthful, lightly tanned face. Deep inside, he felt much older and wearier than would appear from his complexion. Compared to the other westerners around him, he looked conservative. Many of them were rough and ragged, as if they had come straight from the beach bars of Pattaya or Phuket, still in bright shorts and sandals, some in bare feet. The groups of Japanese businessmen stood together in the stale humidity, bound up in their dark suits and ties, whispering guiltily to one another about their exploits. Alex knew how to contain his nerves. He gave the impression he intended to give: comfortable and relaxed. Just another young English teacher returning home from a break at an island resort.

The walkway reached the end of the concourse where an escalator descended into the arrivals hall. The overhead signs directed the passengers to separate passport desks, left for Japanese citizens or right for all others. Alex turned right and joined the snaking line as it shuffled forward. He felt a lightness, a sense of inevitability, as if disembodied. He gripped the rolled leather handles of the holdall tightly in his fist and waited.

When he reached the head of the queue, he stood with his toes on the red line, poised like a diver on a high platform. He gazed steadily ahead and approached the uniformed official as soon as he was called. He set the bag at his feet and handed over his passport. The officer scanned the biometric circuit and flicked through the pages until he found the embassy visa fixed near the back. The tip of his tongue darted out and wet his lips as he read.

'Your visa will expire soon,' he said.

Alex thought quickly. 'I know. I've already applied for an extension.'

'This is a problem. It's not permitted to leave Japan on a visa with less than six weeks remaining.'

The officer paused for a moment, weighing up the situation, then turned and called to his supervisor. Alex began to feel the blood pound behind his ears.

'Your name?' the supervisor asked, checking the identity page of the passport.

'Alex Malloy.'

'Age?'

'Twenty-six.'

'You live in Tokyo?'

'Yes. In Koenji.'

'Your address?'

'3-1-3 Fujimicho, Room nine.'

'Where do you work, Mr Malloy?'

'At the Excelsior School on Shinjuku Dori.'

'Why did you return alone today?'

Alex hesitated. 'I'm not sure I understand,' he said.

The supervisor pointed down at the computer in front of him, the screen hidden from view.

'You purchased two seats on the flight today. One in your name and one in the name of Naoko Yamamoto. Why didn't she accompany you?'

'We . . . we had an argument. She decided to come back on her own.'

'What did you argue about?'

Alex considered his answer for a moment. 'The weather,' he said.

The supervisor looked up over Alex's shoulder at the long queue building towards the back of the hall. Another flight had arrived and passengers were spilling off the escalator at the far side of the building. He closed the passport and handed it over the counter.

'Next time, get the re-entry stamp before you depart.'

Alex forced his relief not to show. He nodded his understanding and slipped the passport into his back pocket and picked up the holdall. He began to walk towards the customs desks that separated the passengers from the outside world. He could see through the glass exit doors to the barrier where families were waiting expectantly, bored taxi drivers lined up beside them patiently holding up handwritten name boards.

He looked along the rows of customs desks to select the one with the shortest queue and chose the desk at the far end. There were four customs officers searching through a suitcase on the inspection counter, an Australian couple watching awkwardly as their clothes and underwear were examined. The officers were waving the new passengers on as they joined the line, not wanting to snarl up the crowd as it funnelled towards the exit. Alex slipped in with them and walked past the desk.

He was ten metres from the door, the cool air breezing against his skin, when the dog handler passed behind him. From the corner of his eye he saw the German shepherd take a curious look in his direction and sniff the air inquisitively, its wet nose twitching at the end of a long muzzle. He kept moving. Beyond the doors, people were hugging their loved ones and walking down the concourse towards the express train platform that would take them back into the city. Alex was striding towards them, the holdall in his right hand, his head up, eyes fixed on the outside world. The handler paid out the leash and allowed the dog to move closer to the scent, following its instinct. Alex heard it give a soft whine as it moved towards him and then stood up on its hind legs with bared teeth and bristling fur, straining against the tether.

The handler stopped and leaned his body back to rein in the snarling dog. Alex stood frozen in place, watching with horror as it began to bark, low and husky at first, then loud enough to bring down the building.

# 1

'COME ON,' HIRO SAID. 'I'LL SHOW YOU THE OTHER JAPAN.'
They left the bar and walked along the overhead rail tracks and
past Shinjuku station. It was nearly 1 a.m. on Friday night, and
the rainy season had broken. The clouds that had threatened
the city for days were pouring down and water was steaming up
from the pavements. Alex tugged the collar of his raincoat
tightly around him and held his briefcase over his head for protection as they crossed the junction and headed deeper into
Kabukicho. The streets were full of plastic umbrellas, all heading down into the inevitable red-light district with its arcades
and concealed entrances. There were strange faces and strange
sounds in a kind of whirl that tricked the eye.

Wolf-eyed hustlers lingered on the corners like comic-book
thugs, waiting to prey on the groups of young girls who shoaled
around them. They reached out and took the girls' arms if they
strayed too close, making offers and enticements Alex couldn't
understand. The girls all wore the practised look that said they
had seen it all and were bored and the world held nothing new
for them.

They all watched Hiro Ozawa as he passed by, imperious
beneath the protection of his black umbrella. He was wearing a
dark suit and French collars under a cashmere overcoat,

handmade shoes that were polished to mirrors in the lights of the arcades. He was sharp and neat, with an air of superiority, as if he knew life had no choice but to surrender everything he wanted. It was the same with the other brokers and traders he worked with, a satisfaction which to strangers could be mistaken for arrogance. Alex had wondered lately just how mistaken they were.

They walked on, under the giant video screens that hung outside the department stores and down into the maze of side streets where Nigerian gangs paid backhanders to control the doors. Hiro stopped at a bar with dancing girls and looked up at the sign.

'This is the place,' he said.

Alex peered past the pink and yellow lanterns hanging over the window. The place was full of sleazy-looking older men watching girls dance under bright spotlights.

'Not a chance,' Alex said. 'This is everything I try to avoid.'

Hiro put an arm around his shoulder to urge him on. 'If you don't like this place, I know another close by. You can pay to watch two girls fuck in a mirrored room. What's wrong with you, *gaijin*?'

Alex watched the furtive touts peer from the doorways. They glared at him with the dark scowls they reserved for all foreigners – the *gaijin* they treated with undisguised contempt. Alex expected it from the low-life inhabitants of Kabukicho, but it was difficult to accept from an old friend. He shook Hiro's arm from around his neck; he could smell the alcohol thick on his breath.

'If you want to do that, you're on your own,' he said.

Hiro pretended to look hurt. 'How often do I get to see you these days, Alex? Why are you always so stubborn? At least I'm being honest with you. If I took you to one of those other places you wouldn't know until you were already inside.'

'Don't worry,' Alex said. 'I can smell them from fifty paces.'

There were crowds of salarymen milling around, promising

themselves one last drink before the trains stopped running for the night. Alex could tell his friend wasn't going to let up, and he couldn't leave him drunk and alone. He looked at Hiro with a straight face.

'Call Naoko,' he said.

'Naoko?' Hiro pronounced her name as if saying it for the first time. 'Why do you want me to call *her*? She would kill me for coming to a place like this.'

It was the reaction Alex was hoping for. Either they could go somewhere less sleazy, or he would get to see Naoko after all.

'I'll make you a deal,' he said. 'We go back to Golden Gai and drink there, or you call Naoko and tell her to come down. Then we can go in and I'll buy you all the drinks you want.'

Hiro's expression didn't change, but Alex could see his mind working. 'There's no way she'll come here. Not a chance. Anyway, she's out of your league.' As an afterthought, he added, 'And she's *jaja uma*.'

Alex frowned. 'What's *jaja uma*?'

Hiro smiled knowingly. 'Trust me,' he said. 'You don't want to find out.'

Alex stepped forward. 'Go on, Hiro. Call her and tell her I'm here. Then see if she comes down.'

The challenge hung between them for a moment. Hiro opened his mouth to argue but then thought better of it. He held his hand up as if it was an easy win and took the phone from his pocket.

'Whatever you want, *gaijin*,' he said. 'Whatever you want.'

They shook the rain from their coats and took a table at a booth near the stage. A line of girls gyrated out of time above them, the spotlights colouring their faces. Curls of smoke hung in thick layers overhead. Hiro called the waitress and ordered whisky sours. She was wearing string underwear and heels she couldn't control. Alex reclined against the worn velvet upholstery and looked around. The place must have once seemed edgy and decadent, but now everything was just shabby and sad. When the waitress brought their drinks and set them on the table, Hiro held out a ten-thousand-yen note for a four-thousand-yen round. She leaned in to take the money and he placed a hand on her thigh and ran it up to her backside. He was whispering something in her ear that Alex couldn't hear over the music. The waitress brushed his hand off and backed away. She looked like she wanted to slap him, but Hiro made an innocent face as if it was an accident. When she leaned in again he slid his hand up her leg once more and held it there. Eventually, she just grabbed the bill and walked off, her expression one of weary resignation. Hiro's eyes followed her all the way back to the bar.

'Why the fuck did you do that?' Alex shouted.

Hiro laughed. 'I just told her I wanted a feel in return for a tip. She's happy enough.'

'I never knew you were such a fiend. Not until I came here and saw it for myself.'

'What did you think? That I spent my time writing haiku and making the tea ceremony?'

Alex stirred his drink with a plastic straw. 'That sounds more fun. I'm sure the waitress would agree with me.'

'You used to love nights out like this when we were students.'

'That was a long time ago. You can't treat people like that just because you're drunk. Not everything you see is for sale.'

Hiro laughed and tossed his head back haughtily. 'Why would I take moral lessons from you?' he said. 'Your track record is hardly blemish-free. You're the only lawyer I know who's been struck off.'

Alex tried to smile at the insult, even though the accusation was true. 'That's why I had to come all the way to Japan,' he said. 'I needed the distance to escape that particular claim to fame. I'm not a failed lawyer here. Now, I'm an education specialist.'

Hiro took a moment to savour his friend's torment. 'I still don't know how it happened. I mean, how does a graduate from one of the best law schools in London lose his job and end up teaching English in Tokyo?'

Alex sipped his cocktail and winced. Hiro had ordered them strong.

'I don't know,' he said. 'I'm just lucky, I suppose.'

'It must have been serious. They don't strike lawyers off for nothing.'

'Whatever happened, I left it behind in London. Just remember that you've promised to keep it to yourself. I don't want my bad reputation following me.'

'That must be why you're always so sensible now. Why you never get drunk any more.'

'I am drunk,' Alex said.

'But you never let anyone see it. You never act any differently.'

Alex shrugged. 'I just like to hold myself together.'

Hiro leaned across the table. 'You can't hold yourself together all the time, *gaijin*.'

There was silence between them for a while. Hiro watched the girls move across the stage, his eyes flicking hungrily from one to the next. He had been so different, Alex thought, back in London, when they had first met. He was calm and quiet, almost introverted, when he was younger, before he realized he had ended up on the winning side in life and quickly learned the new rules. Learned that money was power. Now, it seemed he was ruled by his appetites; the more he could have, the more he wanted. It was becoming harder to reconcile the person now, buttoned up in his expensive suit, with the bookish student Alex had first known. Still, it was natural for things to change. It probably happened to all friends eventually, he thought. Even the briefest recollection of his final few months in London was enough to make Alex wish for the company of the old Hiro again. The last thing he needed in Tokyo was more chaos.

11

He watched his friend down his cocktail and call the waitress for another. Soon, that was gone and replaced by a third. Hiro's face was growing heavy with alcohol now and he was fading as company. Alex wondered what he was trying to prove. He knew better than to keep up. His untouched drinks collected on the table before him as he watched the ice melt in his glass and waited.

Hiro saw Naoko first. Alex noticed the change in his expression, the way his mouth tightened as he looked up and stared back through the bar. She was standing in the doorway, waiting for her eyes to adjust to the dark as she took off her coat.

She was tall for a Japanese woman, with straight shoulders and narrow hips. She stood upright and elegantly balanced, her strong features set on a delicate face. Her eyes were narrow and Asiatic and her hair was blue-black, hanging almost to her waist. One corner of her mouth was slightly crooked, turned upwards, as if something about life seemed perpetually to intrigue her. She was wearing a green dress, the one she had worn the night they had first gone out together, and there was a silk wrap around her shoulders. Her eyes shone fiercely in the lights as she approached. Alex knew most Japanese women would die of shame before they walked into a Kabukicho bar alone but she wore her composure bravely, betraying nothing as the men in the shadows turned to watch her as she passed.

She took a seat in the booth, and Alex felt her hand touch his beneath the table as she sat. She ordered a vodka tonic.

'It's good to see you again, Naoko,' Alex said.

'It's good to see you too,' she said politely, as if greeting an old friend. She turned to Hiro, immediately registering how inebriated he looked. 'So this is where you drink yourself stupid at night while your mother is sick and waiting for you to visit?'

Hiro said, 'Please, Naoko. You've only just arrived and you want to argue already? It's not my fault you go to see her every day. You make me look bad.'

His tone was imploring, but Alex could see she had no intention of backing down.

'I don't go every day,' she said. 'I go just enough to make sure she is okay. All she ever talks about is her precious son, and look where you are.'

Hiro turned to Alex. 'My mother says I'm a bad son and a bad man. She wishes she had Naoko as a daughter.'

'I'm there for her whenever she needs me,' Naoko said.

Hiro's eyes darkened. 'If my mother thought I would rush home to her, she would be sick every night. Anyway, she just wants to talk about how much you both hate men.'

Naoko looked at him squarely. 'How much we hate men like you.'

There was a long silence. Naoko's words seemed to grow harsher the longer they were left unacknowledged.

Hiro turned to Alex. 'I told you she was *jaja uma*.'

Naoko's face flushed with anger. 'Don't ever call me that again,' she said.

'Why not?' Hiro sneered. 'We both know it's true.'

He finished his drink and placed the empty glass on the table. 'It's no fun with you here, Naoko. No fun at all.' He stood up and walked away with a wounded look, moving unsteadily as he made his way past the stage, out through the exit and on to the street.

Alex turned and watched him leave. 'I knew this was a bad idea.'

'It was your idea to call me and ask me to come,' Naoko said.

'I mean coming to a dive like this.' He waved a hand around at the tacky surroundings. 'He's been acting weird ever since we arrived. Sometimes I think he does it all for show.'

'Oh, he's a real mama's boy at heart. Don't let his tough-guy act fool you. He'll forget about it all when he comes back.'

Alex looked towards the door. 'I don't think he's coming back,' he said.

They took their coats and left the bar and walked along the narrow street towards the lights of Shinjuku. The girls outside the massage parlours whispered for business as they passed. Alex called Hiro's number but there was no answer. He could see Naoko knew she had gone too far but was too proud to admit it. In an alley off the main square, they found him asleep in a doorway, his coat wrapped tightly around him. Alex tried to wake him but there was no way he was going to stir. Naoko stood and watched, refusing to show any sympathy.

'We can't leave him here,' Alex said.

'He can rot there for all I care.'

'You don't mean that. He's my friend. I'll have to take him home with me.'

Naoko thought for a moment. 'His mother's house is closer. We could take him there. She'll be pleased to see him. Even in this condition.'

Alex stood and wiped the dirt from his hands. 'You think that's a good idea?' he asked.

'Why not?' she said. 'At least someone will be happy.'

They hailed a cab and placed Hiro between them, his head nodding gently as they drove through the junctions and traffic signals towards the highway. They followed the road east towards Asakusa and crossed the Sumida river. The driver pulled on to a side street flanked by a line of disused warehouses and scrubby patches of waste ground. Naoko paid the fare and Alex pulled Hiro from the cab. He heaved him out and settled his dead weight on the wet kerb.

The building was a block of twelve grey apartments above a grocery shop and an all-night laundry. Beside the entrance, two broken vending machines stood in a pool of water, one tipped against the other. There was no lift, just a rusted iron fire escape that wound up one side. Alex pulled Hiro's arm across his shoulders and hefted him up the steps to the landing and propped him against the door. Naoko rang the bell and motioned for him to wait by the stairs. Hiro's mother was old and frightened of foreigners, she said. Lights came on through the windows as he walked back down the landing and waited. The rain was coming down hard now. After a few minutes, Naoko came out and closed the door quietly behind her. They walked down the fire escape, her heels ringing on the metal treads.

'He's sleeping now,' she said. 'At least his mother is glad to nurse him.'

'Sounds good. I wish I had someone to nurse me.'

'You're drunk too, aren't you?'

'Me? I'm fine.'

'You must be a little bit drunk. That's why you asked Hiro to call me. That's why you take crazy chances.'

'You came to meet me,' he said. 'You're taking the same chances that I am.'

Naoko opened her umbrella and stepped from the cover of the stairwell. Fat raindrops shuddered against the fabric. She tilted the umbrella to one side to check no one was watching them from the window above, and they began to walk towards the high road.

'Hiro's definitely going to suspect something's happening now,' she said.

'Why don't you just tell him? It's been long enough. I don't like keeping secrets from my friends.'

Naoko shrugged. 'He keeps secrets. You keep secrets.'

'Like what?'

'Like why you're really in Tokyo. Like who you really are.'

Alex shrugged. 'I'm just an English teacher.'

'All of Hiro's other friends from London are bankers and stockbrokers. What happened to you?'

'You're so smart. Why don't you take a guess?'

Naoko slowly turned the canopy of the umbrella above her. 'I think you're running away.'

Alex laughed nervously. 'Running away from what?'

15

'I don't know. Something you don't want anyone to know. Maybe something bad. Something intriguing.'

At least Hiro had kept his word, Alex thought. She obviously knew nothing. 'I wish I had a good story to tell you,' he said. 'I really do. But I still don't see why that means you won't tell Hiro about us.'

'Trust me,' she said. 'This way is better for both of us. You're only here for a short time. Then you'll go back to London and I'll have to stay here on my own. That's why it's best not to get too attached.'

She said it in her usual matter-of-fact manner but Alex could sense the challenge implicit in her words. He felt the temptation to tell her she was wrong, that he could never go back, even if he wanted to, but he stopped himself before he spoke out and regretted it later. Some things were best left unsaid.

'Hiding in the shadows doesn't come naturally to me,' Alex said. 'I just don't like it.'

Naoko stopped and looked at him with raised eyebrows. 'Except when it suits you,' she said.

She stepped closer to him under the cover of the umbrella and wiped the drops of rain from his face with delicate fingers.

'Come on. It's Friday night, and I've had a busy week. I'm hungry. You can buy me a late dinner.'

# 2

It was gone 2 a.m. The restaurant was empty but still open despite the hour. The owner was sitting alone on a stool in the doorway, reading the racing news. An old dog lay curled up at his feet, watching the rain as it sheeted down from the edge of the canvas awning. The owner looked pleased to have customers so late and showed them to a table in the window and bowed as he pulled out a chair for Naoko. She took a seat and lit a cigarette from a pack of Seven Stars. There were red paper lanterns hanging low over the tables and the walls were plastered with flyers advertising upcoming bouts in the sumo hall. There was a smell of burnt spice and soot ground into the furniture. The owner lit the gas burner in the centre of the table and brought them plates of marinated meat and vegetables and a bowl of kimchi. Naoko asked for a pitcher of beer and poured two glasses. She held the pitcher high so the foam spilled over the sides and ran down on to the table. It was the Tokyo way, she said. Seven parts beer to three parts froth.

Alex looked out at the deserted streets, the weeds springing up through the cracks in the pavement, the old buildings on the verge of tumbling down.

'I never knew Hiro's mother lived somewhere like this. It's not what I imagined at all. I always thought he grew up in a mansion block in Shirokane or someplace like that. He's always given me that impression.'

'That's what he'd like you to think. But this is it. This is where we're both from. My parents lived in the flat upstairs from Hiro's mother, at least until they moved out to Tachikawa for some peace and quiet. Hiro and I went to the same high school together. I've known him all my life.'

'That kind of friendship is rare. In London people are always moving around, so it's hard to stay in touch.'

'Believe me, it's even rarer in Tokyo. Here it feels like you never really know anyone at all.'

'At least it explains why he's so focused on making money now.'

Naoko placed the strips of beef on the grill with long chopsticks. They seared instantly in the heat and she served them on to the plates.

'He had a hard time as a kid. I had to protect him at school from all the talk about his family. The kids in his class were pretty cruel. His dad left when he was very young. His mother told him he had died so they could avoid the shame of being abandoned. Hiro was the only kid at school with just a mother. There wasn't even a word for "single parent" back then. It was unheard of. When he was at college he found out his father was still alive and living in a small town outside Tokyo. He just hadn't wanted a wife and son. Hiro keeps trying to get his mother to move out of here to someplace more comfortable, especially now she's getting old. But she won't ever leave. It's like she has to stay here and punish herself until the end.'

'I never knew any of this.'

'It's a mystery to me what men talk about when they're together.'

'There's no mystery. We just avoid anything personal, that's all.'

Naoko took a mouthful of food and chewed carefully. 'What about you? What are your family like?'

'Nothing like that. They were just normal, I suppose. Both my parents were teachers. They're retired now.'

'They must be proud of you. Following them into the family profession.'

Alex kept his eyes down to the table. 'I wouldn't say that exactly.'

When he had finished eating he took his chopsticks and stuck them upright in the remains of the rice in his bowl. Naoko reached across the table and pulled them out.

'You shouldn't do that,' she said. 'It's bad luck. It means someone has died.'

'I'm sorry. I didn't know.'

She smiled and her eyes glinted in the faint red light. 'That's so English of you. Saying sorry all the time. Apologizing is a national sport in England, I think.'

'And shopping is a national sport in Japan.'

'Maybe window shopping,' Naoko said. 'Anyway, I've decided not to be Japanese. I'm going to be something else. Something I choose.'

'Like what? You can't just pick a nationality.'

'Why not?' she said. 'I think I will be the Republic of Naoko. I'm even going to have my own flag.'

'A country of one? Sounds lonely to me.'

'Not really. I'm going to outlaw loneliness. I can do that because I'm president. President for life.'

Alex sipped his beer. 'Your republic, your rules.'

When they had finished, they paid the bill and thanked the owner as they left. There was a line of taxis parked at the rank outside, the drivers asleep with newspapers over their faces to shut out the streetlights.

'Are you coming home with me?' Naoko asked.

'Do you want me to?'

'Of course. But you have to leave early.'

'Why?'

She looked down at the tips of her shoes. 'Mr Kimura is coming over in the morning.'

'Again?'

'He's my boss, Alex. I can't say no. He just wants to drop off some paperwork. He's harmless. He's just old and lonely and likes to have company.'

'I doubt he's as harmless as you think.'

Naoko knocked on the window of the taxi at the head of the line. The driver woke up with a start and wiped his eyes, his collar standing crooked against his neck. Naoko closed her umbrella and held the taxi door open.

'Are you coming or not?' she asked.

Alex paid the driver and they walked up the steps to the entrance of her building. Naoko checked the mailbox in the lobby but it was empty except for some junk mail and a flyer from the new pizzeria. She pressed for the lift and they rode up together to the twelfth floor. She opened her front door slowly so as not to wake her neighbours, and they both kicked off their shoes in the entrance hall.

'*Tadaima*,' Alex said into the darkened flat. 'We're home.'

'*Okaeri nasai*. Welcome back,' Naoko replied, and went into the kitchen and switched on the lights.

The apartment had windows on three sides. It was large for a Tokyo flat, with a view over the rooftops of Mejiro. It was a corner room, all white, with pale furniture and high ceilings and a glass-walled balcony. A long steel bookcase stood in the middle of the room, dividing it in two: the bedroom on one side and the living room and galley kitchen on the other. Naoko took a bottle of plum wine from the fridge, moving as silently as possible.

'Do you creep around like this all the time?' Alex asked. 'Or just when I'm here?'

She poured two glasses and handed one to Alex, watching him over the rim as she took a sip. 'You know what my

20

neighbours are like. They look at me sideways when I pass them in the lobby as it is. If they thought I had a foreign man in here, it would be the talk of the building. Also, Mr Kimura knows the manager. It's how I got the lease. If he were to find out, I would be in big trouble.'

'I don't know how you can stand to live this way. Locked up in a gilded cage.'

'Well, not everyone wants to live like you,' Naoko said.

'And how do I live?'

She swallowed a mouthful of *ume-shu* and smiled at him playfully. 'Like a bum.'

In the living room there was a large framed picture newly hung on the wall above the sofa. It was a screen print in red and black ink of a young Japanese woman staring serenely from the canvas, her body twisted into an impossible yoga position. She was standing naked on one leg, holding the other ankle over her head. A lit cigarette protruded from the cleft of her vagina.

Alex stood before it in silence, examining the piece carefully. Naoko nestled on to the sofa and tucked her feet beneath her.

'Do you like it?' she asked. 'It's a print from the new exhibition we're having at the gallery. The artist is called Masakazu. I've known him a long time. He gave it to me as a gift.'

'I'm not sure I understand it,' Alex said.

'I don't think there's a lot to understand.'

'Does it have a title?'

Naoko smiled knowingly, predicting his response. 'It's called *Fifty Views of Mount Fuji in the Rain.*'

'Wow,' he said. 'Of course it is.'

'You can't be so dismissive, Alex. This is my career. I have to believe in it to be successful.'

'I prefer these,' he said, and pointed to two small photographs standing on the bookshelf. They were bright arrangements of flowers in a desert landscape. A spray of snow willows against dark, volcanic sand and a bowl of camellias in a bone-white dune. They were both overhung by skies rippled with rags of cloud.

'You like them?' Naoko asked.

'Much more than the other one.'

For a moment, she looked embarrassed. 'They're mine. I took them when I was at art school.'

Alex stood and looked closer. 'You never told me you were a photographer. They're really good.'

'I studied photography. That was my ambition when I was young. But then one thing or another got in the way so I settled for working at the gallery.'

'Don't you still want to try to make your own work instead of selling everyone else's?'

Naoko stood up and looked at them over his shoulder. 'I wish it was that easy,' she said. 'Come on. I'm going to take a shower. If you ask nicely you can wash my back.'

Naoko lay face down on the bed. Alex traced a finger over the ink lines of the tattoo that covered her hips and flank. Two golden peacocks fighting in a forest of bamboo. The tattoo started inside her thigh and ran up across her torso to cover one side of her ribcage. The colour was unfinished in places, with only the black outlines complete. It was minutely detailed with intricate patterns and vivid reds and purples that faded into one another. Alex found something new in it each time he looked. He felt the soft down of her skin beneath his fingertips.

'I've never liked tattoos,' he said, 'but I like yours. It's unique.'

'You think so?'

'The first time I met you, I never imagined that you had something like this. I was amazed the first time I saw you undressed.'

Naoko's voice was full of sleep. 'Sometimes I wish I had just got a heart or a butterfly. Something simple.'

'That would be too obvious. I don't think that would suit you at all. I was told that tattoos are uncommon in Japan. They're seen as antisocial.'

'They are.'

'But you went ahead and got the biggest, craziest design I've ever seen.'

Naoko smiled at him. 'But only you get to see it. I don't show my body to anyone else, so no one knows it's there.'

'Really? You've never shown it to anyone?'

'Just you.'

'So it looks like you have secrets, too?'

Naoko laughed sarcastically. 'I suppose so,' she said.

'Are you ever going to get it finished?'

'I don't think so. If you knew how painful it was, you wouldn't ask. It was done the old-fashioned way, with a sharpened bamboo point instead of an electric needle. It hurt like hell.'

Alex squeezed her body beneath his hands. 'What's wrong? Can't you handle a little pain?' he said.

Naoko shook him away and turned over. 'You wouldn't know. You've never had a tattoo.'

Alex reached up and patted his shoulder. 'No,' he said. 'But I have this.'

The skin across his shoulder and back was smooth and stretched over the bones where it had been burnt, almost to the point of melting. The scars had a pale red sheen from the skin grafts running down the left side of his back and the inside of his arm, from shoulder to wrist.

'This was painful enough.'

'It was the first thing I noticed about you,' Naoko said. 'I saw it through your shirt on the night we met. I think it looks masculine. Like you've been through the wringer.'

'I think I went through it a couple of times.'

'That must have been a terrible experience,' she said, and lifted herself on to one elbow. She leaned across and delicately kissed the scar tissue on his shoulder blade where the grafts were heaviest.

Alex drifted away for a second, as if remembering. When his focus returned he tried his hardest to look unfazed. 'Put it this way, I'd prefer not to do it again if I can help it. It was pretty bad.'

'Bad enough to run away from?'

He turned to her, his expression full of serious intent. 'You like to let your imagination go wild, don't you?'

She could see it was foolish to insist. She bent down and held his face in her hands. 'Let me kiss your eye,' she said.

'Why?'

'Because it heals all things.'

She reached out with the tip of her tongue and Alex felt it run across his eyelid.

'Does that feel better?' she asked.

He felt the weight of her body on his, the slightness of her, the tautness of the muscles across her slender back.

'Yes,' he said, and smiled up at her. 'Much better.'

Later, while she was sleeping, Alex got up and stood at the balcony doors, watching the night. Clouds had gathered over the city and swirled like paint mixed in water, obscuring the buildings in the skyscraper district. Below lay a square of waste ground where an old house had stood, only the foundations still visible in the moonlight. He remembered how they had watched from her window as a demolition crew had dismantled the building piece by piece and taken it away. He'd been amazed that a building could be turned into an empty space so quickly. Efficiency was the Japanese way, Naoko had told him, and he'd laughed and said that destroying things was a skill westerners would never be beaten at.

He turned to watch her now, lying on her side, the faint streetlights drawing patterns on her skin as she slept. He quietly made his way into the kitchen and filled a glass with water, sipping it as he wandered from the kitchen into the living room, walking on the balls of his feet so as not to disturb her. He idly flicked through a magazine on the coffee table and then picked up one of her framed still-life photographs from the bookshelf and held it up to the light creeping in through the curtains. Even though he knew nothing about art, he could see that she had talent. The flower arrangements and the landscapes they were set in were striking. To be so gifted but unable to use that gift must be such a bitter pill to swallow. He held the frame closer to the soft blue beam to see it better.

On the reverse of the frame, Alex noticed the corner of a folded piece of paper protruding from the wooden back that sealed the photograph inside. It appeared to have been pressed inside the frame for safekeeping.

He loosened the clips that held the photograph in place and removed the panel. Lifting it away, he saw that he was right: there was a printed sheet of paper folded behind the image. He lifted it out carefully and held it up to the light. There were rows of intricate Japanese characters printed in dense, vertical lines of text. It looked like an official document, with some kind of seal at the head of the paper and a series of stamps in red and black ink along one edge. He could see Naoko's signature at the foot of the page but, apart from that, the only section he was able to read was a date: 27 March 2004. So it was a ten-year-old sheet of paper. But he still had no idea why it was hidden inside a photo frame.

He laid the document back inside the frame and sealed it shut. As he turned to replace it on the bookshelf, he noticed the back of the frame was covered in a pattern of skin whorls and palm lines, printed in a thick, dark impasto. The pattern was dry and crusted on to the delicate wooden grain and it flaked away in patches as his fingers ran across the surface. Alex lifted his fingertip to his nose and breathed in gently. Immediately, he could smell the rich, iron scent of blood.

He lifted the frame up to the light to see better. There were patches of dark, bloody palm- and fingerprints dried on to the backing, like the sinister hand painting of a child. The explanation must be innocent, he thought. Any other possibility was too crazy to consider. He placed the photograph back on the bookshelf and went into the bedroom. He looked down at Naoko, still sleeping soundly beneath the white cotton sheets. His eyes ran along the length of her arm and down to her hand, lying at her side, turned palm up. Near the centre of it, he could make out a small, round wound. It had dried and scabbed over but was still painful-looking, deep and angry like a vicious stigmata. He wondered how he hadn't noticed it before.

Naoko stirred gently as he watched her, and then lay still. It was 5 a.m. and the dawn was beginning to break outside. Her boss, Mr Kimura, would be arriving soon and Alex knew he needed to get going. Now he knew Naoko was no different from anyone else. Everybody has something to hide, after all, he thought. He considered waking her for a moment, but then changed his mind.

The sun was up when he left the station at Koenji. The early-morning flights were passing overhead, and he could hear their engines whine as they made the descent to Haneda. The streets had been washed clean in the night and there was a sharp citrus smell on the breeze. Groups of workmen were hanging strings of electric lights in the trees along the roadside and the shop-fronts were all decorated for the start another festival.

His room was in a guesthouse in the backstreets behind the railway crossing. It was a low-rise suburb, outside of the Yamanote line, where all the upmarket addresses grouped together. There was no traffic, just corner after corner of narrow streets, the buildings all pushed up against one another. Drying poles with laundry were suspended from every balcony, and mattresses hung from the windowsills, airing in the sunlight.

The guesthouse was on five levels, with ten bedrooms and a communal kitchen and bathroom. The landlady lived in a cottage at the end of the garden and came in each day to clean.

She was a widow from Kyushu and spoke no English, except to ask for the rent money on the first of each month. Alex saw the other tenants only occasionally, in the kitchen or when he passed them on the stairs. Some were permanent and others just passing through. There were two Russian girls, *Village of the Damned* blondes, who were hostessing. Others did bar work. But, for most, the fall-back position was teaching in the language schools. 'Specialist in Humanities', their visas said. None of them were specialists in anything, Alex guessed; otherwise, they wouldn't be here. He opened the front door and climbed the steps to the fifth floor, where the rooms were built into the eaves of the house. He unlocked his door and let himself in.

His room was small and bare, with wooden walls and a window covered by a bamboo blind. There was a tatami floor and an old teak dresser and a smell of warmth and cheap incense. Dust motes floated in the slatted light. When he unrolled his futon mattress and spread out his bedding it took up three quarters of the floor space. Old postcards were pinned to the walls beside a faded map of the Japanese islands, the seams held together by tape, left by unknown tenants who had lived there before him. Alex had stayed there since his first night in the country and, although he had thought about finding somewhere more permanent, the plan had never become a reality. It was just as well. In his experience, it seemed an invitation to misfortune to put down roots.

He took off his clothes and lay down and tried to sleep, but his mind was too restless. He lay on his back and thought about the night, about Hiro and the bar in Kabukicho, about Naoko. There was a weightless sensation in his stomach, like wheels lifting off a track. Alex had promised himself he would avoid all personal entanglements in Japan, especially the ones that gave him this feeling of impending danger. With Naoko, he could definitely sense obstacles fast approaching around unseen corners. But when he pictured her face, that crooked smile, he knew his promises to himself were pointless.

27

He pushed the thought away and turned over, pulling the sheet up over his head. There were only three hours until he was due back at work.

# 3

ALEX KNEW HE MUST BE DREAMING. HE WAS SHIVERING, HIS *jaws rattling against each other inside his aching skull. He could feel the hardness of the frozen tarmac beneath him where he lay; his hands were like ice but his back was burning, a relentless, piercing sensation like a constant scald. He could see the spectral silhouettes of trees above him, the snow flurrying down through the tangle of darkened branches. He tried to move, to push himself up on to one elbow, but his body refused to obey.*

*Voices around him, phasing over each other in tones of panic. A face appeared above him, unfamiliar and terrifying in its demeanour. Blue emergency lights strobed in the darkness, reflecting back from a high-visibility jacket as the face leaned in and searched inside Alex's eyes for signs of life.*

*That was when he remembered the car, remembered driving through the junction and the look Patrick had flashed him from the passenger seat. The look of horror as they collided with their inevitable fate. He wondered where Patrick was now. He tried to turn his head to see if he could spot him among the crowd of paramedics and onlookers that had gathered above him, but his neck was encased in some kind of padded restraint, nylon straps binding it across his forehead. Maybe he should call out to him, Alex thought, but his tongue seemed to have swollen horribly inside his blood-filled mouth. He kept hoping that Patrick would appear in his eyeline, smiling, just so he knew that he was safe and unharmed.*

*The thought of injury brought his focus back to the searing pain down one side of his spine. The flesh felt like it had been flayed from his body, ripped from the bones as if flensed by the blade of a butcher's knife.*

*More faces crowded above him. More voices.*

'Is he alive?'

'He still has a pulse.'

'Can he hear us?'

'No idea. His back looks like a bomb went off behind him.'

'He's full of shrapnel from the other vehicle. It impacted straight through the driver's side door. All that metal folded in and practically minced him. He must be in agony.'

'Look at the colour of him.'

'Iris dilation minimal.'

'Can you give him something? For the pain, I mean. I have ketamine in my kit.'

'Has he taken anything already? The other one's as high as a kite.'

'If they're junkies, I can't risk it.'

'He was driving an expensive car.'

'That doesn't mean he's clean.'

'Look in his pockets.'

'Wait. I've found something. Two small bags. Some kind of powder. I don't know what, but it's not legal.'

'He's got a spoon and a hypo in here as well.'

'That's you fucked, son. No meds for you. You're going to have to do this by gritting your teeth.'

'No iris dilation.'

'What?'

'He's unresponsive. He's going.'

'Shit. Okay. Let's move him. Quickly.'

*The pain was immense. Overpowering in its relentlessness. Alex desperately needed relief. There was nothing else in the world he wanted more. He began to see more faces as he was raised up on the stretcher and lifted towards the ambulance. He looked for Patrick, searched desperately for a glimpse of his face, but in the crowd around him he could see only strangers.*

# 4

IN THE MORNING, NAOKO TOOK THE METRO BACK TO ASAKUSA. She bought green tea and rice balls from the grocery beneath the apartment and carried them into the bedroom. There was a thick, earthy smell of stale alcohol in the room so she pulled the curtain back and opened the window. She left the breakfast tray beside the bed so it was there when Hiro woke up and went out to the balcony.

Hiro's mother was called Yukiko. She was sitting on a low wooden chair in the sun. Naoko poured her a cup of green tea and sat down beside her. Yukiko thanked her and took the cup and blew on it gently. She was listening to old show tunes on the radio and singing along under her breath. Yukiko was starting to look old now. Her hair was grey and cut short and she was wearing a thick cotton housecoat, despite the humidity. Her face was deeply lined, probably from all the smiling, Naoko thought. She should have been depressed more often. She definitely had reason to be. There was a wire cage hanging from the wooden rafter above the balcony. A songbird stood on a perch inside, busy and proud, with a yellow head and a puffed-out grey chest.

'When did you buy yourself a bird?' Naoko asked.

'Hiro bought it for me. To keep me company.'

'What's it called?'

Yukiko laughed at the thought. 'Why would you give a bird a name?' she said.

They heard Hiro come out of the bedroom. His eyes were red and bloodshot. He had a bathrobe draped around his shoulders and an old-style pair of house slippers on his feet. He yawned deeply when the fresh air hit his lungs and bent down and kissed the top of his mother's head.

'What happened last night?' he asked.

Naoko gazed up at him from her chair. 'You were drunk, as usual, so we brought you here to sleep it off.'

'Who's we?'

'Alex and I. You don't remember?'

Hiro leaned against the balcony railing. 'Refresh my memory,' he said.

Naoko could see he was playing dumb. She had known him far too long to fall for his tricks. 'Your memory is just fine,' she said. 'It's your liver you should worry about.'

'What did you do after you left me?'

'Nothing much. We just said goodbye and went our separate ways. You have your friend to thank for getting you here.'

'He's a true gentleman. That's what the girls in the bar were saying about him. And handsome as well. The feeling was mutual, from what I can remember.'

Naoko sipped her tea, refusing to take the bait. 'I see your memory's coming back now,' she said.

'It's starting to.' Hiro ran a hand through his hair. It was messy from sleeping. 'I'm going to take a shower,' he said.

Naoko carried the dishes to the kitchen and started to rinse them. A framed photograph hung on the wall above the sink. It was an old picture of their coming-of-age ceremony, the colours faded by the sun. Naoko was wearing a brightly patterned kimono and *zori* sandals; Hiro was uncomfortable in a new suit. They both looked serious and innocent. It seemed like a lifetime ago.

Hiro came in from the bathroom and opened the fridge. He took out an apple and started to peel it with a knife. The peel unfurled in a single strand.

'I lost my wallet last night,' he said.

'No, you didn't. I have it in my bag. I came here to return it.'

'Why did you take it?'

'To pay for your taxi home. I'm not nursing you and paying for the privilege.'

'What would I do without you?' Hiro said, and wrapped his arms around her from behind.

Naoko touched a hand to his. Her head was turned to the window, so he couldn't see her face.

'Tell me about Alex,' she said.

Hiro took a step back, pulling his hand from under hers. 'I knew it,' he said. 'At least I can still read you after all this time.'

She turned to face him. 'I'm just curious. Most of your friends are asshole bankers. It's unusual to see you with someone real. Someone who has feelings.'

Hiro threw the peel into the bin. 'What do you want to know?'

'Tell me the first thing that comes into your head,' she said.

He didn't hesitate. 'That's easy. I don't want you seeing him.'

'I'm not seeing him.'

'Then stop playing games, Naoko. I know you. I'm not picking up the pieces again. I know how close you've come to hitting rock bottom before. I know because I'm the one you always turn to when you need help. Alex is a bad choice for you.'

'Why do you have to be so dramatic? I'm interested, that's all. Nothing's happening.'

Hiro watched her with a steady gaze as he took a bite of the apple and it crunched between his teeth. He chewed thoughtfully. Naoko turned back to the sink and carried on washing the dishes.

'His room was across the hall from mine when I did my exchange year,' he said. 'I lost touch with him when I left London and came back to Japan. Then one day I got a message to say he was in Tokyo, working as a teacher. I was shocked, to be honest. I never imagined him doing something like that. He went straight from law school to a position in one of the big firms. The kind of stellar career everyone always dreams of. The kind they don't mess up. He seemed different when I first met him here. Older, and more solitary. Kind of beaten down. I had no idea what had happened so I asked some mutual friends back in London.'

Naoko stopped washing the dishes. She kept her face to the window. 'And what did they say?'

'I'm not supposed to tell you anything,' he said. 'He doesn't want his misdemeanours following him six thousand miles to Tokyo.'

'It's only me,' Naoko said, trying to look bashful. 'What difference does it make if I know something about one of your friends?'

Hiro took a last bite of the apple and tossed the core away. 'I heard he was in some kind of trouble. Big trouble. With drugs.'

'Alex?'

'That's what I was told by people in London. They said that he had a serious problem. That he was involved in a car accident and really screwed everything up. He was driving high and lost control of the car, and a passenger was killed.'

Naoko tried to hide her shock. 'This doesn't sound like Alex. He seems so reserved.'

'His calmness is new-found, believe me. He never used to be like that. Apparently, the accident was why he lost his job. Why he ended up here. His family disowned him when they found out about the drugs and then he had nowhere else to go.'

'And Alex has confirmed all of this himself?'

Hiro shook his head dismissively. 'He had to tell me that he'd been struck off as a lawyer and lost his job. He knew he had to be honest about that much, at least. But the rest he won't talk about. He keeps it all inside, hidden away, where it can fester. I try to get him to open up, but he's not that kind of person.'

'What kind of person is he?'

'You want me to tell you?' Hiro said, his face becoming serious. 'He's stubborn and proud. That's a dangerous combination. He hasn't got the sense to avoid trouble. It follows him around. It always has done. He's my friend but it's no coincidence that every situation he's involved in turns sour eventually. He doesn't mean to ruin everything he touches, but he can't help himself. It's like a gift he was born with. I know you too well, Naoko. Someone like Alex isn't meant for you. He's not like you and me.'

'I'm nothing like you,' Naoko said, her voice full of disdain.

'Don't kid yourself. You're just as protective of your lifestyle as I am. Probably more so. Look where we come from and look how far we've managed to go. Don't forget – I know everything you had to do to get where you are now. How much you've sacrificed. Don't throw that all away. I remember how unhappy you were, and I don't want to see you go through that again. Promise me you'll stay away from him. You owe me that much.'

Yukiko came in from the balcony. Her smile dropped when she sensed the tension in the room. 'What's wrong?' she asked.

Naoko tried to smile, but it formed weakly on her lips. 'Nothing. We were just talking about work. That's all.'

'Why don't we all go out?' Yukiko said. 'It's such a lovely day, and it's so rare for me to have you both here. We can go for lunch in the park.'

Naoko bowed apologetically, her face cast down to the floor. 'I can't today, Yukiko-san. I have to meet clients in an hour.

Please forgive me. I promise I will call you next week and we can go out together then.'

'Of course,' Yukiko said. 'I will look forward to it.'

Naoko took her coat from the rack by the door and called out goodbye as she left. She walked down the metal staircase and out on to the street. A seed of doubt had been planted inside her now. She could feel it beginning to take root and grow already. When she looked up, she could see Hiro at the rail of the landing, looking down. He didn't call or say anything, just kept watching her as she walked to the corner. His eyes followed hers, an overbearing expression set on his face, the one she had hated since she was a girl.

# 5

It was Hiro's fault they had met in the first place. Naoko remembered it clearly. It was the cherry-blossom season and the evenings were starting to grow warm. The company Hiro worked for had chartered a boat to take clients cruising around Tokyo Bay so they could ply them with cocktails and pitch the latest investments. The boat was a traditional *yakatabune*, with a closed deck and low tables arranged around the cabin for entertaining, the kind that foreigners found exotic. The kind that made them spend money. A gentle breeze blew across the water and a yellow spring moon hung over the curve of the Rainbow Bridge. New passengers boarded in groups as the boat docked at piers along the bay.

Hiro wanted her to meet a group of Japanese currency traders at a table near the bow, eating from ornate platters of yellowtail and swordfish sashimi. Their wives knelt beside them, slightly removed, watching in obedient silence as the men argued about their tennis scores, laughing at each other like excited schoolboys. At the head of the table was a man in his forties, overweight and breathless, the buttons on his shirt straining from his bulk. His younger companions were trying hard to impress him. From his sour expression, it appeared they were failing. Hiro said his name was Togo Nishi, that he was the new head of risk management.

'What happened to the old head?' Naoko asked.

Hiro shrugged. 'He couldn't take the pressure any more. They found him hanging in his office last week.'

Hiro introduced her to the table, taking special care when he came to Nishi. Naoko bowed to each in turn. She saw how Hiro revelled in it, showing her off like a trophy. He sat at an empty place at the table and motioned for her to kneel beside him. Naoko was almost shocked to find herself doing as commanded, lowering herself quickly and tucking her dress beneath her. Nishi selected a piece of tuna, thick and pink as a tongue. He set it down in a saucer of soy to let it marinate. His hair was receding above a broad, round face, smooth and bloodless as a doll's.

'Hiro tells me you work for the Kimura Gallery,' Nishi said. 'Shoji Kimura is a member of my golf club. I've played with him a few times. He likes to cheat.'

Naoko smiled vaguely. 'Kimura-san must be thirty years older than you. I'm sure he needs all the advantage he can get.'

'I was planning on calling him, actually, but perhaps you can help me. I've just bought a beach house in Fukuoka and I'm having it decorated. I want to buy some artwork for the place, and Hiro tells me you're quite the expert. He assures me that my money would be safe in your hands.'

'Of course, Nishi-san. It would be my pleasure to help in any way I can.'

'I understand that your gallery specializes in modern work, but I don't want anything pretentious. I want something that I know will keep its value. Not something that people will laugh at behind my back.'

'We only represent the most prestigious new artists. I can assure you all the work we show is of the highest quality.'

'I'm looking to invest in something traditional. I like erotic pieces, *shunga* especially.'

He took the tuna from the dish and sucked it from the tips of his chopsticks. The soy stained his lips the colour of chocolate.

His boldness brought some interested glances from his entourage. Naoko could sense he was trying to shame her.

'I will try to find something suited to your taste, Nishi-san.'

'And then you will come to Fukuoka with me to supervise the hanging . . . ?'

He let the question linger and stared at Naoko as if she were included in the price of anything he might buy. His subordinates seemed impressed, but their wives glared at her with undisguised scorn, as if she were deliberately inviting the attention.

'It's just that it's such a long journey. I'm not sure Kimura-san would cover my expenses . . .'

Nishi waved away her objection. 'Money is of no concern. You would be my guest.'

She wanted to tell him she would rather drown herself than spend a second with him being treated as a concubine, no matter what the expense. She looked to Hiro for assistance, but he avoided her eye. She realized he had used her as bait so he could enjoy the patronage of a superior. She felt cheap and hated herself for having to play along. She hated Hiro more because he was usually so quick to assume the role of her protector. Now, it was obviously more beneficial for him to set her up as a sacrifice. Naoko felt exposed and knew she had to tread carefully.

'Why don't you come to the gallery next week?' she said. 'Then we can make all the necessary arrangements and work out the details.'

'You seem nervous, Ms Yamamoto. Do you not think I would be a generous host?'

'I'm sure your hospitality is exemplary, Nishi-san. My concern would be my suitability as a guest.'

He reached into his jacket pocket and took out a leather cigar case and selected a fresh Cohiba. He sucked the end and waited for one of his employees to light it. Heavy clouds of milky smoke puffed out before him. He knew that to press the matter further would make him look weak.

'Very good,' he said. 'Please call my assistant to set up a meeting.'

Naoko stood up and excused herself. The wives eyed her with contempt as she backed politely away from the table. Naoko could tell none of them had ever worked for a living. They reeked of ostentatious spa resorts and country-club fundraisers. She turned to leave.

'Such a beauty,' Nishi said to Hiro in perfect English. 'Magnificent but difficult. Exactly my type. Well done for bringing her.'

Naoko turned back to face him. 'I can speak English,' she said quietly.

He took a drag on his cigar and let the smoke trickle from one corner of his mouth, staring at her with his small, imperious eyes. 'I know,' he said, and waved a hand towards the others at the table. 'But they can't.'

There was a viewing platform at the stern, open to the night. The stars were beginning to shine over the bay as they motored past the island at Odaiba. Naoko looked down from the rail into the black, oily water. It rippled in the breeze like the surface of a shattered mirror. She envied how Hiro had been allowed to reinvent himself, not be a prisoner of his roots. Independence was what she craved and what she was perpetually denied. She felt like a fly trapped in amber. She was alone at the rail, watching the water pass below, when she felt someone come and stand beside her. He cleared his throat to speak.

'*Sumi masen*,' he said, pronouncing each syllable carefully.

She looked up into a pair of blue eyes, wide set and intelligent. She guessed from his manner he was another *gaijin* from the trading floor, trying his luck with every woman that came into view. He had the same startled look as most westerners new to Tokyo, as if the scale of the place was still a source of anxious surprise. He looked at her and gave a hopeful smile.

'*Oshiri o tabetai*,' he said.

41

Without thought, Naoko's hand instinctively swiped out in an arc towards his face. Her palm landed square on his left cheek and he gripped the hand rail to steady himself. From his shocked reaction, she could tell he had no idea what he had just said. Over his shoulder, she could see Nishi sitting with Hiro and the others, but they were too engrossed in conversation to have noticed. She was surprised by her impulsiveness and instantly regretted acting on it. It seemed to belong to a side of herself she had long since tried to abandon.

'I'm sorry,' she said. 'Are you okay?'

He was massaging the skin on his face. A red welt was steadily appearing. 'Do you do that to everyone who asks if you want a drink?' he said.

'Is that what you think you just asked me?'

He looked confused. 'Wasn't it? Those are the only Japanese words I know.'

'Who taught them to you?'

'My friend Hiro. He says he knows you.'

'Then I suggest you find a better teacher.'

He began to realize he had been set up and tried to work out how to save the situation but quickly decided too much damage had been done. She watched him as he turned to walk away. He was tall, with pale skin and broad shoulders, his hair the colour of warm sand. He moved without guile, walking with a certain dignity as he made his way back into the cabin. She felt bad for him, for his misplaced effort. Hiro looked over at the westerner with a knowing glance. The pleasure written on his face was too much for Naoko to bear. She hated to give him the satisfaction.

'Wait,' she called out. 'I owe you an apology. A drink would be great.'

He looked back at her and smiled without triumph. 'I thought I had offended you?'

'You did. So now you can make it up to me.'

'Are you sure you're not going to swing for me again? It looks like you have a hair trigger.'

She looked puzzled. 'What does that mean?'

'Hair trigger? It means you're easily provoked and not afraid to fight back.'

Naoko flashed a shy smile at being so quickly deduced. 'You're not the first person to say that,' she said. 'Maybe you should just speak to me in English. You're safer that way.'

He went to the bar and returned with two glasses of rum punch. There was something about him that was reassuringly calm and solid. A subtle humility that stood out in the room full of overconfident wealth.

'My name is Naoko,' she said.

'Alex Malloy. Nice to meet you.'

'How long have you been in Tokyo, Alex Malloy?'

'About two weeks.'

'You're lucky. It's a sign of good fortune to arrive during *hanami*. The flowers are only out for such a short time.'

'That's what everyone tells me.'

'You're one of Hiro's colleagues?'

Alex shook his head gently. 'No. We're old friends.'

'You don't work in finance?'

'Would it make me more interesting if I did?'

She looked over towards Nishi's table. 'Absolutely not,' she said. 'So why did you decide to come to Tokyo? Had you visited before?'

'No. I just looked on the map for the furthest place from London. I needed to spend some time as far away from home as possible.'

'You weren't scared about moving somewhere so un-familiar?'

'Terrified. That's why I had to do it.'

'I think that's brave.'

'Or stupid. I knew Hiro was here, and I always remembered the stories he used to tell me about Tokyo. I thought I should come and see the city for myself.'

'Sometimes good things only happen to you if you take a

chance. I hope it works out for you. Do you have plans for your time here? Places you'd like to visit?'

'Nowhere in particular,' he said. 'I just want to stay out of trouble.'

They moored in front of the park at Urayasu to watch the blooms on the cherry trees that grow close to the bay, their branches hanging over the stone embankment and touching the water. Gulls wheeled overhead, their eyes trained on the tables below. Other boats with other parties anchored alongside, the guests drinking and talking together on the viewing decks. Naoko was sure they were all saying the same things, trying to find the same business opportunities. *Shamisen* music played gently over their conversations. It all seemed so staged.

The crew brought dishes of skewered shellfish and earthenware jugs of *ginjo-shu* for the passengers. People walked down the gangway to the quayside and stretched out on blankets laid out under the trees. There were lanterns in the branches, casting a yellow glow over the waves that washed against the shore. A gust of wind came up suddenly and the boats rocked together and clouds of pink and white petals flew from the trees like confetti. Cheers went up from the crowd as the blossom floated overhead on the breeze. She could see Hiro flirting with a secretary in the shadows. Alex went to the bar for more punch and left her alone at the stern.

She smelled the pungent scent of Nishi's cigar smoke before she heard him approach. He looked at least three drinks past his limit, fuelled with the false courage of a man who believes his time has come. He slurred as he spoke.

'I think the blossoms are beautiful this year,' he said. 'But you are so much more eye-catching than anything else here tonight.'

She could see he was trying to be charming. 'Thank you, Nishi-san,' she said.

'You must be aware that I can't stop looking at you.'

'I wasn't told that my invitation meant I was on show.'

He reached out a bloated hand and tried to place it on her waist. 'I think you should remember who I am,' he said.

She shook him away. 'I think you should remember your manners.'

'If only you were a little softer, you could be living in a beautiful ocean-front villa.'

Naoko laughed at the presumption. 'Only if I've paid for it myself,' she said.

Nishi heard Alex returning. He turned and looked at him with sour disapproval. 'You can't possibly prefer that *gaijin* to me?' he asked.

'I would prefer a slow death to you.'

His face began to fall in defeat but then he seemed to remember himself. 'I'll make you regret that. Kimura will receive a call from me in the morning.'

Naoko watched him slink unsteadily away. She was certain he wouldn't remember any of this when he woke and, even if he did, there was no chance of him complaining. To tell anyone of her refusal would mean losing face, and she knew bullies like Nishi valued their status as winners above all else.

'Who was that?' Alex asked.

'Just a prospective client,' she said. 'But he can't afford to turn his dreams into reality.'

'He looked pretty upset about it.'

'Too bad for him,' she said.

'Shall we go down to the park to see the cherry blossom?'

Naoko shook her head. 'I've seen it a thousand times before.'

'You're not enjoying yourself?'

'I feel a little seasick, to be honest. I'm not much of a sailor.'

'Do you want to get out of here?' Alex asked.

In the distance, standing out against the darkness of the bay, the giant Ferris wheel at Yokohama turned like a delicate, filigreed web, illuminating the night sky. Beneath it was an amusement park with a roller coaster and a haunted mansion.

She hadn't visited since she was a girl. Naoko looked up at him and smiled conspiratorially. She felt intrigued. He seemed open and unguarded, not like the Japanese men she met, with their rules and constrictions. Their predictable betrayals. She thought of the English childhood of her imagination: governesses in oak-panelled drawing rooms and winter shooting parties. She could sense he was well bred but had somehow fallen on hard times, like an ocean liner abandoned at dock. There was a faint voice somewhere calling danger. Naoko couldn't deny she heard it, even though it was barely louder than a whisper. Her conscience told her to listen, but her instincts smothered it with a sense of reckless adventure.

'I want to go there,' she said, and pointed out across the water. 'I want to go to the fairground and ride the big wheel.'

'I hate heights,' Alex said. 'I can't even stand on a chair.'

Naoko smiled at his honesty. 'I promise I'll look after you.'

'You want to tell Hiro that we're going?'

The voice whispered to her once more. She struggled with herself for a moment, but the warning was futile. Her curiosity was too strong.

'No. There's no need,' she said. 'Let's leave him guessing.'

# 6

THE SUN HAD SOFTENED THE PAVEMENTS UNDERFOOT AND bleached the colour from the leaves. The city slowed to a crawl in the heat. There was a haze of pinkish smog colouring the cloudless sky and the faces of the people walking on the wide boulevard were covered by surgical masks against the pollution.

Alex saw her as she stepped from the escalator and into the ticket hall at Yurakucho station. Naoko stopped to check her make-up in a photo-booth mirror, turning one way then the other, and came out through the barrier with bright, weightless steps. She was wearing a white summer dress printed with purple anemones and soft leather sandals.

'Did you wait long in this heat?' Naoko asked.

'When it's you I'm waiting for I don't really mind.'

The sun was low to the west and cast long evening shadows from the roofs of the tall buildings. The air looked cooler there so they crossed the street and walked in the shade. Bicycles passed by in an orderly procession, ringing their bells as buses roared near. Naoko was hurrying them both along.

'It's only seven thirty,' Alex said. 'We have an hour before the film starts.'

Naoko looked at him apologetically. 'There's been a change of plan. My friend has invited us to join her for dinner at a new restaurant. The place is supposed to be amazing.'

'I'm confused. I thought you didn't want me to meet your friends?'

'It's different with Megumi. She's my assistant at the gallery, so she knows how to keep a secret. You'll like her. She's from a wealthy family. Very old money. Her father owns two office buildings in Nihonbashi. She's bringing her boyfriend, so you'll have to be on your best behaviour.'

'Who's her boyfriend?'

'I don't know. I've never met him. Megumi is still quite young so we don't share everything, I suppose. I don't know how she got a reservation on a Saturday night. I've heard it's very exclusive.'

'You could have warned me,' Alex said, pointing at his chain-store suit and tie. 'I came straight from work.'

'Don't worry. You look fine. Anyway, I think the restaurant has a dress code.'

They turned down a side street of tall wooden houses built along a narrow canal and over a low bridge surfaced with cobbles as smooth as marble. There was a small neighbourhood shrine tucked away, almost hidden from view behind high stone walls. It looked old and untended, overgrown with wreaths of twisted vines. Alex stopped to look, but Naoko walked on. She turned back as he called out for her to wait.

'Let's take a look inside,' he said.

'We're late, Alex. I don't even think it's open. It's practically falling down.'

'Come on. It will only take a few minutes.'

She started to walk on, but stopped. 'You really want to?' she asked.

'This is probably my only chance. I'll never come here again.'

They crossed the street and walked up the steps to the gate at the front of the compound. It was hanging half open, forgotten among the elegant doorways of the surrounding houses. The shrine was a low wooden-framed building with long, carved eaves and a roof of ornately patterned copper. The roof shingles were green and weathered with age. An iron bell hung from the gables by a thick rope and tall cypress trees blocked out the noise of the city. Inside the compound there was only the sound of birds calling back and forth in the high canopy.

They walked to the front of the shrine and stood side by side at the rail.

'You're supposed to choose a blessing from the box,' Naoko said. 'Then you can tie it to the tree over there and wait for it to come true.'

She pointed to an old camphor tree, its branches hung with hundreds of pieces of paper that fluttered in the wind like crisp, white leaves.

'They're called *omikuji*,' she said. 'They bring good fortune, or money, or love. It's sort of a superstition. Only old people believe in them now.'

The *omikuji* were stored in a tall ebony chest. They were filed by type, with a number painted on the front of each drawer in *kanji* characters. Naoko took a small metal can and shook it until a stick dropped out of a hole in the bottom. The stick had a number which corresponded to a drawer. Naoko opened the drawer and took out a rolled-up length of paper. She handed the can to Alex, and he did the same.

'Which one did you get?' she asked.

'No idea,' Alex said. 'I can't read it.' He handed the strip of paper to Naoko.

'It's a blessing for travel,' she said. 'Maybe you'll take a journey soon.'

'What about you? What did you get?'

Naoko unrolled the paper and gave an excited laugh. She showed the scroll to Alex. 'This is for success in business. How lucky is that?'

'I thought this was all superstition?'

Naoko read the fortune again. 'Not if you get the one you want.'

At the camphor tree they folded the papers lengthways and looked for a space to tie them. Naoko pointed to a branch that was bare, and Alex reached up and tied them on with a folded knot. Naoko clapped her hands and clasped them before her face for good luck.

They went back inside the shrine building. A wooden chest stood beyond the rail with an open top and a heap of old five-yen coins lying inside, each with a hole at its centre.

'What's the money for?' Alex asked.

'Now you have to pay for your blessing,' Naoko said. 'Like everything else in life, it doesn't come free.'

'Why a five-yen coin?'

'It's the luckiest one.'

Alex took the change from his pocket and threw in all the five-yen coins he had. 'I don't mind paying extra. I need all the luck I can get,' he said.

'We make our own luck in life, surely?'

'I wish it was that simple. Sometimes everything goes wrong despite your best intentions.'

Naoko turned to him. 'I want you to tell me, Alex. Tell me what went wrong in London. I want to hear you say it.'

'Whatever it is you're looking for, you won't find it by trying to probe me.'

'Why do you have to be so evasive? Why won't you talk to me?'

'I am talking to you. Some things are best forgotten, that's all. Tell me you don't have anything in your past that you'd prefer to forget.'

Naoko breathed out heavily. 'That's not fair. We're talking about you. At least, we're trying to but you're always hiding.'

'Isn't that why we chose each other, Naoko? You're able to hide what you want from me because I'm not Japanese. I don't see all the tiny details about you that they see. All your faults and secrets. And you don't see mine. That's why it works between us.'

'You think so?'

'The past is a dangerous subject,' Alex said. 'Sometimes it's best left alone.'

They walked to the rear of the main building and along a gravel path through a grove of wild rushes to a pond at the corner of the compound walls. A waterfall streamed down a boulder at the far side of the pond and a row of moss-covered stones led across. The waterfall emptied into a bamboo pipe that filled up and tipped into the pond and then swung back and filled again. The pond was full of carp sunning themselves and splashing their tails as they fought for insects. The evening sunlight streamed through the high branches and reflected back from the surface of the water.

'Let's walk across to the waterfall,' Alex said.

Naoko shook her head. 'No way. I'm not dressed for it. Anyway, we need to go now, or we'll be late.'

Alex jumped on to the first stone and turned and held out a hand for her. 'Hold on to me. I won't let you fall.'

Naoko took a step back. 'This is stupid,' she said. 'Why do you want to see a waterfall in a temple garden? What difference does it make to you?'

'I'm curious. It's different for you. You grew up around all of this, but it's all still new to me. I want to understand it.'

She pointed to the bamboo pipe, filling and emptying in an unbroken rhythm. 'It's just a lot of rocks and water. There's nothing to understand.'

'I don't believe that,' Alex said, and jumped across to the next rock. 'What happened to the Republic of Naoko? What happened to doing things your way?'

She turned and started to walk along the pathway and called back over her shoulder. 'Doing things my way doesn't pay the bills.'

The restaurant was called Go. A giant sculpture of crystal and blown glass hung in the lobby, suspended from the ceiling by a single wire. It was positioned over the entrance, all angles and sharp edges, as if designed to unsettle the guests that passed beneath. The host greeted them coolly and examined the reservation list. When he found their names his demeanour changed and he bowed and showed them inside. A waitress led them through the busy dining room to a private table at the back. Megumi and her boyfriend were already there, drinking chilled sake from wooden cups.

She was just in her twenties, Alex guessed. Shorter than Naoko, with narrow shoulders and slender arms. She had thick black hair with a low, straight fringe, and wide eyes. She radiated an obvious air of confidence, despite her youth.

'So I finally get to meet you,' Megumi said. 'Whenever I ask Naoko about her private life she changes the subject. Sometimes I think that maybe she's ashamed.'

'That's not true,' Naoko said. 'I like to keep my mind on my work, that's all.'

'This is Shinichi,' Megumi said, and pointed across the table to her boyfriend. He was tapping a message on his phone, too engrossed in the screen to look up. His hair was dyed blond and spiked with black roots and there was a cigarette tucked behind his ear. He barely responded as he was introduced.

Megumi turned to Alex. 'So how long have you been a teacher?' she asked.

He gave an embarrassed half-smile. 'Is it that obvious?'

She looked him up and down quickly. 'You're far too young to dress like that for fun.'

'It's the language-school uniform. We all have to wear it. The schools only let us take it off when we sleep.' He glanced over at Shinichi, in his T-shirt and ripped black jeans. 'I thought there was a dress code,' he said.

Megumi lowered her voice. 'There is. But his father is part-owner.'

The meal was *kaiseki*-style, with each dish served in antique lacquerware bowls. When the food was laid out it filled the table. There was snow crab and *manju* dumplings, turnip in white miso, fried monkfish with lotus root, and eel served on steamed *komatsuna* greens. Megumi asked for more sake, and the waitress brought another bottle.

'Are you coming to the private view next week?' Megumi asked. She was wearing a pendant shaped like a heron on a platinum chain and she rolled it between her fingers as she spoke. 'I think you'll enjoy it. It's a great chance to see Naoko as she works the room.'

Naoko gave a quick laugh, trying to sound relaxed. 'I think we will both be too busy for guests.'

Alex could see she was becoming flustered. The force of her personality was usually enough to control these situations, but Megumi appeared immune. She seemed to grow more at ease as Naoko became tense.

'Alex has to come,' she said. 'It's the perfect time to introduce him to everyone. I imagine Mr Kimura will be delighted to meet him.'

Naoko shifted her eyes from one to the other. She had the look of someone unused to being backed into a corner. Finally, Megumi reached out a hand and placed it on her arm.

'I'm only teasing,' she said. 'You're always so serious, Naoko. Honestly, Alex, I don't know how you manage to control her.'

The room was busy with conversation, the diners talking across one another like mating birds. Megumi pointed out people around the room, using her indiscretion as the perfect cover. There were artists and collectors. An ex-sumo champion. Girls from the fashion houses drinking white burgundy with their clients' husbands. Megumi seemed to know the personal history behind every face. At the head table was the chairman of the largest airline in Asia. With him was an actress who had been forced to retire now her looks had faded. She was wearing her hair *kepatsu*-style, with a grey silk kimono and thick *obi*, like a widow. She served him dutifully from the dishes in the centre of the table while he watched silently, his hands resting on his belly. Behind them, through the picture window, the summit of Mount Fuji seemed to float above the city like a ghostly projection.

When the waitress began to clear the table, Megumi said she was going to the bathroom and beckoned Naoko to go with her. Once they had gone, Shinichi came alive. He leaned closer to Alex across the table.

'Do you think it's obvious to everyone that they hate each other or just to us?' he asked.

Alex was surprised at the intimate tone. '"Hate" is a strong word. I think they're just competitive.'

Shinichi shook his head doubtfully. 'That's just wishful thinking. Megumi is obsessed with her work. It's all she ever talks about. It's as if nothing else matters.'

Alex shrugged. 'She seems confident enough. I'm sure she can handle it.'

'Don't be fooled by appearances. She cries herself to sleep most nights when she thinks I'm not listening. There's a lot of pressure that comes with ambition. That's probably why I've never had any.'

He took a cigarette from a packet on the table and lit it and offered one to Alex. He looked surprised when Alex refused.

'You'll have to start if you want to fit in with the Japanese. Tokyo is a paradise for smokers.'

'It's the one vice I was never able to pick up,' Alex said. 'I managed most of the others.'

Shinichi looked inquisitive. 'You prefer this?' he asked, and reached into his pocket and took out a small plastic bag and tossed it on to the table. There was a bundle of fresh-looking weed inside.

Alex looked at it lying there in plain view on the table. He felt uneasy and checked around him quickly. The waitress was making her way over to them.

'I'm not sure it's a good idea,' he said.

Shinichi remained still as she approached, unfazed by any

danger. Finally, he reached towards the bag and pushed it closer to Alex. 'Take it,' he said. 'If you have to put up with as much grief as I do, you must need it.'

Naoko came out of the bathroom stall and washed her hands. She checked her make-up in the large mirror and straightened her dress. When the door opened and a middle-aged woman entered, Naoko recognized her instantly. She turned away and took a paper towel from the dispenser and began to pretend to blot her lipstick so the paper obscured her face.

The woman stopped on her way past and turned to look at Naoko's reflection. She smiled without hesitation.

'Excuse me,' she said. 'It's Eriko, isn't it?'

Naoko didn't meet her eye.

'It is you. I'd recognize you anywhere. It's been such a long time.'

Naoko took the paper from her mouth. 'I'm sorry,' she said. 'You must have me mistaken for someone else.'

The woman was in her fifties, wearing a loudly patterned dress that was too tight and heavy chandelier earrings. Her lips and teeth were stained purple with wine.

'I'm sure it's you. Don't you remember me? Hisako Ota? You were one of the best who ever worked for me.'

The woman's voice was loud and indiscreet. There was no way to quieten her down without being complicit, so Naoko stood her ground.

'My name is Naoko Yamamoto,' she said frostily. 'I don't have any idea who you are.'

'But I know who you are. I still have enquiries for you even now.'

Naoko made sure her words were firm and certain. 'I have no idea what you're talking about,' she said.

The smile dropped from the woman's lips. 'Oh, I see. You're too good now, are you?'

She looked like she was going to argue further but Naoko

faced her down. Finally, she turned in disgust and walked into a bathroom stall and closed the door. Megumi came out of the next cubicle, her expression revealing nothing. Naoko knew she had heard it all.

'Who was that?' Megumi asked.

Naoko shook her head blankly. 'I have no idea,' she said.

It was past 1 a.m. when they left the restaurant. The streets were lit in a deep cobalt glare from the electronic hoardings high above. The light had an eerie quality that cast no shadows, bright enough to beat back the night. They waited for taxis and Naoko insisted the others take the first one. She stood with Alex as it pulled away. He could feel her tense and rattled beside him.

'Are you working tomorrow?' he asked.

'Yes. I have to start early.'

'Then I'll take you home.' He looked for a taxi among the traffic.

'Not tonight, Alex,' she said. 'I feel like being on my own, if you don't mind.'

'You didn't have a good time tonight?'

'I'm just tired. Sometimes it's exhausting being with Megumi.'

'I thought you two were friends?'

Naoko's eyes flashed with annoyance. 'We are,' she said.

Alex took the bag from his pocket and held it in a cupped hand. 'Have you seen what Shinichi gave me?'

He was expecting her to be amused, but Naoko's face filled with anger when she realized what it contained.

'Shinichi gave that to you? And you took it?'

'He just threw it on the table. I didn't buy it from him.'

'That's not the point. He's going out with my assistant. Now he'll tell Megumi that you take drugs, and then who knows who she'll tell. Don't you see?'

She started to walk away but Alex grasped her by the arm to hold her back.

'No. I don't see. I didn't ask him for it. Don't you think you're overreacting?'

She pushed his hand away. 'I don't care what you do, Alex. Your choices are your own. But this is a serious matter in Japan. If you get caught you'll be in big trouble and that will reflect badly on me. Shinichi has a rich father to bail him out but you're alone here. I thought you were smarter than this, but it looks like I was wrong. From what I've heard about your past, you should have learned your lesson by now.'

Alex felt his skin tighten as the blood left his face. 'What have you heard about my past?' he asked.

Naoko stared into his eyes with a sneer of indignation. 'I know why you're here, even if you refuse to tell me yourself. There are other ways to find things out. I heard all about what happened to you. All about the drugs and the accident you caused.'

He took a step towards her. 'Who told you this?'

'Who do you think?'

'Hiro.'

'He knows all about you screwing up your life. He's concerned that I don't let you do the same to mine. He knows I don't need any more trauma in my life. I can't stand it.'

'Neither can I.'

'I'm not sure this is working any more. Maybe we're bad for each other.'

'You don't really believe that?'

'How can I trust you when you won't be open with me?'

Alex reached out and took Naoko's arm again. He turned her hand over so her palm was exposed. The half-healed wound was plain to see in the streetlight.

'What about you, Naoko? Are you really being open with me?'

She tried to close her hand but Alex pushed her fingers back and held them. A rush of heat seemed to come to her face and her eyes darkened with anger. She lashed out with her free arm and dragged her nails along the side of his neck, the skin tearing in deep gouges along their path.

He quickly released her arm and held a protective hand to his neck.

'Jesus, Naoko. Calm down. This is all getting out of hand.'

She looked at the raw tracks on his neck and a brief flicker of shame came to her eyes. She quickly forced it away and replaced it with defiance. There was a taxi approaching and Naoko stepped out on to the street and waved it down. The driver stopped and opened the rear door for her.

'I'm going home,' she said. 'I suggest you do the same.'

She climbed in and the door closed. Alex watched as the taxi pulled away into the flow of traffic. He could see her through the rear window as the cab disappeared into the distance. She didn't look back.

There was sweat running down the length of his spine beneath his shirt, and Alex loosened his collar and tried to breathe. He stood for a while watching the world move around him, holding a hand to his neck to stem the bleeding. People on the street gave him a wide berth as they passed so he turned and started walking down towards the crossing, staring at the pavement ahead of him as he went.

He wandered for a while, going nowhere in particular, heading down into the side streets where the air was cooler. When he began to tire, he looked up and saw the old temple, the gates open and the courtyard deserted. He stepped inside and walked along the gravel path and stood beneath the camphor tree. He found the branch where he had tied the *omikuji* and reached up and pulled them down. He untwisted both of the paper strips and looked at the inked blessings in the moonlight. He had no idea which was his and which Naoko's so he tore them both into small pieces and stuffed the scraps into the pocket of his jacket. So much for her belief in superstition, he thought.

It was calm and peaceful in the garden, the water in the pond gently lapping against the rocks. Alex walked to the pond's edge and looked across at the waterfall, the bamboo pipe gently filling and emptying on the far side. He gathered himself up and jumped from rock to rock. The boulders were wet and he took his time, the carp swimming up slowly to examine the intruder above them, rolling over each other lazily and eyeing him in the faint light. Alex took the bag of grass from his pocket and sprinkled the contents over the water. At least the fish could have some fun.

At the waterfall, he stood and listened to the water as it sluiced down, tipping the weighted bamboo pipe and pouring into the pond. It looked as if it had been there, rocking back and forth, for a thousand years. There was a wind chime hanging from the branches of an orange tree above him and it rang out in the breeze. He stood and watched for a while but soon he had to admit that Naoko was right. It was just a lot of rocks and water. None of it made any sense to him at all. The whole country seemed to be a puzzle that no one had the grace to explain. For the first time since he had arrived in Tokyo, Alex had no idea what he was actually doing there.

# 7

ALEX LET THE CLASS LEAVE EARLY. THE STUDENTS HURRIED from the room, handing in their homework assignments as they left. It was the end of the week and even the most diligent ones had been watching the clock for the last ten minutes, eager to get out and start their weekends. They were undergraduates from the university taking an English course to please their parents or gain extra credits from their tutors. Most of them were fluent already so it was an easy class to teach. All they were really interested in was the latest news of western film stars and sports teams. Once they had filed from the room, Alex closed the door behind them and stacked the papers on his desk and began marking.

The Excelsior English School was in an office building on the main highway at the edge of Shinjuku. Alex's classroom was on the tenth floor, with a window that overlooked a billboard advertising pay-day loans. The window shook in its frame when trucks switched gears on the slip road heading north. Classes were scheduled from 11 a.m. until 10 p.m., Monday to Friday, and a half-day on Saturdays. No one wanted to learn English on Sundays.

His phone buzzed in his jacket pocket and he reached for it, hoping it was Naoko. It had been a week since they had gone out to dinner with Megumi and he had heard nothing from her. He knew that this was the night of the private view at the gallery, the big event she had been concentrating on for weeks now, so the odds she would call today were slim. But he clicked on the screen, full of hope, anyway. He gave a rueful smile when he saw Hiro's name appear.

*What are you doing tonight, gaijin? Come and meet me for a drink.*

He tapped out a reply.

*Not tonight. I have to work late.*

There was a desk covered with marking to catch up on. Alex knew he had been neglecting his work since he had argued with Naoko. It had been a week of uncountable nouns and past participles, the classes merging seamlessly with one another. Alex knew he was distracted and his lack of enthusiasm was starting to show. The worst choice he could make now was to be dragged into one of Hiro's late-night adventures.

He wasn't surprised when Hiro messaged him back quickly.

*I haven't seen you for weeks. Just one drink. I'm paying.*

For a moment, he considered giving in and agreeing to meet. Naoko knew he was alone in Tokyo but she still hadn't bothered to call. He had tried to kid himself he didn't care but, deep down, he was still holding out hope. He knew it would look thoughtless to be with Hiro when she called.

He sent his final reply.

*Another time, Hiro. Take care.*

He put his phone away and continued with his marking. Through the walls, he could hear the other teachers stack chairs and switch off lights as they rushed to finish for the week. Alex took his time. At least work was a good way to keep his mind occupied.

There was a knock and the door opened before Alex could give his permission. Craig Wyndham strolled into the room, wearing a chalk-striped suit and a silver tie clip. Everything about him screamed that he'd been in Tokyo too long. He was the longest-serving teacher at the school and the owner had decided this meant he should be their supervisor. The responsibility had gone straight to his head.

'How was your week, Malloy? I saw you were running late again this morning. Anything I can help you with?'

His assistance was offered in the most loaded way possible. Alex knew showing weakness was not going to result in sympathy. It was what Craig had been wishing for for months now. He had always been uneasy around Alex. They were a similar age, older than the other teachers, and Craig seemed to view him as a threat.

'Thank you, but everything's fine,' he said. 'I was just feeling a little under the weather today, that's all.'

'Not too many late nights, I hope. We're paid to keep our minds on our work, after all.'

'I'm down with the sunset and up with the dawn, Craig. You know me.'

Craig sat at the table at the front of the classroom and leaned on his elbows, tapping his fingers together in a show of patient authority.

'I thought I did, Malloy. I've always seen you as one of the most dependable members of my team. But lately, I've seen a change. A loss of focus, shall we say?'

'I've had one bad week. Doesn't my track record count for anything?'

Craig looked at him with a smug expression fixed on his waxy face. He adjusted one of his monogrammed cufflinks. 'We're each only as good as our last lesson.'

Alex struggled to contain himself. He knew that staying silent was the wisest course of action but his contempt felt too poisonous to hold inside.

'Let's be honest. You don't like me, Craig,' he said. 'You never have. And I don't like you either. We come from the same place so I know all about stuffed shirts like you. But who the hell else do you have around here to carry any weight? You'd be lost without me, and you know it.'

'Don't get cocky, Malloy. Everyone is replaceable. You know that.'

Alex stood up. 'If you could live without me, Craig, I'd already be gone. So unless there's anything else, I think I'm done here . . . ?'

Craig Wyndham stared mutely from the classroom chair. Alex picked up his bag and pulled on his raincoat. He was waiting to see if Craig had any of the courage he pretended to possess in front of the younger teachers. He was sure that it was all an act and, as he opened his classroom door and stepped out into the hallway, he wasn't proved wrong.

His chest was tight with adrenaline when he left the building and walked out on to the street. The night-time city was beginning to come alive around him. It felt wrong to go home and be alone with his thoughts but Alex knew Naoko wouldn't take his call. The exhibition at the gallery took precedence over everything. He was aware of that. But there was another way to release the stress.

He took out his phone and tapped out a message.

'You've got that smell on you,' Hiro said.

'What smell?'

'Girl trouble. What happened? Did you fall for one of your students?'

They met in a *ramen* shop next to Ikebukuro station. The place was a long narrow counter with ten seats facing the kitchen and *noren* flags over the door. The room was filled with steam and the rich smell of pork broth. Hiro dipped a *gyoza* into his noodle soup and soaked it before swallowing it in one bite.

'Nothing like that,' Alex said. 'It was just some girl I met in a bar.'

'What did she do? Steal your pay cheque?'

He could sense Hiro feeling him out. It felt strange to have a conversation with such an old friend that skirted the truth so blatantly. He knew he would come clean about Naoko if he was just asked directly, but he wasn't going to offer up the information as a gift. That would just give Hiro a false sense of superiority and he was in no need of any boost in that respect.

'Trust me. My salary isn't worth stealing. It was just an argument about nothing. You know how it happens.'

Hiro pointed at him with his chopsticks. 'I don't know why you put yourself through all this grief, *gaijin*. Is it really worth it? Why come all this way to settle down?'

'Well, it's out of my hands now,' Alex said.

Hiro sucked up long strands of *ramen* from his bowl. 'Luckily for you, I know just what you need.'

Alex felt uneasy at the look in his friend's eye. 'Why can I hear alarm bells ringing?' he asked.

'Just relax,' Hiro said with a smirk. 'Wait until you see what I've got in mind for us tonight.'

The bar was like a dark cocoon. It was decorated with black suede ceilings and crocodile banquettes, all washed in low amber lighting. Two girls were sitting on high stools at the bar drinking cocktails through straws. Both wore short dresses and knee-high boots.

'This is Kyumi, and this is Yuko,' Hiro said. 'They're occasionals.'

'What's an occasional?' Alex asked.

Hiro put his arm around Kyumi's waist. 'Ask them. They don't bite. Well, the small one does a little.'

Alex watched as Yuko took a hand mirror from her bag and checked her make-up. Her skin was deeply tanned and her hair was backcombed and peroxide blonde. She wore pale contact lenses and false eyelashes with beads of mascara at the ends. Her nails were long and pink and heavy with plastic jewels. When she held her glass she had to hold it with both hands.

'Do you like them?' she asked. 'I only had them done today.'

'Of course,' Alex lied. 'I like them very much.'

She held her hands out proudly in the dim bar-room light. 'Where are you from?' she asked.

'London.'

'I've never visited. I've heard that everything looks old and the Underground is dirty.'

Alex thought about it for a moment. 'That's what I like about the place,' he said.

Yuko told him she wanted to open her own beauty salon but she had no way to raise the money. She said it was fine because she wasn't in any particular hurry. Her parents owned a *bento* shop in Shinagawa and worked so hard they were always ill. She was content to do nothing now, while she was young, she said. She was their only daughter so she was going to wait until her parents finally gave in and died. Then she would have all the money she needed.

Their table was ready so they followed the waiter back through the bar to a private cubicle at the end. Both girls walked pigeon-toed, as if they were playing dress-up, their heels scraping along the ground. The waiter slid open the paper door and they left their shoes outside in a row. Hiro was laughing hard at his own jokes and the girls were calling him names and making shows of mock-offence. His hands were all over Kyumi, pulling her close to him, but she didn't resist. Through the plate-glass windows, Alex could see trains running like clockwork toys in the distance, the lights shining haloes on the glass. Yuko sat close to him and placed a hand on his thigh. She had that Japanese quality of looking nineteen and thirty-nine at the same time.

'So what's an occasional?' Alex asked.

Yuko took her time to answer. Finally, she said, 'It's no big deal really. Tokyo is an expensive city and Tokyo girls have expensive tastes. We like the stores in Ginza and Shibuya and it's difficult to afford to shop there so we find boyfriends to help.'

Alex pointed across the table. 'Like Hiro?'

'Yes,' she said. 'And older men or married men who are sick of their wives. Men who can't take their eyes off the young girls they see on the streets every day. We go on dates with them and laugh at their jokes and, in return, they buy us gifts.' Her voice was flat and even, as if she were describing being a Sunday-school teacher.

'Do you sleep with them?' Alex asked.

'Of course we do,' she said. 'Why else would they buy us gifts?'

'So what's the difference between an occasional and an escort?'

'There's a big difference,' she said, slightly indignantly. 'Escorts take cash and have clients, but we have boyfriends and only accept gifts.'

'That seems like a narrow distinction to me,' Alex said.

The table was littered with half-empty glasses and food no one was eating but the girls called on the intercom and ordered more. They excused themselves and left for the bathroom.

Alex turned to Hiro. 'I can't believe you made a date with two hookers.'

'Didn't you listen, *gaijin*?' Hiro said, and started to laugh. 'She's only an occasional hooker.'

'You're unbelievable.'

'Stop worrying. They ordered everything expensive on the menu. Surely we deserve something in return?'

'She's a princess. They both are.'

Hiro tapped a finger against his temple. 'You're letting all this trouble go to your head. Relax and enjoy yourself. I guarantee that, whoever this girl of yours is, she's doing the same right now.'

Alex knew he was right. Maybe it was time for Naoko to feel let down for a change. He looked around the crowded bar.

'Let's get out of here,' he said. 'This place is just a lot of smoke and noise and lights.'

Hiro stood up and finished his drink. 'Exactly like Tokyo, my friend.'

They paid the bill and hailed a cab outside on the street. Hiro took the front seat and gave the driver directions to Shin-Okubo. He looked back at Alex and winked. The girls were sitting close and texting each other, singing along with the J-pop on the radio.

The taxi pulled up outside the love hotel and Alex looked up at the pink neon heart flashing on top of the building. The girls still had their blank, seen-it-all expressions, even inside when they saw the black satin sheets and gold fixtures and the king-sized bed that crowded the room. A giant TV hung on one wall between a pair of ornate mirrors but there were no windows.

'It's like a bad Blaxploitation movie,' Alex said.

Hiro pulled Kyumi down on to the bed and rolled her up in the sheets, and she was giggling and play-fighting drunk. Yuko took Alex by the hand and led him into the bathroom and closed the door. She pushed him down on to the tiles surrounding the sunken bathtub, kissing and holding his face. He reached out and felt the smooth skin of her thighs beneath his palms and moved his hands higher and hitched up her short dress. She pushed her long pink nails through his hair and started to unbutton his shirt.

'Don't move too quickly,' she said. 'Or they'll break.'

Alex closed his eyes and tried to lose himself. He breathed in the smell of her skin and buried his face into the cleft of her breasts. She took his hand and placed it inside her underwear and he caressed her warm, shaved flesh. She began to talk to herself in a low Japanese whisper.

As she talked, Alex heard another voice, softer but more insistent, inside his head. He tried to shake it off but the distraction was overwhelming. Yuko was still speaking quietly to herself and Alex lifted a finger to her lips and she stopped and looked down in confusion.

'What's wrong?' she asked.

'Nothing. It's fine.'

He kissed her stomach and ran his hands on to her backside. He searched for the feeling, but it had disappeared and he knew there was no way to get it back. The harder he tried, the further it slipped away. He opened his eyes and now he was sober, making out with a strange girl in a tacky love-hotel bathroom. He desperately wished he was somewhere else. Yuko felt the mood change and backed away.

'Don't you want to?' she asked.

'I can't,' he said, and began to button his shirt.

'Don't you like me?'

'Of course. But I don't really know you.'

'Are you going to fuck me?'

He looked into her pale, fake eyes. 'No,' he said.

She paused for a moment, thinking, and then asked, 'Do you have a girlfriend?'

'Kind of.'

'What does that mean?'

He stood up and looked around for his jacket. 'It means that it's complicated.'

'It's always complicated,' she said.

'If I do this, I know I'll regret it later.'

She began to straighten her dress. 'Do you love her?'

Alex looked at her for a moment. 'Yes,' he said finally.

'Have you told her?'

'No. Not yet.'

'Why not?'

'She's never given me the chance.'

'Is she *jaja uma*?' Yuko asked.

'What the hell is *jaja uma*? Why do I keep hearing this?'

'It means a wild horse. A horse no man can tame.'

'That certainly sounds like her,' he said.

Yuko looked like she was going to say something else, but then stopped. She opened the door and waited for him to leave.

As the door closed behind him, he could hear her begin to cry softly to herself.

He was waiting for the lift in the corridor when he heard Hiro coming down the hall. He was barefoot, wearing a *yukata* tied loosely at the waist, his hair messed up and lipstick on his neck and cheeks.

'What the fuck are you doing? She's sobbing in there.'

Alex pressed for the lift again. It was stuck on the basement floor. He avoided meeting Hiro's eyes.

'I can't do it,' he said.

'Why not? I've got money, if that's what you're worried about.'

'It's not that.'

'Then what is it?'

'I'm not like you. That's all.'

'And what am I like?'

'If I do this, it will all be over between us.'

Hiro waved a hand between the two of them. 'You mean us?'

Alex shook his head. 'No. Naoko and I.'

There was silence for a time. Alex pressed for the lift again and he heard the mechanism kick into life and the cables begin to rise. He kept pressing the button to try to make it come faster.

'So I was right,' Hiro said. 'You two have been lying to me. How long for?'

'It wasn't my idea, Hiro. I wanted to tell you.'

'How long?' he asked again.

'A while now. About four months.'

'Well, you're not the only one who can keep a secret, Alex. I guessed there was something going on. Ever since the night you met. I knew I should never have introduced you.'

'Why didn't you say anything?'

'I didn't want to do anything to make it real.'

'It is real.'

The lift arrived and the doors opened. Alex stepped inside and pressed for the ground floor. Hiro placed a hand against the frame, his face bright with anger.

'No, it isn't. And it never will be. That's why I brought you here tonight.'

Alex bristled at his friend's words. 'Was that the plan all along? You arranged all of this so I would fuck that girl and you could tell Naoko?'

'It's what's best for both of you.'

'Why did you tell her what happened to me in London?'

'It's my job to protect her.'

'From me?'

'From everyone.'

'Why didn't you ask me first? I would have told you the truth.'

Hiro jabbed a finger at him. 'No, you wouldn't, Alex. You've had months to tell me but you insist on keeping silent.'

'I've never lied to you. The story you told Naoko was all lies.'

'I know you were involved with drugs. Tell me that's not the truth?'

'It's not the whole truth.'

'You killed someone in a car accident, Alex. How can I let Naoko be with a person who would do that and then run away? That's about as low as you can get.'

Alex shook his head gently. 'Believe me, Hiro. It was much worse than that.'

'You'll never be good enough for her. Why don't you just accept it?'

Alex took his friend's hand and pushed it from the metal frame, and the lift doors started to close.

'The thing is, Hiro, you're wrong.'

'Wrong about what?' Hiro asked.

Alex watched him back away into the hall but didn't answer.

The doors sealed shut and the lift began to drop with a shudder. He heard Hiro shout the question again, his voice echoing through the lift shaft as he descended. Wrong about everything, Alex thought.

## 8

*Snow blanketed the streets. Flakes of uneven white, crooked as teeth, were twirling slowly out of the bitter sky. Tracks of deep grey slush ran in parallel on each side of Denmark Hill. Alex drove carefully, two hands on the steering wheel, feeling the delicate traction of the car as he cornered on to Sunset Road and headed down towards the deserted park. London lay before him, veiled in cloud.*

*Lights were strung tastefully in the front window of his parents' house, framing the thick, dark green of the Christmas tree, sparsely hung with ornaments. It was a narrow Victorian terrace with a dark blue door and tall bay windows, the panes dotted with moisture where the warmth had melted the snow before it could take hold. He parked by the garden wall and took the bag of gifts from the boot of the Audi and walked up the garden path and let himself in. The same patterned carpet that had always greeted him still lay in the hall. The same worn bannister and frayed doormat.*

*He heard his father call out to him heartily when he heard the door open.*

*'Is that Dr Malloy?'*

*Alex put his best front on. 'No. It's just me,' he called back.*

*His father came out into the hallway as Alex was hanging his* coat on the stand. 'Alexander,' he said. 'Merry Christmas. How was the traffic?'

He came forward, raising his arms as if for a hug, and then remembered himself. He reached out and shook his son's hand politely.

'Traffic? There wasn't any,' Alex said. 'It's the best day of the year to drive.'

The hallway was bathed in pools of colour from the stained-glass fan light. His father smelt of Scotch and soda and musty woollens. His hands were like ice. He'd been outside, sneaking a taste of whisky in his shed again, Alex guessed. There was no way alcohol would be allowed in the house, not even on Christmas Day.

'Did you bring Patrick with you?' his father asked, looking back over Alex's shoulder as if the door would open at any moment.

'I thought he would already be here,' Alex said.

His father was still gripping his hand. 'I'm sure he won't be long. Come in and say hello to everyone.'

The family were in the living room, waiting for lunch to be served, just as they were every year, gossiping and sharing tales of obscure relatives back home. Great-aunts and cousins were sitting on every available surface, while children ran from room to room. Festive tunes played softly on the radio. Alex greeted everyone in turn and set his gifts under the tree. One flock-papered wall was hung with thirty years of school photographs, massed ranks of boys arranged before the granite colonnade of Saint Dominic's College. His father was on the front row of each, wearing the same corduroy jacket and flannel trousers. He looked like a stern, patrician version of Alex, although there was no way his father would ever admit to the resemblance. The mantelpiece was laden with Communion photos and cards illustrated with Nativity scenes. There was a framed picture of Patrick in his graduation gown, but nothing of Alex, not that it bothered him much. He'd long since ceased to care.

*His mother sat on a high-backed chair in front of the open fire, turning her ankles out towards the flames. She waited for him to bend down to kiss her on each cheek. She was wearing a thick apron over a tweed skirt and a grey cardigan, her skin translucent and tight across the bones of her face. Her lips were pinched beneath the violet lipstick she wore only on this day.*

*'I looked out for you all through the service this morning,' she said. 'I didn't see you.'*

*'I tried to make it.'*

*'Oh, Alex. When was the last time you attended? You or your brother.'*

*'If I want to spend time in a darkened room, there's a perfectly good pub at the end of my road.'*

*She pursed her mouth in distaste. 'One day you'll need the comfort of your faith. You mark my words. Especially after working in that godforsaken Square Mile. I noticed the car you're driving looks very expensive. It must make a hole of its own in the ozone layer.'*

*'It's a company car,' Alex said. 'I didn't get to choose it.'*

*'Bought with the ill-gotten gains of some corporation or other, I suppose.'*

*'I'm a junior tax lawyer, Mother. I don't steal from collection plates.'*

*At least his parents had always been consistent, he thought. Their lifelong belief had been that learning served a purpose only if put to the use of others. They had wanted him to be a barrister or human-rights lawyer, impoverished and noble, not squandering the education they had provided for the tawdry return of a decent salary. A convenient opinion, Alex had always thought, for a career teacher who'd married the headmaster's daughter.*

*Alex had realized young that he had come too late ever to win his parents' approval. Patrick was almost ten years his senior and had exhausted whatever affection they may have had. It had been made clear to him that they hadn't planned for a second son, especially with his mother nearing forty when he arrived, too set in her ways to indulge a child. But that had never really caused Alex concern. He had always understood that the adventure of life lay outside their horizons.*

*They ate lunch at the table in the kitchen, sitting elbow to elbow, jammed in like beggars. His parents made no mention of the empty chair as they ate, despite their obvious disappointment. They had long ago learned to hold their emotions like Spartans.*

*Finally, his mother said, 'Perhaps he's been called into the hospital on an emergency. That would be like Patrick. Thinking of others on a day like today.'*

*At least they had their illusions to fall back on, Alex thought. It was wishful thinking, but it seemed to relieve the tension. By the time his father lit the pudding Patrick still hadn't arrived. Alex excused himself as the table was being cleared and went out to the car. He knew the truth of his brother's absence was far from selfless.*

*Patrick's flat was on the third floor of a terrace near Battersea Park. Fold-away buggies were propped in the hall and piles of unopened mail were sorted neatly on the stairs. Alex rang the buzzer and stood back from the porch to look up. The windows were dark. Clouds had formed into thick banks overhead. The snow was sheeting down now, coming in heavy gusts, almost sideways on the wind. Alex had to shield his eyes from the flurries of wet, stinging flakes. He rang again and again until he knew Patrick would have to acknowledge him. Finally, the lock clicked open and Alex pushed his way inside and climbed the flight of narrow stairs.*

*The flat was almost bare. There were indentations in the carpet where the furniture had recently stood. The rosewood sideboard his parents had given as a wedding present was gone and bright patches of paintwork stood out on the walls where pictures had been removed. He called his brother's name and his voice echoed back from the bare surfaces.*

75

*There was no answer, so he went from room to empty room until he found Patrick in the kitchen, sitting alone on the only remaining chair.*

'Hi, Alex,' *he said.* 'Make yourself at home.'

*He was wearing a dress shirt unbuttoned at the collar with the sleeves rolled up to the elbows, his overcoat and scarf draped over his shoulders like a pensioner. His hand was trembling slightly as he ran it through his thinning hair.*

'Everyone missed you at lunch,' *Alex said.*

'I wanted to come. I really did. Every time I tried to leave the house I just couldn't face it. What did you have?'

'Goose. As always.'

'Was it dry?'

'As sawdust.'

'At least some things don't change.'

*Alex looked around at the empty room.* 'What happened here?'

'I had to sell some things. I was short of money.'

'What about Monica?'

'She left. I came home last week and found her gone. She said she would give me until the New Year to sort myself out but she must have decided to bail early.'

'Where did she go?'

'I don't know. She won't answer my calls. But she left a note, which was nice.'

*He tried to laugh but lacked the energy. Sweat was beading on his forehead, despite the cold.*

'Jesus. You look terrible,' *Alex said.* 'Do you need to go to a hospital?'

*His brother shook his head weakly.* 'I'm a doctor, Alex. What are they going to tell me that I don't know already?'

'That you're killing yourself.'

'I don't need a hospital. I need money.'

*Alex shook his head firmly.* 'No,' *he said.* 'I'm not helping you to get drugs.'

*Patrick looked up with wide, pleading eyes. His mind seemed to be working at a furious speed. 'I'm not going to get high. I just need something to stop me feeling so sick. You can ration it out to me bit by bit. I haven't got anywhere else to turn.'*

*'No way.'*

*'I'm asking for your help.'*

*Alex hesitated. He could sense the danger in giving his brother what he wanted but it was sickening to see him in such a raw state.*

*'Even if I say yes, where can you get anything on Christmas Day?'*

*'I know someone who'll deliver.'*

*'And then what happens? You can't carry on like this.'*

*'Just help me now, Alex. Then I'll go wherever you want. I promise you.'*

*'How much money do you need?'*

*Patrick's face flushed with eagerness, as if he could already taste it. 'How much have you got?'*

*Alex thought it over. 'I'm really not sure about this,' he said.*

*'I'd do it for you,' Patrick pleaded. 'You know I would.'*

*They waited in the kitchen, Patrick looking weary with anticipation, checking out of the window each time he heard a car pass by. It had started with prescription pills. Just a few Valium to help smooth out the pressures on the ward, the long night shifts and jet-lagged days. The endless procession of sickness and death. Soon the pills grew stronger and the doses higher, until he discovered pethidine. Then everything began to go very wrong. He had always been the responsible older brother, free from parental scrutiny when they were growing up because of his age and academic achievements. The education their parents had provided hadn't included the survival instincts required to avoid his current predicament. Alex knew how devastating it would be for them to see their elder son so broken down. But then he also knew they weren't entirely blameless either. Even as a child, Patrick had borne the weight of the family's ambitions. It was always obvious that him becoming a doctor had been their parents' wish. They had pushed him into medicine as a way to show that their prejudices had always been correct. But Patrick had never been cut out for it. It had seeped into him over the years by a slow osmosis, like water eroding stone. At least it had made the family happy. It certainly hadn't done any good for him.*

*When the buzzer sounded, Patrick hurried to the entryphone and clicked the front door open and waited. He tried to act composed but couldn't contain his excitement. The unhurried pace of the feet creaking on the wooden staircase seemed excruciating.*

*He came into the flat as if it belonged to him. It wasn't far from the truth, Alex thought. He had probably taken enough of Patrick's money in the last year to put a down payment on the place. He wore a heavy puffa jacket buttoned under his chin and white trainers fresh from the box. He looked young and healthy, as if he had never had any inclination to sample the product he sold. He stopped when he saw Alex and flashed him a dark look.*

*'Who the fuck is this?' he asked Patrick.*

*'No one you need to worry about.'*

*'You didn't tell me you had company when you called.'*

*'He's my accountant,' Patrick said. 'I'm putting him in charge of all of my future transactions.'*

*'Very funny. Where's the cash?'*

*Alex stepped forward and reached into his coat pocket. 'That's fifty pounds,' he said, fanning out the notes before him. 'How much does that buy?'*

*'It's in twenty-pound bags.'*

*'So we'll take three,' Alex said.*

*'Not much of an accountant, are you?'*

*'Surely there's a discount for weight?'*

*He shook his head. 'Three bags is a long way from weight.'*

*Alex nodded towards his brother. 'Come on. Look at him. He must have paid all your bills for the last year.'*

*'It's twenty pounds a bag,' he said, taking his time to enunciate clearly.*

*Alex took out his wallet and added a ten-pound note to the money in his hand.*

*'There's no more after this. Do you understand? I want you to stop selling to my brother. If he calls you, ignore him. Or I will become someone you will need to worry about.'*

*He looked Alex up and down for a moment, sizing him up to decide if there was any disrespect he needed to challenge. He could see Alex was serious but not threatening. He took the money and handed over three small bags of powder.*

*'Fine,' he said. 'He's your problem now.'*

*When he was gone, Patrick settled back into his chair. It seemed to take a long time. His eyes were fixed on Alex's hand.*

*'Here's what we're going to do,' Alex said. 'I'll give you enough to straighten you out for now but I'm keeping the rest with me. And you're going to hand over the needles and other paraphernalia. That way, you can only get more when I think you need it. When you're done, we'll go over and see the family for an hour or two. We'll tell them you've been finding a cure for cancer or something. Then I'm taking you home with me so I can keep an eye on you until we can find someplace where you can get some help. No arguments.'*

*Patrick nodded eagerly, barely listening. 'Okay. Whatever you want.'*

*Alex tapped out a fraction of the powder from one bag on to a scrap of paper. He folded the paper and handed it to Patrick and bundled the bags inside the pocket of his overcoat. He waited as his brother went into the bathroom and locked the door. He had no desire to see how a doctor administered his own dosage.*

\*

*The roads were deserted as they drove past the common, the lane markings obscured by a blanket of snow. Alex followed the deep tyre tracks leading down the long hill back to his parents' house. They would be squeezed in together in the small living room now, he thought, watching a black and white film or arguing over a board game.*

*'I'm sorry about this,' Patrick said. 'I wasn't sure if I could get to the New Year without killing myself.'*

*He was wrapped up in his coat and scarf, even though the heater was turned up. He had lost his sickly pall and his eyes had regained some vitality.*

*'I don't want your apologies,' Alex said. 'I'm never doing this again. I won't help you kill yourself in small steps just to stop you doing it in one go. This has to be the end, Patrick. You have to get help now.'*

*'I know. I wish I never got started. Seven years of medical school should have taught me something.'*

*'As soon as we find a place for you at rehab, you're going. Just like we agreed.'*

*Patrick held up his hands, as if in mock-surrender. 'I'll go. I'll go.'*

*There was something insincere in his tone that was jarring. 'You promised me,' Alex said. 'That's the only reason I helped you.'*

*'It's not that simple. I'm a doctor, Alex. I'll get struck off.'*

*'That doesn't matter. I want you as a live brother, not a dead doctor.'*

*Patrick turned in the passenger seat to face Alex. 'But what about Mum and Dad? It'll kill them if they find out. It's funny. Everyone would have predicted it would be you in my place. Maybe that's why they were so hard on you. Trying to save you from a fate they always assumed I was never in any danger from.'*

*'I need you to promise me you'll end this.'*

'I want to,' Patrick said, smiling slowly to himself. 'I'm just not sure I can any more.'

Alex watched him, his arms clutched to his chest and his nose running. 'If you don't promise me now,' he said, 'I'm stopping the car and . . .'

He noticed Patrick's expression harden as something caught his eye. An incredible noise. The side of the Audi caved inwards on impact as the tow truck hit it at a right angle, the chassis folding in on itself like a hinge closing. Metal screeched against metal and the windows shattered into thousands of tiny granules that sprayed over the interior. The air seemed to disappear, sucked from lungs into a vacuum like a light bulb imploding. The crushing force of the air bags deploying. Rolling. Snow. Blood and darkness. Silence.

# 9

THE KIMURA GALLERY WAS LIT UP BY FLOODLIGHTS THAT cast a glow across the square. The façade was white marble, with plate-glass windows either side of a set of brass-framed double doors. The entrance was covered by a striped awning that extended out to the kerb with a uniformed doorman welcoming guests. Alex walked up to the main window and cupped a hand against the glass. Inside, immaculately groomed people stood talking in groups while silent waitresses moved among them with trays of drinks and canapés. Alex scanned the room from face to face until he found Naoko.

She was standing in one corner beneath an oversized action painting, a group of men in evening wear gathered around her. She was wearing an antique lace dress with a chrysanthemum pattern, her hair curled and lying across her shoulders. She looked serious and intent as she listened to the older man who was addressing the group, his hands gesticulating as he talked. She was holding a glass of champagne, clutching it close to her chest like a shield. When the older man finished his speech, the group began to laugh enthusiastically. Naoko remained still, with her legs crossed elegantly beneath her, her body taut, as if poised to move. She seemed smaller somehow, her usual presence reduced, as if diminished by her surroundings.

Alex approached the doorman standing behind the velvet rope in the entranceway. He held out a hand for Alex's invitation.

'I don't have one,' Alex said.

He shook his head. 'Then you can't come in. This is a private event, for invited guests only.'

'I'm here to see Naoko Yamamoto. She works here. I can see her inside.'

The doorman stood his ground. He kept the velvet cordon in place and politely moved Alex aside to allow the next set of guests to enter. Alex was trying to think of an alternative when he felt a tap on his shoulder and turned around. It was Megumi.

She gave him a quizzical stare. 'I thought you weren't coming?' she said.

'I wasn't going to, but then I changed my mind. I just want to see Naoko.'

Megumi raised an eyebrow sceptically. 'She doesn't know you're here, does she?'

'Please, Megumi,' he said, trying not to sound desperate. 'I just want to talk to her for a few minutes. That's all.'

'She's working, Alex. If you do anything to upset her, it will be bad for me.'

'I came all this way because I have something important to tell her. It will only take a few minutes, then I'll go.'

Megumi thought it over for a moment. 'Just don't tell her it was me,' she said.

The gallery was decorated with vases of bougainvillea and white lilies. The guests stood before the artwork, talking in hushed tones and milling from group to group. There was a high mezzanine above the main gallery, where soft white spotlights shone down, carefully picking out the smaller pieces and casting out shadows from the corners.

Alex looked for Naoko in the crowd. He could see the group

she had been standing with but she was no longer there. He peered around the room but she had disappeared among the strange faces. As he searched, he felt a moment of indecision as his recklessness started to desert him. He suddenly wished he hadn't come. The air conditioning chilled his skin as his resolve drained away. He turned to leave.

He saw her across the room, standing beside a plinth bearing a crystal-encrusted *maneki-neko*. She was lifting a champagne glass to her lips as a Japanese man touched a hand to her hair and drew his fingers gently down and rested them on her shoulder. She smiled softly at him as he talked.

Alex approached without thinking.

She saw him as he pushed his way through the gathering. Her eyes widened at the realization of his presence and her face seemed to show a thousand different emotions. She shrugged the man's hand away quickly.

'Alex,' she said without surprise. 'How nice to see you.'

The man inched away and surrendered his space. Alex ignored him.

'I need to speak to you.'

'Can't it wait . . . ?'

'I only want five minutes of your time. But I can see why you don't want me here.'

Naoko was struggling to keep her professional demeanour. She glanced quickly to her side. 'This is Masakazu Sato,' she said. 'He's one of the artists exhibiting tonight. Masakazu, this is Alex Malloy. Alex is my English teacher.'

Masakazu's eyes darted around inquisitively. He could sense the charged atmosphere and seemed intrigued. He extended a hand and Alex took it automatically, Naoko's denial of him stinging to the core.

'What do you think of the show?' Masakazu asked.

The change in subject left Alex flustered. 'I . . . I haven't seen anything yet,' he said. 'I've only just arrived.'

'And you haven't even got a drink. Please, allow me.'

Masakazu disappeared into the next room, where a bar had been set up on a table draped with heavy white linen. Naoko's calm was replaced with quiet fury now they were alone.

'What the fuck are you doing?' she said. 'Are you high?'

She was struggling to contain her emotions and the strength of her words. People standing close by glanced towards them curiously.

'What was he doing with his hands on you?'

Naoko shook her head in pity. 'He doesn't like girls, Alex.'

All of his certainty had vanished and he felt washed up and stranded. He wanted to tell her about Hiro, that what he had told her was all wrong. He wanted to say that he was sorry, that this was a mistake, but his pride blocked any chance of an apology. He couldn't back down now.

He looked at her defiantly. 'You say I never tell you anything – well, here I am.'

Naoko was incredulous. 'Now?'

'Why not?'

'Does it look like I have time to talk?'

'You had time to throw accusations at me the last time I saw you.'

'Don't mess this up for me, Alex.'

'Fine,' he said. 'I'm leaving.'

Naoko held his arm as he turned to walk away. 'You can't go now,' she said through gritted teeth. 'It will look like there was a problem and that will only make it worse.'

Masakazu was returning, his face lit up as if he had finally found something to amuse himself with. Megumi was walking beside him. Naoko gave a false laugh as they appeared.

He handed Alex a glass of champagne. 'I know Naoko is very captivating,' Masakazu said, 'but I hope you'll find a moment to look at some of the beautiful work in this amazing show. She's spent months organizing it.'

'I'd love to,' Alex said. 'It looks very interesting, although I have to admit I'm no expert.'

'You'll have to see Masakazu's new installation upstairs,' Naoko interrupted. She gestured towards her assistant. 'Megumi will take you. I think you'll be very moved by it. Come back and find us when it's over.'

Megumi led him up a spiral staircase and through a blackout curtain into a darkened room. There was a Super 8 projector playing from the back of the room and Alex could see the silhouettes of heads picked out in the darkness. The sound of *taiko* drums echoed from the speakers.

The screen showed a static camera shot of a teenage girl in a cheap hotel room, the film scratched and grainy. The girl had short dark hair and dry lips and her eyes were glassy and pinned. She was wearing a cut-off T-shirt and denim shorts. The furniture in the room looked worn and dirty and frayed curtains were pulled across the window, the daylight bright around its edges. There were several middle-aged Japanese men standing around, wearing cheap shirts and nylon slacks, some holding video cameras and others taking notes. The girl moved towards the camera and unbuttoned her shorts and stepped out of them and pulled the T-shirt over her head. She stood naked, listening to some inaudible off-screen instructions before she bent down and the camera followed her. On the greasy hotel carpet there was a kind of plastic garment bag with a hose attached. The girl wiped the hair from her eyes and stepped into the opening and crouched as the bag was pulled over her head and the zipper fastened. The air began to drain from the bag as it was pumped out through the hose, the plastic beginning to pucker around her frame. She remained crouched as it sealed tightly, the plastic forming over the contours of her body. The men in the room stood over her and she looked up at them through the frosted material as the hose was removed. The camera adjusted as she sucked the plastic over her mouth and looked down the barrel of the lens.

Alex looked at Megumi in the darkness. He cleared his throat to speak but failed to find any words.

Megumi glanced up at him and squeezed his arm protectively.

The girl didn't struggle. She just blinked rapidly as she stared out in close-up from the screen.

Everyone in the gallery stood, watching silently. Someone walked in front of the camera and it refocused, picking out the cigarette burns on the hotel carpet. Alex felt Megumi's fingers tighten around his arm. The *taiko* drums beat on.

The thick plastic had soon stopped moving over the girl's mouth. Small beads of moisture had formed on the inside of the bag as her breath condensed. Her eyes began to roll slowly back into her head.

No one in the hotel room moved. The feet surrounding the girl's cocooned body remained still. The sound of the film reeling through the projector rattled away, counting out the time in a sinister rhythm. Then a hand dipped into the frame and tugged at the zip and the bag opened and ballooned as it filled with air. The girl spilled out on to the floor listlessly. Her face was flushed and her mouth wide open as she sucked down oxygen. The men stood above her and continued to film as she heaved deeply and stared up at the camera. She tried to smile as the film tailed out to blackness.

The house lights came up and a soft peal of applause passed through the audience.

'I thought this night couldn't get any weirder,' Alex said.

'You didn't like it?'

'Like it? I think that was the most disturbing thing I've ever seen.'

Megumi shrugged. 'Masakazu has already sold it to a gallery in Berlin.'

'Who was the girl?'

'She's here somewhere,' Megumi said, glancing around the room. 'She arranges these events every weekend. Apparently, they're very lucrative.'

'You mean she does this for money?'

Megumi looked puzzled. 'Why else would she do it?'

'Sometimes I don't think I understand a thing,' Alex said.

'About this film?'

'About this country.'

They left the screening room and stood out on the mezzanine, looking down over the railing to the viewing space below. The voices of the crowd carried up through the ductwork and merged into one dull noise. A waitress passed and Megumi took two glasses of champagne. Alex placed his empty glass on the tray as she left. He motioned down at the gathering below.

'Do you know all of these people?'

'Some of them. They all look the same after a while. Rich people tend to blend into each other seamlessly.'

'Do they all spend money?'

'No. Just a few. Mostly they're here to watch each other and pretend to enjoy artwork they have absolutely no understanding of.'

'You sound like you don't enjoy this job very much.'

Megumi stood up from the balcony railing and looked at him squarely. 'Enjoyment isn't the point. Once you've started something, it's important to be successful. Otherwise, how could you live with yourself?'

Alex sipped his champagne. 'Is that why you and Naoko are so competitive with each other?'

Megumi looked momentarily flustered. 'Is it that noticeable?' she asked.

'I imagine she's a hard act to follow. She's very dedicated.'

'Do you have any idea what it's like working with her?' Megumi said, becoming animated. 'Can you imagine having to walk in her shadow and act dumb while she gets all the attention? Sometimes I feel like the girl in that film.'

'You're still young. You have lots of time yet.'

'Maybe I don't need that much time. There are things I've found out about her that I'm sure Naoko doesn't want anyone to know. But it's going to come out. I'll make sure of that. Then

everyone will finally see that she doesn't belong here. In the meantime, I always have you to help me.'

'I'm not sure what you're saying?'

'I've thought about this a lot,' Megumi said. 'And the only way for me to progress in my career is for something bad to happen to Naoko.'

Alex was confused. 'Something bad? Like what?'

'Like this.'

Megumi stepped forward and pressed her hand to Alex's chest. She slipped her fingers inside the buttons of his shirt and dug her nails into his skin. He instinctively grabbed her wrist and pulled her arm away, twisting it as he took a step backwards to remove himself. Megumi cried out and sank down as her knees buckled. She dropped her champagne glass and it shattered on the wooden floor below.

The room fell silent. Every face in the gallery turned towards them.

Alex was still standing above her, gripping her wrist. He released it and she held it against her body, clutching it as if she had been badly hurt. Two security guards began to make their way up the spiral staircase but Megumi waved them away.

She didn't look up but very deliberately said, 'I think you had better go.'

Alex was sure he could see the trace of a smile on her lips. He looked down at the shocked expressions in the crowd below.

'Don't worry,' he said. 'I'm leaving.'

# 10

HIS INSTINCTS TOLD HIM TO GET AS FAR AWAY AS POSSIBLE, SO
Alex started walking over the junctions and crossings of Ebisu,
the streets dark and humid and empty. There was no logic
to the sequence of events, no matter how many times he tried to
replay them in his head. He stopped under a streetlight and
tried to call Naoko but there was no answer. He tried once
more and again it went straight to voicemail. He wondered what
Megumi was telling her now, what version of events she was
fabricating that worked to her favour. He couldn't believe he'd
been so dumb.

There was no way he could leave this unresolved so he looked
for a taxi and told the driver to go to Mejiro. He would wait for
Naoko there, he thought, and then explain everything once she
came home.

When he arrived at her building, the lights were off in most
of the windows and the lobby was deserted. He took the lift up
to the twelfth floor and checked the landing was clear before he
approached her front door. He felt along the top of the door
frame until he found the spare key Naoko kept there and let
himself in.

He called her name from the entranceway but there was no
answer. He took off his shoes and walked into the living room.

Everything looked different without her there. Her clothes were spread across the furniture in the bedroom where she had tried on different outfits for the party and her make-up was scattered over the coffee table. He wondered if she was still at the gallery, if she was looking for him. There were footsteps out in the corridor and Alex froze and waited, standing stock-still in the dark. The sound receded and a door opened and closed at the end of the landing and then the silence returned. His heart was racing and he tried to force himself to relax. It was nearly 3 a.m. so Naoko had to be home soon.

He walked into the bedroom and took off his jacket and shirt and lay down on the bed in his jeans. He looked up at the ceiling. He could feel his eyes grow heavy as the adrenaline ebbed away and left him hollow and empty. He tried to force himself to stay awake. He could hear the crows outside on the waste ground shrieking and fighting for food. It was still dark when he woke.

Naoko was sitting above him, across his chest, her knees digging hard into his ribs. He saw the mascara on her cheeks, like black war paint. She was still wearing the dress with the chrysanthemum pattern, hitched up, and her hair was scraped back from her face. He was still half asleep and he found his hands were resting on her thighs and he felt the flesh beneath his palms. He smiled at her but she didn't smile back. She looked down at him with dark, wet eyes and pressed something sharp into the softness of his neck below his jaw. He saw the muscles in her shoulders tighten and he looked down and saw the wooden handle of the knife held firmly in her grip.

'It's just me,' he said. 'I didn't steal anything.'

He tried to sit up but she forced him back with the angle of the blade. He coughed to clear his throat and felt the metal jagging against the stubble on his neck.

'Everyone saw what you did,' Naoko said.

'It wasn't how it looked.'

'Megumi showed me the bruises on her wrist. You did it deliberately, didn't you? To get back at me.'

Alex tried to raise his hands but she pressed the knife harder.

'She's lying,' he said. 'I didn't touch her. I swear.'

'The whole gallery saw you.'

'Nothing happened. I'm stupid, but not that stupid.'

'What do you mean?'

'You're worth a thousand of her, Naoko.'

He looked at her, the black make-up streaked down her face, and saw the flicker in her eye as her perspective changed. He could feel his heart beating and felt hers in time through his fingertips. The muscles and tendons were wire-tight beneath her skin. She gripped the knife with her arms extended and pushed harder into his neck.

'If you're good to me, I will give you one hundred per cent good in return. But if you're bad, I will give you one thousand per cent bad. Believe me.'

'I would never do anything to hurt you, Naoko.'

'You must think I'm a fool.'

'That's not true.'

Naoko leaned further on to the knife, edging it a fraction deeper. The tip of the blade seemed desperate to puncture the skin.

'Just tell me you weren't high when you came to the gallery tonight.'

'Of course not.'

'I can't believe I even have to ask you that.'

'You don't.'

'You humiliated me,' she said. 'In the one place I told you was important to me.'

'It wasn't like that, Naoko.'

'You can fuck up all you want to in your world. I just don't want you to fuck up mine. You have no idea of the sacrifices I had to make to get here.'

He felt the knife dig into the softness of his throat. For a moment he thought she was going to do it but she breathed out and released the pressure from the blade. Her shoulders slumped wearily as she pulled the knife away from his neck and let it hang beside her.

'I know whatever you had to do, it hasn't made you happy,' he said.

'Who in life ever gets to be happy?'

'Everyone who really wants to.'

'You believe that?'

'Good things only happen if you try.'

'And bad things happen if you try too hard.'

'You know I didn't touch Megumi, don't you? You know I would never do something like that to you.'

'But why would she lie? What does Megumi have to gain by making a crazy scene?'

'I don't know,' Alex said. 'We were chatting and she was acting normally. Then I started talking about you and she just lost it. She said she had found out something that you didn't want anyone to know. She was talking like a madwoman.'

Naoko looked down at him with a suspicious scowl. The aspect of her face accentuated the Asiatic cast of her eyes.

'What had she found out?'

Alex held his hands up in a gesture of surrender. 'She didn't tell me, Naoko. And I didn't have time to ask.'

'But what did she say? What were her exact words?'

'I don't remember. I couldn't really follow what she was saying.'

'Try to remember!' she shouted frantically.

Alex tried to sit up but a look of panic overtook Naoko and she pressed him back down on to the bed. She swung the knife towards him and Alex saw the metal blade flash close before his eyes as she held it to one side of his face. The sensation of the sharp edge on his skin revolted him and he pushed her away, bolting upright as she fell backwards, her skull cracking against something dense, a chair or table, as she fell. The knife skittered off across the floor.

Then he felt the burn across the crest of his cheekbone where the skin was tightest, the coldness of the exposed nerve endings and the blood as it pulsed down his face and neck. He held his hand to the wound and it slicked along his fingers, his palm tight against his face. He couldn't stop it coming. He stepped over her and walked into the bathroom and stood before the mirror.

'You're crazy,' he said. 'I thought you were bluffing.'

She looked up at him from the floor, her hair raked out and blood smeared down the lace of her dress.

'What's bluffing?' she said.

The blood ran down his forearm and dripped from his elbow on to the floor. There was a slice across his face from cheek to ear, the wound open like a mouth about to speak. Alex felt as though he could stand there fascinated for ever. He forced himself to turn away.

'I can't believe you did it.'

'It was an accident, Alex. You moved too quickly.'

'I'm leaving,' he said, and started to look for his shirt.

'Where will you go?'

'I don't know. Anywhere. Somewhere less dangerous than here.'

Naoko stood and moved towards him and he could see the seriousness of the situation register on her face.

'You can't go,' she said. 'There's been too much noise already. Stay and I'll take care of you.'

He sneered at her. 'I think you've done enough for one night.'

Naoko picked up the shirt and jacket he was looking for and opened the window and tossed them outside. Alex watched them flutter down to the waste ground twelve storeys below. She ran to the entranceway and grabbed his shoes and threw them out as well.

'There,' she said calmly. 'Now you have to stay.'

Alex turned and swept an arm over her dresser and cast off the mirror and her make-up and then picked up an ashtray from the coffee table and threw it against the framed print on the wall. The glass shattered in a spray of jagged fragments that showered down on to the wooden floor.

He stood with his fists clenched white-knuckle tight, his body shaking with rage. Naoko came towards him and tried to reach up and take his face in her hands. He gripped her by the wrist and held her scarred palm open.

'Maybe this is the big secret Megumi has discovered about you?' Alex shouted and pushed her aside. He walked to the bookcase on the opposite side of the room, his footsteps reverberating through the structure of the building. He picked up the landscape photograph in its heavy frame and tore the wooden back away. The document was inside, folded carefully, exactly as it had been before. He took it from its hiding place and unfolded it. It was meaningless to him.

'Or maybe this is it? I don't know. It seems that you have just as many secrets as everyone else.'

'Please give it to me,' Naoko said, her eyes washed with tears.

'Tell me what it is.'

'It's nothing.'

'Tell me.'

She hesitated. 'It's a birth certificate,' she said. 'You can destroy anything else here but not that. It's all I have.'

Alex held it up before her in both hands. He tried to find the resolve to tear it in two, anything to hurt her in return, but he couldn't do it. He threw it to the floor and watched as she fell to her knees to retrieve it.

The blood was coursing down the side of his face and neck and he went into the kitchen and pressed a towel to the wound. He looked out of the spyhole in the entranceway. Lights were coming on in the neighbouring apartments and doors were already cracked open as people looked out to find the source of the commotion. He unhooked the security chain and was about to turn the lock. Naoko ran in short, quick steps and held him back. The tears had given her eyes a burning clarity.

'Stay, Alex. Please. You can't go out like that. Let me clean you up. I know what you need.'

She touched her fingers to his face where the blood was still streaming down from his cheek and on to his neck and chest. She tried to clean it away but only smeared it on her hands and on to the scars on his shoulders and arms. He looked down at the fresh blood flowing over old wounds.

'You don't know anything about me,' he said.

He hesitated for a moment, then turned and unlocked the door. Faces peered from the doorways as he walked along the landing. He opened the fire-escape door and took the steps down twelve flights to the lobby. Then he was out of the building, barefoot and shirtless in the Tokyo dawn.

Rain was cascading down the gutters and into the storm drains. Alex walked past rows of shuttered shopfronts and stopped by the entrance to the park. He was dazed and nauseous and needed to think. The gates were locked so he hoisted himself up on to the surrounding wall and climbed over.

There was a wooden bench beside the baseball diamond and he sat there and tried to work out how it had started. It was too much to compute. The vagrants who lived near the bandstand came out of their blue plastic shelters to see who the stranger was at that hour. They stood around him and stared at the cut on his cheek and the blood splattered down his face and made guesses among themselves without asking for an explanation. They offered him a drink from the gallon bottle of *sake* they shared and Alex accepted. The *sake* was tepid and stale but it seemed impossible to refuse something from a group of homeless men.

One of them stepped forward and pointed to the cut on his

face and the scars on his back in a gesture to connect the two.

'*Onagi mono, desu ka?*' he asked.

'No,' Alex said. 'Not the same thing at all.'

'You want medicine?'

Alex shook his head. He thought about the chain of events that had brought him there. 'No,' he said. 'The last thing I want is more medicine.'

The man didn't understand. He reached into his backpack and handed Alex an old, stained T-shirt. Alex thanked him and slipped it on.

The sound of a siren blared out from the road beyond the park and the blue flash of emergency lights strobed through the dark branches. The homeless men froze momentarily, waiting to see if it was coming nearer. The electronic squeal built to a piercing crescendo and then started to recede as it drove past the park gates and down towards the highway. The vagrants were relieved and began to drift back up towards the cover of their shacks, but Alex realized what it meant. He thought of Naoko, still in her room with the knife, and began to feel his panic mount. He knew he would never forgive himself if he left her alone and she did something really stupid. He began to sprint back to the entrance and climbed the wall and ran back along the rain-drenched road towards her building. When he turned the corner, he could see the police car parked at the foot of the steps outside the main doors, the lights still flashing, with no one inside. He ran through the lobby and took the stairs to her floor three at a time.

Naoko bent down and reached under the dresser. The blade of the knife was still smeared in blood and the imprint of her fingers were marked out in relief on the wooden handle. She pulled it out and walked over to the bed, stepping carefully over the broken glass and upended furniture. Books and clothes lay in piles, as if a strong wind had blown them into drifts at the edges of the room.

She lay on the bed, her chest still heaving, and tried to calm herself. She closed her eyes and pushed her face into the pillow but she could smell the warm scent where he had been sleeping. She sat up and pulled the pillow from the case and threw it across the room.

A sound of voices out in the corridor and footsteps approaching. A frenzy of yelping and scratching from her neighbour's dog as it tried to ward off strangers. Her buzzer sounded and Naoko got up and went to the entranceway. She opened the door without looking out through the spyhole.

Two uniformed policemen were standing with solemn expressions, their coats dripping water on to the landing carpet. They were both wearing clear plastic rain protectors over their caps, their collars turned up to their ears. Naoko looked at the prying stares of her neighbours, some in night clothes, standing in half-opened doorways, watching her with curious pity. She was still holding the knife in her hand, her dress torn and ragged and streaks of blood on her face and arms.

'We've had a report of a disturbance,' the first officer said, his eyes peering past her to the chaos inside her room. 'Can we come in?'

She stood aside and they entered without removing their boots. She followed them into the living room.

'Are you hurt?' the second officer asked.

'No. I'm fine,' Naoko said.

He reached out a hand and waited for her to pass him the knife. She held it out at arm's length and he took it carefully, holding the handle between his forefinger and thumb, and placed it on the sideboard.

'What happened?' he asked.

Naoko paused for a moment as she saw the scene through the officers' eyes. She tried to think. There was a chair lying beside her on the floor and she set it upright and slowly took a seat. How could she explain her dishevelled appearance? How could she explain the noise of the disturbance and the chaos of broken furniture in her flat? Most importantly, Naoko knew, was how to explain the blood-stained knife. To tell the truth to the police would be to condemn herself. That would mean losing her job and her home and everything she had worked for. Alex was gone and she was all alone now. She had to do what was best for her. A different explanation of the night began to piece itself together in her mind. The patrolmen stood above her, waiting. Then the words started to come in an unbroken flow and she found herself unable to stop. The officers listened intently as she spoke, their expressions becoming ever more serious with each sentence. When they began to look at one another with the worried glances of concerned parents, Naoko knew she had gone too far.

She was still talking when Alex came into the room, wide-eyed and breathless. There was miscomprehension in his eyes as he took in the officers' presence, his mouth open slightly and his hair slicked against his forehead from the rain. Then a look of resignation as he understood events had moved beyond his control.

Naoko watched him as he stood in the doorway, the cut on his face still pulsing blood as one of the officers drew his baton and swung, once to the elbow and once to the knee, taking his legs from underneath him.

# 11

THE CRIME DIVISION OFFICE WAS ON THE TENTH FLOOR OF Ushigome police station. Officers looked up from their desks as he passed. Their eyes tracked him and Alex knew he would do the same if their places were reversed. He held his expression and returned the stares. He was the only westerner he had seen since they had brought him in and his wrists were bound, both hands crossed in front at an awkward angle. The patrolman opened the door to an empty interview room and ushered him inside. Alex took a seat at the far side of the desk.

'Wait here,' the patrolman said, and began to close the door behind him.

'Who am I waiting for?' Alex called out.

'Senior officer.'

'I don't know what you want to interview me for. Why don't you just speak to Naoko?'

The patrolman looked at him quizzically. 'She's the reason you're here,' he said.

When he had gone, Alex sat and waited. There was silence in the room and, beyond the walls, the rumble of the morning traffic. He stared at the row of dirty brown patches on the wall opposite, left there by heads that had sweated nervously against the paintwork.

*

The senior officer introduced himself as Inspector Saito. He wore black-framed glasses and there were liver spots on his arms and hands. He eased himself into a chair and arranged his papers on the desk and closed his briefcase and set it beside him. He moved with the conscious efficiency of a veteran, every action neat and precise. He was accompanied by a young female officer wearing a stab-proof vest over her uniform and a pistol holstered at her waist. She was young and wore her hair cropped close to her skull. She seemed used to walking in Saito's foot-steps, her small frame accentuated by the bulk of her body armour. The inspector introduced her as Officer Tomada. She took a seat in the corner of the room and rested a clipboard on her knee.

Saito opened a file and produced a single typewritten sheet and looked it over. He turned it and slid it across the desk. Alex could see it was written in Japanese, in an official bold type with a government seal, but he had no idea what it said. He looked up at the inspector and waited for an explanation. Saito took a pen and reached across the desk to place it on the sheet. He motioned for Alex to sign.

'I can't read it,' Alex said.

The inspector motioned again. He indicated with his finger the red X in the signature box.

Alex pushed the sheet back across the desk with a definite weight to his movements so the inspector was sure of his intentions.

'I can't sign it if I can't read it,' he said.

Saito shrugged slowly, as if it was the answer he had been expecting. He took the paper and passed it to his assistant. Her face flushed as she started to read, her voice directed down-wards so Alex had to strain to listen.

'On the morning of August 13, you wilfully and grievously assaulted one Naoko Yamamoto at her place of residence. This assault caused physical harm and mental distress and resulted in extensive damage to her property. You have assaulted Ms Yamamoto on several previous occasions, also resulting in injury . . .'

Alex shook his head and tried to speak but the officer continued. The inspector watched, impassive, as she read on.

'In the early hours, you accessed Ms Yamamoto's property without her permission and refused her requests for you to absent yourself. You displayed violent behaviour and made several threats against her safety. An argument ensued, during which you became verbally and physically aggressive. Ms Yamamoto was fearful of her safety and in attempting to protect herself you were accidentally injured . . .'

Alex stopped shaking his head and slumped down in his chair, his eyes closed. He began to laugh at the absurdity of what the officer was reading.

Saito held up a hand to interrupt her. 'Do you disagree with this statement?' he asked.

'This is all bullshit,' Alex said. 'I don't know who told you any of this.'

Saito held out a hand and Officer Tomada passed him the document. He placed it on the desktop. 'This statement was given by Ms Yamamoto.'

For a moment, Alex thought it must be a trick. 'I don't believe you,' he said.

'That is of no importance. It only matters whether *I* believe *you*. What in this document do you disagree with?'

Alex looked the inspector in the eye. 'All of it. I disagree with all of it. I want to speak to a lawyer.'

Saito shook his head. 'There are no lawyers and no telephone calls here. I have the right to hold you for twenty-one days before the law requires I charge you or let you go. Now, if this isn't the truth, you need to tell me what is.'

Alex turned and looked out through the glass portal in the door. He felt the vibrations of the traffic through his chair, the real world beyond the room. He looked at the skin on the backs of his hands turning pale as the circulation was stemmed by the restraints.

'I'm sorry,' he said, 'but I'm not saying any more.'

Saito pointed a finger at him. 'What happened to your face?' he asked.

Alex considered his answer. 'I fell.'

'Where?'

'At the station.'

'Which one?'

He tried to think but his mind was blank. 'Does it matter?' he asked.

Saito stood and walked around the desk and sat on the edge. He took Alex's face in his hands and angled it towards the ceiling light. He stared down at him as he examined the cut.

'Why is it stitched so badly?'

There was a row of adhesive sutures holding the skin together, the cut raw and angry beneath.

'It was all I could afford,' Alex said. 'I was bleeding all over the back of the patrol car so they took me to Keio hospital. I told the doctor I didn't have medical insurance and he wouldn't touch me. A nurse did it. She said it was the best she could do for free.'

Saito twisted Alex's head from side to side to catch the light. He pressed his fingertips to the tender flesh and Alex grimaced at the touch.

'It will leave a scar, I think.'

'Probably. If they had taken the handcuffs off, I could have done better myself.'

'Tell me how it happened.'

'I already told you, I fell.'

Saito returned to his seat. He pushed his glasses up on to his head and rubbed the bridge of his nose as if the effort had caused him pain. He closed his eyes and spoke calmly.

'If Ms Yamamoto did this without provocation, then she is in a lot of trouble.'

Alex knew the inspector was right. If he started telling the truth about what had happened, the situation was only going to get worse. He wanted it all to be over as quickly as possible. That meant keeping quiet.

He shook his head in resignation. 'I can't speak out against Naoko,' he said. 'This isn't her fault.'

'Then whose fault is it?'

'It was just a trick that someone played on us at the private view at her gallery. I went back to her apartment to try to talk to her and there was an argument. It got out of hand and I admit I was angry and I was shouting but I don't want to make a complaint. I just want to go to work. I'm late already. In my country . . .'

The inspector held up a hand to interrupt him. 'We are not in your country, Malloy-san. Japan is a safe society and we are proud of that safety. This isn't England or America, where drug-taking and violence are allowed. Do you understand?'

Alex nodded.

'The allegation made against you is very serious.'

'If you speak to Naoko again, maybe she'll remember things differently. Maybe she was confused and angry the first time you spoke to her.'

The inspector looked unconvinced. 'You accessed her apartment without permission.'

'I know where she keeps the spare key. I didn't break in.'

'But you entered her property alone and she found you there when she returned home. You agree with this?'

Alex sensed a chasm opening up. There was no other way to answer without lying. 'Yes,' he said. 'But I didn't want to hurt her or threaten her. I just wanted her to listen to me.'

'The penalty for this is fifteen months in the foreigners' prison at Fuchu. Give me a reason not to refer this to the prosecutor right now.'

There was a bitter, metallic taste in Alex's mouth. He tried to think of a way out but it seemed senseless to fight against the current any longer. He felt the energy sap from the room. After a time, the inspector stood and slowly gathered his papers from the desk and placed them inside his briefcase. He shut the case and locked it and opened the interview-room door. The sounds of the police station filled the room.

Alex looked up from the floor.

'Why did I go back?' he said.

Saito stopped in the doorway and waited for him to continue. The bright strip light reflected back from the lenses of his glasses, obscuring his eyes.

Alex's voice was clear as he spoke. 'If everything you said is true, why did I go back when I knew the police were at her apartment?'

'What do you mean?' the inspector asked.

'Speak to the officers who arrested me. I wasn't at Naoko's flat when they arrived. I'd left thirty minutes before but I came back when I knew they were there. I could have just kept running and they wouldn't have found me but I wanted to go back. How does that fit with your version of events?'

Saito remained impassive. Alex could see him consider how this changed matters. He spoke briskly to the female officer in Japanese and turned to leave.

'Am I being charged?' Alex asked.

The inspector shook his head. 'No need.'

'What happens next?'

'We will detain you and investigate further.'

'How long will that take?'

Saito didn't answer. Officer Tomada stood and bowed to the inspector and they both watched as he left the room.

# 12

THE GALLERY WAS OPEN WHEN THE TAXI DROPPED HER AT THE kerb. The shutter was up over the window and the caterers were clearing away tables and chairs and linen from the party. Naoko buried her nerves as she crossed the threshold and made her entrance.

She had briefly considered calling in sick but she knew that would only create more problems. Once the officers had finished taking her statement, she had dressed hurriedly and rushed to be on time for work. The swelling on the back of her head was a solid lump now and her hands were bruised from hitting the floor so hard. There were only two directions to choose. Naoko could see that. The first was to curl up in a ball and give up. The second was to keep her grip. She knew which she was going to take.

Megumi was in the main room, talking on the phone. She looked as if none of the previous night's drama had affected her at all. She hung up when she saw Naoko approach and tried to look innocent but the effort showed on her face.

'Good morning, Naoko,' Megumi said. 'How are you?'

Naoko knew it was best to act while her resolve was still strong.

'Tell me what happened with you and Alex one more time.'

Megumi paused. 'I already told you last night,' she said. 'I told you the truth.'

'Alex denied it when I challenged him.'

'He's a liar, Naoko. Of course he did.'

'Then tell me again.'

'He came on to me and tried to kiss me and I refused. Then he got really mad. He was drunk and angry at you for some reason. I'm not going to twist myself into knots trying to figure it all out. I've got nothing to hide.'

Naoko didn't say anything. She stood firm and tried not to show any reaction.

'You do believe me, don't you?'

'I want to. There's just something about it that doesn't feel right.'

'Mr Kimura believes me,' Megumi said.

'Where is Kimura-san? Is he here now?'

Megumi shook her head. 'He's taking his wife to Ginza for lunch. He's going to come in later.'

'Is he angry about last night?'

'What do you think?'

Naoko knew it was best to get the news out in the open as soon as possible. If she waited, it would only be discovered outside of her control.

'They arrested Alex,' she said, trying to sound as neutral as possible.

'What do you mean? Who arrested him?'

'The police. I came home and found him in my flat, waiting for me in the dark. There was a situation and Alex was arrested.'

'A situation?'

'It was just an argument that got out of hand. One of the neighbours called the police and they took him away. It's what he deserves.'

'This sounds serious, Naoko. What will happen now?'

'They will give him a warning and let him go or maybe

give him a small fine. You know how lenient they are with foreigners.'

Naoko opened her bag and took out her wallet. She passed Megumi a five-thousand-yen note. 'Why don't you go to the deli and buy coffee and pastries for everyone. I'll look after things here.'

Megumi kept her smile but a look of distaste passed over her eyes. She folded the note into quarters and closed it inside her fist.

'Of course,' Megumi said. 'I won't be long.'

Naoko watched as she walked out on to the pavement and crossed the street. That was the hardest part over with, she thought. Megumi would start calling everyone she knew as soon as she was out of sight. At least then she wouldn't have to worry if her private life was being discussed behind her back. That was a certainty now.

Naoko took a seat at her desk and began to check her emails but she was too tense to concentrate. She was trying to figure out what she was going to say to Mr Kimura when her phone rang.

'Hello?'

'Is that Ms Yamamoto?'

It was a woman's voice, clipped and direct. Naoko knew from the first syllable it was the police. She adjusted herself quickly for a formal conversation.

'Yes,' she said. 'How can I help you?'

'This is Officer Tomada from Ushigome police station. I'm calling on behalf of Inspector Saito. The inspector is investigating the complaint you made earlier. He would like to arrange for you to come to the station for a meeting.'

Naoko tried to hide her surprise at the mention of inspectors and investigations. 'May I ask why?' she said. 'I gave a statement this morning to your officers.'

'The inspector will be able to answer your questions when you attend the station, Ms Yamamoto.'

'So this is just a formality?'

The officer paused at the end of the line. 'I think it would be best for you to discuss this with Inspector Saito,' she said.

'When would he like me to visit?'

'If you could come on Monday at 11 a.m., the inspector will have some free time then.'

'Monday? Why is it necessary to wait two days? I was under the impression that this matter would be resolved today.'

'This is a serious allegation, Ms Yamamoto. It will take some time to investigate thoroughly.'

'I thought this would be concluded with a warning?'

'I think it's best if you come at eleven on Monday. It will only take an hour, or two at the most.'

Naoko knew she had no choice. 'Very well then.'

'Thank you, Ms Yamamoto.'

Naoko hung up. Her hands were shaking. She picked up her bag and quickly walked along the corridor and stepped into the toilet. She locked the cubicle door behind her and perched on the edge of the seat and lit a cigarette. From somewhere overhead she heard a voice saying: You've really screwed up now, Naoko. Now you deserve everything you're going to get.

Her hands were still trembling so she gripped one inside the other but it still wouldn't stop. She puffed on the cigarette until the end glowed red and pressed it on to the palm of her hand and watched the skin bubble and sear. She could feel her anxiety ebb away as the pain increased. She held it there for a long time.

When the burning had stopped, she stood for a few minutes with her hand under a stream of cold water. There was a perfect circle burned into the skin. Surrounding it were the scars of other identical wounds, most long healed, patterned randomly like the map of a lunar landscape. Naoko felt the sting of her blistered flesh under the icy water. She tried to think how best she could cover the burn before she went back to her desk.

# 13

IN THE HOLDING AREA THEY UNLOCKED THE RESTRAINTS AND Alex massaged the life back into his hands. The skin was grey and numb and each joint cracked as he flexed them into position. The guard pointed to the locker room and motioned for him to empty his pockets and undress. He stood naked as they bagged his belongings and handed him a blue canvas uniform, the fabric stiff and heavy and the seams torn open.

After his fingerprints had been scanned, he was led in front of a wall chart to have his mugshot taken. The technician shouted and grew angry when he couldn't follow the instructions and shoved him into position and kicked his feet on to the footprints painted on the floor. Alex braced himself for a beating.

'You like the yellow cabs?' the technician sneered.

Alex had no idea what he meant. The guard looked on, leaning, bored, against the wall.

'Some Japanese girls are like yellow cabs,' the technician said. 'Any foreigner can ride in them.'

Alex knew better than to react. He stood and faced forward as the flash popped, holding the name board close to his chest.

Through door after door, waiting at every stop to be buzzed in, he was led down into the cell block, a murmur of low voices filling the corridors. A line of men, gnarled and ugly, stood

110

waiting to be processed, and they watched him suspiciously as he passed. He saw some Korean and Filipino faces mixed in with the Japanese but no westerners. He could smell the stench of fear mixed with sweat and mould and rotting food, all masked behind a layer of cheap disinfectant. The officer stopped at a cell at the end of the block and unlocked it and showed Alex inside. Six Chinese men were squeezed into a room barely big enough for four, each dressed identically in blue uniforms with numbers stencilled on the legs, cramped together on the cement floor with their backs against the wall.

The cell had no beds or chairs, just a steel toilet bowl in the corner and a bright strip light in the ceiling, protected by a wire cage. Every surface was chipped and gouged and scrawled with graffiti. The door closed behind him and the lock clicked into place. Alex found a space on the floor and settled himself down with his knees raised, his chin resting on his arm. A layer of dust, fine as ash, swirled around him as he moved.

One of the men, tall and stringy, with a birthmark that filled one eye, stared across the cell. He had a ragged haircut and sunken cheeks where his teeth were missing. The men spoke to each other in rapid Cantonese, arguing as if trying to concoct an alibi or apportion blame. They lowered their voices to a whisper each time a guard passed by in the corridor outside.

The hours drifted past. The cell became rank from bodies perspiring in the hot, windowless room. Everyone seemed dazed, on the verge of falling into unconsciousness from the heat and the tedium. Only the discomfort of sitting unsupported on the cement floor kept Alex awake. As the day ebbed away, his thoughts kept returning to the party at the gallery and the argument at Naoko's apartment. Nothing that happened justified him being arrested. Alex knew that. He thought he should feel reassured by the knowledge that he was innocent, the balance of natural order being in his favour. But there was an unmistakable doubt that this would end up working against him.

In the late evening the door finally clicked open and the guard called for the people in each cell to gather in the corridor. The Chinese men all stood as one and stumbled out, dazed and numb. Alex followed them. The hallway was full of uniformed prisoners standing closely together, stretching and massaging the circulation back into wasted limbs. He took his place and waited. When the guard had checked that all the cells were empty he called the line forward, each man walking six inches from the one in front. They filed along the corridor, calling their numbers to the guard as they passed, and made a left turn into a long, narrow washroom with banks of metal water troughs at the centre.

Alex copied the others. He stripped off his uniform shirt and rinsed his face and neck, tossing handfuls of water over himself to wash the sweat away. He drenched himself thoroughly and rinsed out his mouth, then dried himself and made way for the next man. In the locker room, he was handed a thin futon mattress and a rough blanket and followed the line back to the cells. The Chinese spread their bedding out on the floor, jostling one another for the best sleeping positions. Alex took the place that was left beside the toilet bowl and arranged his futon and blanket.

Before locking them in for the night, the guard placed a tray in the middle of the cell and issued instructions Alex couldn't understand. The Chinese nodded and bowed to the guard as if this routine was familiar. The door was locked and then the overhead light flickered off behind the wire cage and a green safety light blinked on. Seven plastic containers and seven bottles of water were stacked roughly on the tray, each containing a portion of rice and fish with a serving of pickled vegetables. The meal looked stale and cold but Alex was starving. He reached out a hand to take a box from the tray and immediately sensed the atmosphere change.

A hand jabbed forward and snatched his wrist and for a moment he was caught unguarded. He turned and looked into fierce eyes behind the deep-crimson birthmark. The hand gripped him tightly and Alex froze as the others gathered up the food and began to tear open the packaging. He shook his arm free but the man moved to block his way, his hands clenched into fists. He stared from behind the plum stain around his eye, breathing heavily through flared nostrils, poised, ready to fight. The others were huddled together, looking over blankly. One of the men took a water bottle and tossed it on to Alex's futon. He called out to his friends in Cantonese and they laughed and continued eating. Alex felt the sweat-slicked uniform cling to his body and his stomach turn over with hunger and fear. He took a step forward.

A fist struck him on the cheekbone where the cut was still fresh. There was a burning sensation as the stitches tore against the wound. He felt arms clench around his chest and grip him from behind. He ripped himself free and tried to turn but stumbled. A blanket was thrown over his head and pulled tightly around him and he was forced to the floor, the cement winding him as he landed hard. He was struggling to breathe and unable to push himself up, one arm locked beneath his body, the other pinned to his flank. He tried to kick out but his legs were trapped, his voice muffled by the rough material over his mouth.

As the blows from fists and feet rained down, Alex tried to squirm free, but there were too many hands forcing him back. He felt a rib crack beneath sharp knuckles and a stamp on his stomach doubled him over like a branch snapping in a storm. He could hear rasping voices and muted laughter. He wasn't sure when he finally blacked out.

# 14

THE CURTAIN WAS PULLED AROUND THE HOSPITAL BED. BEYOND IT, nurses were talking quietly and a buckled wheel squealed as a trolley rolled along the ward. His lips were dry and cracked, one sealed against the other. Pain was evident in every part of him, muffled by the warm, nauseating glow of medication. The sheets felt creased and damp beneath his body, a cannula impaled in his left hand like a parasitic insect gradually feeding in morphine. Outside, the sky was a brilliant blue. The snow on the window ledge was patterned with delicate tracks where resting birds had landed.

He could see the feet of the man in the next bed through a narrow crack in the curtain. They were pale and still, the skin waxy and lifeless. He stared at them for a long time, willing them to move, listening to the sound of the ventilator as it bellowed softly. He had no idea who they belonged to.

The curtain parted. His father looked surprised to find him awake, and hesitated, shifting back then forwards on his heels, unsure of himself. Finally, he called for a nurse. He was still wearing the stiff collar and striped tie he had chosen for Christmas lunch.

'You're awake,' he said, standing at the side of the bed. 'We can thank the Lord for that. It was a hell of an accident *you were in. We didn't know if you were going to make it.'*

*Alex slowly opened his mouth to speak. His tongue was swollen, his teeth aching in his jaw. 'How long have I been here?' he asked.*

*'Two days,' his father said.*

*'What happened?'*

*'You got hit by a breakdown truck. It was towing a car and the driver lost control in the snow. It hit you at full speed, right in the driver's side door.'*

*'They won't tell me how badly I'm hurt. The nurses keep telling me to worry about that later.'*

*'Well, maybe you should listen to them.'*

*'Tell me, Dad.'*

*He touched a hand to Alex's shoulder. 'You're going to be fine. It'll take some time to get completely better, though. You've got a broken leg, a ruptured spleen, two chipped vertebrae. And there were severe burns on your back and arms.'*

*'The truck driver?'*

*'He's fine. He had a concussion but it's not serious.'*

*'Patrick?' Alex asked hesitantly. He realized he'd been avoiding speaking his brother's name.*

*His father blinked rapidly. Tears began to moisten his eyes. 'Don't worry about that now,' he said.*

*'You sound like one of the nurses.'*

*'They're right. Some things are best left until later.'*

*'Where is he?'*

*'He's gone, Alex.'*

*'Gone?'*

*'He's dead.'*

*Alex looked away. Above him, the heating pipes rattled. Somewhere, a telephone was ringing. The pain in his back and shoulders was immense.*

*'In the crash?'*

*'No. They pulled him from the wreckage with just cuts and bruises. He collapsed in the examination room before we got here. They said it was a brain haemorrhage. He was asking for*

*details of your condition before you went into surgery. He was only alone for a few minutes and when the nurse returned she found him unconscious. He didn't feel any pain at all.'*

*'How is Mum taking it?' Alex asked.*

*His father shifted uncomfortably. 'Not well.'*

*'Is she here?'*

*'She won't come.'*

*'Why not?'*

*He checked back over his shoulder. 'Where's that nurse? It's been five minutes since I called her.'*

*'Why won't she come, Dad?'*

*'She's at Mass.'*

*'She blames me?'*

*His father leaned closer to the bed and lowered his voice. He sounded practical and forthright, just as he had in his days as a teacher.*

*'The police . . . Well, they said Patrick had heroin in his bloodstream when he died . . . and they had checked your clothing at the scene and found some strange things. A hypodermic and some other unusual items. They say there was heroin in your possession. They want to interview you as soon as you're well enough. As you can imagine, your mother's very upset. She seems to think that you got Patrick mixed up in something. I keep trying to talk to her but she won't listen. In fact, she's unhappy that I'm here now.'*

*Alex turned his face away and looked out through the window. The world had somehow changed now, in just the few moments since he had last laid eyes on it. The buildings and the streets were the same, the traffic stopping and starting and the people walking in busy crowds on the wide pavements. But what had appeared familiar now seemed hostile and forbidding. The weight of the situation seemed overpowering, as if there were some great force dragging on his feet, pulling him down unstoppably. He had no desire to fight. None at all. All he felt was an overwhelming desire to sleep.*

# 15

THE PRISON YARD WAS A VOID AT THE FOOT OF USHIGOME police station. It was a concrete pit dug out of the earth ten metres below ground level and covered with ribbons of razor wire. The officers working in the building towering above stared down from their windows at the men caged there.

Most of the yard was in shade. The sun slanted high over the roof and shone on a section at the far corner. Alex was aching and battered, moving with the humility of the defeated. He wanted to feel the sun on his face but he could see he wasn't welcome. A group of Japanese prisoners were sitting on the benches, smoking and talking casually, the guards standing easily around them. The corner of the yard where the sunlight fell was theirs exclusively.

The Koreans were grouped together in the shadows by the water fountain. The Chinese were huddled together tightly so they couldn't be heard. They all dragged hungrily on the ration of two cheap cigarettes handed out at the start of morning exercise. Alex stood with his back to the chain-link fence and watched a crow fly far above the razor wire, beating its wings against the head wind coursing between the buildings.

'Hey! Russia-jin!' a voice called out to him.

Alex looked over warily. A Japanese prisoner was approaching, stepping cautiously around the shallow pools of rainwater that lay in the yard. He listed to one side as he walked, one leg refusing to straighten beneath him. Alex turned away, trying hard to ignore him.

'Hey! Russia-jin!' he called out again.

'I'm not Russian,' Alex said, without looking round.

'You look Russian.'

'I'm English.'

'Suit yourself, Russia-jin. Do you want a cigarette?'

Alex shook his head. 'I don't smoke.'

'Then can I have those?' He pointed to the pair of filter tips poking from Alex's breast pocket.

He had a flat face and no brow, his skin pitted with old acne scars. He was about twenty-five, Alex guessed, short-limbed and scrawny, grinning to himself at springing the simplest of traps. He seemed thoroughly at ease, as if he were perfectly at home in his present surroundings. His face was the first Alex had seen that wasn't dangerous or unfriendly.

'Take them,' he said, and handed the cigarettes over. 'I don't have the energy to bargain.'

'I'm Jun,' the man said as he lit one. He spat a loose strand of tobacco from his lips. 'Why are you here?'

'I don't want to talk about it.'

'Why not?'

'Because I don't want to get into any more trouble.'

Jun took a long drag and exhaled through his nose. 'You're already in jail, Russia-jin. What more trouble is there?'

Nothing good had happened since he'd arrived at Ushigome and he could see no reason why that was about to change. Alex turned away and waited for him to leave.

'Why did they arrest you?' Jun said to his back. 'What does a westerner have to do to end up here?'

Alex thought for a moment. 'A speeding ticket,' he said.

Jun gave a snorting laugh. 'A speeding ticket. Very good. At least you're not in his place.'

Alex turned around. 'Whose place?'

'The old guy over there.'

An old man was alone by the latrine, his arms gathered tightly across his chest, as if he were trying to make himself as small as possible.

'Who's he?' Alex asked.

'He's *hentai*.' Jun made a hand gesture like he was milking a cow. 'He was caught groping a schoolgirl on the train. It's his weakness. Now he'll be lucky to get out in one piece.'

'How come you know all this?'

'It's my business to know,' Jun said with a shrug. He lit the second cigarette from the end of the first. 'Like I know about the Chinese in your cell.'

Alex looked up and waited for him to continue. Jun took his interest as an invitation to move closer.

'They're Triad. Not the serious guys, but they're nasty enough. They've just finished sentences at Fuchu and now they're waiting for their deportation orders to come through.'

'Well, I really hope it happens soon.'

'Why? They're giving you some trouble?'

'Let's just say they don't like to share at mealtimes.'

'What are you going to do?'

Alex looked over at the Chinese standing together. Not one of them had strayed from the pack since they had come outside to the yard.

'I'll just have to keep winning them over with my charm,' he said.

'How's that working out so far?'

'Not good.'

'You don't want to talk to them?' Jun nodded over to the guards.

'No. That'll just make my problems worse. One thing I can say for my cellmates is they're smart. They only hit where the bruises don't show.' He lifted his uniform shirt a little to show his tender flank. It was blotted with lurid yellow and purple bruises.

'Maybe I can help you?' Jun said.

'In return for what?'

'Your cigarettes.'

'You've already got them.'

Jun smiled and took a drag. 'Then we already have a deal.'

He turned and limped away across the yard, weaving between the different groups of men, towards the table of Japanese prisoners basking in the sunlight. He stopped and bowed to an older man drinking coffee from a plastic cup. Alex couldn't hear their conversation but he could see the man listen intently as Jun bent close to him. He nodded from time to time to show his understanding but didn't speak, just stared ahead in concentration. When Jun had finished speaking he sipped his coffee and looked up at the sky, deep in thought. Alex observed from across the exercise yard with growing anxiety. He had no idea what was happening.

The older man finally turned and beckoned to a tough-looking prisoner standing at the fence line. He pointed out the Chinese from Alex's cell and the prisoner bowed and strode towards them. They stood as a group when he approached, gathering together for safety like a herd. He came in close and they listened to him in silence as the message was relayed. It took just a few seconds.

Then the bell sounded to end the break period and the guards began to usher the men back inside. They gathered themselves wearily and shuffled back towards the entrance to the cell block. Alex took one last look at the sky before he returned to the windowless room. The crow was still flying overhead, beating its wings against the wind eddying above, a dark silhouette in the bright morning sky. It had made no further progress towards its destination.

The prisoners swept out the cells and returned their bedding to the storage lockers. The guard counted every man back inside and they took their places on the floor and prepared for another day in confinement. Alex watched as the breakfast tray was placed in the middle of the room and the guard walked out to the corridor and shut the heavy door. He remained seated, waiting for the Chinese to make the first move.

They remained motionless, their backs against the wall, watching him in return.

There were seven packages, steam misting the clear plastic lids of the containers. Alex pushed himself up from the floor and adjusted his uniform. The Chinese sat fixed in their positions as he stepped forward and crossed to the centre of the room. He reached down and took a box from the tray and lifted it gently, as if in expectation of some sudden movement or attack. He removed the cover and looked inside. There was a plain omelette and a bread roll with a serving of instant miso in a paper cup. The smell of the warm food drifted invitingly into the cell.

The man with the plum birthmark blinked as he caught the scent and shifted his weight to stand up. A voice from across the cell called out to him and he stopped.

He looked around for assistance from the others but every face was full of caution. He settled himself back down and waited, looking at Alex as he took his place beside the toilet bowl and began eating in quick mouthfuls, spooning up the hot food and tearing bites from the roll. Each man watched him in silence as he ate. No one moved until his plate was empty.

# 16

INSPECTOR SAITO OFFERED HER THE CHAIR AT THE SIDE OF HIS
desk and Naoko bowed to him in thanks. She had worn a
surgical mask for the journey to Ushigome and she removed it
and folded it on to her lap. The chair was hard moulded plastic
and seemed designed to make its user as uncomfortable as
possible. The soles of her shoes hung suspended above the faded
grey carpet.

'Thank you for coming,' Saito said. He turned to the short,
plain-looking policewoman to his left. 'This is Officer Tomada.
She's assisting with your case.'

Naoko gave a polite smile, which the officer didn't return.
'We've spoken on the phone,' she said.

'There are just a few minor questions I'd like to ask, Ms
Yamamoto. I understand this may be hard for you but there's
no alternative, I'm afraid.'

Naoko kept her tone respectful. 'I understand completely,
Inspector.'

Saito was upright in his chair. He had an angular face and
neatly combed grey hair, cut military-style. Naoko could see
that, despite his age, he was lean and trim beneath his crisp,
white shirt. His eyes had the calm resolve of experience.

He began to read out her statement in a measured voice,

speaking evenly, without dramatic inflection. Naoko listened but she needed no help refreshing her memory. She'd done little else but go over it in her mind for the last couple of days. She remained silent but attentive, with an expression she hoped showed sincerity without seeming forced. When he had finished, the inspector leaned back in his chair.

'So the details of this document are correct?' he asked.

Naoko knew she had no other choice. 'They are.'

'On the night in question, Mr Malloy gained access to your apartment without permission. You discovered him there and he refused to leave. A struggle took place and you attempted to protect yourself.'

'That's right.'

'And Mr Malloy has displayed similar behaviour towards you in the past?'

'Yes.'

'And on this occasion you felt you needed a knife to protect yourself from him?'

'I picked up the knife without thinking. I just wanted to defend myself . . . to scare him off. It was never my intention to hurt anyone.'

'May I ask a question, Ms Yamamoto? After the altercation had taken place and he had been injured, why do you think Mr Malloy returned to your apartment?'

Naoko looked down at the paperwork on the inspector's desk. The way it was organized so precisely, compared to the others in the office. She looked across at the groups of young detectives drinking coffee and chatting aimlessly with one another. If her case had been assigned to one of them, she thought, the whole matter would have been dismissed by now.

'I'm sorry, Inspector,' she said, 'but I wouldn't want to speculate.'

'This is very serious. Mr Malloy is facing fifteen months in prison at Fuchu.'

She knew she had to resist the inspector's attempts to unsettle her. She steeled herself inside. 'Every detail in my statement is correct.'

'And you're prepared to testify as such when this matter comes before the courts?'

'If you think that's necessary, Inspector.'

Saito looked at her over the frames of his glasses. 'What do *you* think is necessary?'

'Alex knows he's done wrong. I'm sure he's learned his lesson. Isn't a warning or a small fine sufficient?'

'This was a severe incident, Ms Yamamoto. My officers were called to your home and found you holding a knife that you had used to injure an intruder. A crime has been committed and we have been tasked with investigating it. Therefore, we have to reach a conclusion.'

'But a prosecution seems so severe. I'm very busy. I don't have time to become involved in a court case.'

'My job is to maintain order, not to act as you see fit. Either your statement is correct or it is not. If it is, there must be a prosecution. If not, then you need to tell me now and we will have to take a different course.'

Naoko held firm. She had prepared herself for this moment. 'I have my reputation to think of, Inspector. My future. Everything in my statement is true.'

'It's not your *future* that worries me, Ms Yamamoto.'

'What do you mean?' she asked.

'I checked your records. It seems there are certain events you have made efforts to erase.'

'What are you talking about?'

'You know exactly what I mean. That must have been a difficult situation for a schoolgirl to experience?'

'I don't see how that's relevant.'

'The courts will want to know everything about you in order to establish your reliability. It took only a brief check to discover information that may harm your standing. Do you want this made public?'

'Of course not.'

The inspector gazed at her from behind his thick glasses. His sense of superiority was unmistakable. 'You're an ambitious woman, Ms Yamamoto. A woman who has come far in the world. That requires the ability to protect yourself when necessary.'

Naoko struggled to contain her anger. 'Aren't I the victim here?' she said.

Saito eased back in his chair. 'That's exactly what we are trying to establish.'

They looked across the table at each other, their eyes locked. Naoko was flustered inside but refused to show it. She knew it was suicidal to concede any ground. Officer Tomada shifted in her seat and coughed to break the silence.

'There is an alternative,' she said meekly.

Saito turned to her. 'What do you mean?'

Tomada seemed cowed, as if she regretted intervening. 'I think there may be another way to solve this matter. A way that bypasses the courts but allows for an official conclusion.'

'Go on.'

'Financial reparations could be made. *Jidan*.'

Naoko had never heard the term. 'What's *jidan*?' she asked.

'Forgiveness money. Mr Malloy could admit his guilt in the matter and pay a set amount as compensation. If you're willing to accept, then we would be able to draw our investigation to a conclusion.' The officer hesitated for a second. 'As long as the inspector is in agreement, of course.'

'It would be highly unusual in a case such as this,' Saito said. 'A violent incident would normally have to be put before the authorities.'

Tomada cast a quick look at Naoko. There was a hint of solidarity in her eyes. 'But if the *jidan* payment was set at a high level, Mr Malloy would incur a punishment that even the prosecutor would find satisfactory.'

Naoko could see the opening Tomada was giving her. She

could ask for compensation and then return the money to Alex once the case was settled. She seized her opportunity before it disappeared.

'I think that *jidan* would be sufficient,' she said. 'Of course, the amount would have to reflect the damage Alex has inflicted. I think that five million yen sounds like a reasonable figure.'

Saito leaned forward on his elbows. He touched the fingers of his clasped hands against his chin. 'But five million yen is significantly higher than the amount usually demanded in the *jidan* system.'

Naoko had the upper hand now and she wasn't going to lose it. 'I understand, Inspector. But why don't you make the proposition to Alex? The higher amount would reflect the sincerity of his apology. Surely if he accepts, we can all move on and put this matter behind us?'

Saito took a moment to consider the suggestion. He began to speak and then stopped, his mouth seemingly tangled with half-formed words. It was the first time Naoko had seen him in less than full control. He seemed disappointed with himself, like a hunter who has lost sight of his prey at the crucial moment. Saito removed his glasses and wiped the lenses slowly, the lines around his eyes tensed in deep creases. Naoko avoided his gaze. She fixed her sight on the faded crime-prevention posters tacked to the wall beyond the inspector's shoulder.

Finally, Saito said, 'Very well. I will relay the proposal to Mr Malloy. If he agrees to pay, we can consider the incident resolved.'

Naoko had to make an effort not to show her relief. 'Thank you, Inspector,' she said.

'Thank you, Ms Yamamoto.'

Naoko stood and bowed to them both. She pulled the surgical mask over her face to hide her smile as she left the office and rode down in the lift. She couldn't believe how easy it had been.

*

Her triumph was short-lived. Mr Kimura was waiting for her when she returned to the gallery, sitting at her desk with a look that suggested he had been waiting for some time. He was idly flicking through a sales report, turning the pages with long, manicured fingers.

'Where have you been?' he asked.

'I had a personal matter to attend to, Kimura-san. I apologize.'

'A personal matter?'

'Yes. It's taken care of now.'

Kimura stared up at her with a resignation that was unsettling. His elderly face remained still, his hands resting lightly on the arms of the chair and his thin legs crossed one over the other.

'I'm not so sure that it is,' he said. 'I received a call from Ushigome police station. An Inspector Saito asked to speak to me, regarding the mess you have managed to get yourself into.'

Naoko felt the back of her neck turn dry and cold. 'I'm truly sorry, Kimura-san. I hope you can forgive me.'

'How long have you been seeing this foreigner?'

'Only a few weeks,' she lied.

'In this time, you have taken him into your bed?'

She hesitated at the intrusion. Finally, she said, 'Yes.'

'Even though you are unmarried?'

'It was a foolish moment.'

Kimura's face flushed with distaste. 'The disturbance at the private view was most discouraging. And now this. Megumi has told me her side of the story and it reflects very badly on you.'

Naoko couldn't hide her outrage. 'I think there's much more to Megumi's involvement than she is admitting,' she said. 'This whole incident began with a commotion designed to stir up trouble for me. It's all far too convenient for her.'

Kimura brushed a piece of lint from his suit, as if it had been bothering him for some time. 'Please, Naoko. She is young and naive. She doesn't have the experience that you and I have.

127

You're usually so dependable, which is why I expected more from you. Especially after everything I have given you – your position here at the gallery, your generous salary, your apartment.'

'I have nothing but gratitude for all you've done for me, Kimura-san. I hope that always shows in my work.'

He rose from the chair and adjusted the buttons on his jacket. Everything about him was light and elegant, except his manner, which was faintly cruel. He stepped towards her and touched a hand to her face to sweep back a stray strand of hair.

'These have been troubling times,' he said. 'But the course of life is always unpredictable. The test of character is how we overcome the obstacles that are thrown into our path. That is why I've decided not to take any immediate action. But we need to discuss this further at some point. Firstly, however, there is a business matter that I need your assistance with. I've brokered the sale of a very expensive *ukiyo-e* print for an exclusive client. He wants to finalize the details on Saturday evening over dinner in Ginza. This could be very lucrative for our business and he has asked specifically for you to accompany me.'

'I would be honoured to, Kimura-san,' she said, relieved. 'Thank you for your faith in me.'

Kimura opened the office door and stepped out. 'Saturday at seven thirty,' he said. 'I will send a car for you.'

# 17

'YOU HAVE A DIFFICULT SITUATION,' JUN SAID. 'FIVE MILLION yen is a lot of money. Maybe you should find a cheaper girlfriend.'

It was hot and close in the evening, the humidity rising as the sun began to set. Beyond the tower of Ushigome police station, Alex could hear the muted sound of traffic on the downtown expressway. They were sitting on a low wall at the edge of the exercise yard. Alex did a mental conversion. Five million yen was about thirty thousand pounds.

'I don't understand why she's asking for so much,' he said. 'She knows I haven't got that kind of money.'

'Appearance is everything now. She needs to maintain her good reputation. Money is the best way to show it.'

'I didn't even touch her.'

'Maybe,' Jun said, looking up through the wire surrounding the prison yard. 'But she is out there and you are locked up in here.'

'I just want to get out of here now,' Alex said. 'I'm sick and tired of this place.'

'Do you have any money saved?'

'A few thousand yen. That's all.'

'Do you have any family that can help you?'

Alex imagined making the call, his mother picking up the telephone, the sound of her voice after all this time. He imagined her reaction when she found out where he was. Her bitter satisfaction as her misjudgements were confirmed. It would be a humiliation he would never be able to live with.

'No,' he said. 'I don't have any family at all.'

Jun lit a cigarette and tapped the ash against the side of his slipper. 'In that case, maybe I can be of some use to you.'

Alex turned to him with raised eyebrows. 'Really? How you can you help?'

'We're in prison, Russia-jin. Do you think you're the first person to face this kind of problem? When it comes to borrowing money, this is the easiest place.'

Jun pulled deeply on his cigarette and blew a trickle of smoke from his lips. It hung in the still, wet air. He pointed at the men walking and sitting around in the concrete yard.

'Everyone here has asked for a loan at some point,' he said. 'To pay fines or to help their families while they are locked up. It's the system.'

'So what are you saying?'

'I'm saying I can arrange a loan for you. Five million yen.'

'And I have to pay interest?'

'Just like you would to a bank.'

'Who will be lending it to me?' he asked. 'You?'

Jun nodded towards the group of Japanese prisoners at their usual table. 'Not me. Them.'

'Who are they?'

'Just some old men with money. They're waiting for their trial to start and trying to delay the prosecutor with every trick they can think of. They spend the days here and the nights in the hospital at Keio. Their lawyers have argued they're too old to sleep in the cells. They have a lot of experience playing these games.'

'What are they here for?'

Jun gave a knowing smile. 'You know better than to ask that question, Russia-jin.'

'Are you sure taking money from them is a good idea?'

'Do you want to leave here or not?'

'Of course I do.'

'How long have you been in Japan?' Jun asked.

'About six months.'

'Do you know *uchi soto*?'

Alex shook his head.

'Then I will give you the only Japanese lesson you need.'

He flicked his cigarette out into the yard and leaned back against the chain-link fence.

'*Uchi soto* means "inside outside". You are *soto*. Outside. My family is from Korea, so even though I was born here, I am *soto* also. You and I are no different. No matter how long we live here, we will always be outsiders. Your girlfriend is *uchi*. Inside. She must maintain her standing and her reputation in society or she is nothing. In many ways, life is more difficult for her. But everything she says is true and anything you say is a lie. Remember that. You are guilty anyway. Guilty of being a foreigner. Now you need money and I can get it for you. All you have to do is ask.'

'Are you sure about this?'

Jun shrugged. 'What alternatives do you have?'

Alex let the question hang for a moment. Absolutely none, he thought.

'Okay,' he said. 'Go ahead and arrange it for me.'

They returned to the cell block when the bell sounded and stood for the evening roll call. As they were counted off, the men dispersed in groups and filtered back to the airless rooms. Another evening of waiting lay ahead. At least it would all be over soon, Alex thought.

The safety light washed the cell in green. The sweat-drenched prisoners, their faces pallid as corpses', stirred occasionally, as if they were dreaming on the ocean floor. Alex woke to the sound of voices outside the cell door, the scuffle of feet as new arrivals were checked in during the night. He had no idea what time it was.

He lay back and looked at the cracks in the ceiling. His thirst was incredible. The humidity seemed worse at night, choking the oxygen from the cell and forming in fat droplets on the walls. He had watched how the Chinese saved their water ration to drink overnight and now he had begun to do the same. He reached for the bottle hidden beneath his pillow and took a short sip. It barely wet the back of his throat.

He tried to remember how long he'd been there now. Was it three days, or four? There were no details in the course of daily life to mark the passage of time. Just the hourly grind of events without importance. Keys turning. Doors slamming. Raised voices punctuating the silence. Endless hours of waiting seeping through the corridors. The only thing he knew for certain was he'd been there too long. Whatever he had done to hurt Naoko, whatever fury she had worked herself into, he didn't deserve this.

He turned on to his side to try to sleep and realized he wasn't the only one awake. Two eyes blinked in the pale green light. They had an eerie quality, as if they had been watching him for some time. He stared back for a moment and then looked away.

There was the shuffle of a blanket as it was kicked off, and Alex glanced back. He could see the watcher rise up from his futon and reach over towards the head of the man next to him as he gave a long, nasal gutter of sleep. The watcher was moving with patient stealth, hardly breathing, checking around to make sure no one else could see. He seemed unconcerned about Alex.

He reached under the head of his sleeping neighbour and slowly pulled out a half-full water bottle. He unscrewed the cap and pressed the bottle to his lips, letting the liquid run down his gullet in a single draught. Then he quietly placed the cap on to the empty bottle and tucked it back and lay down again. Alex turned over and closed his eyes. He listened for a few minutes but heard no further movements. He willed himself to go back to sleep. There were too many waking hours to be spent in the cell as it was.

In the morning, they were roused by the 6 a.m. bell and began to stir. The foul stench of rancid bodies soured the air. Alex felt as if his bones had been crushed to dust on the solid cement floor. He rubbed his eyes and stood up. His cellmates began to fold away their bedding.

The birthmarked prisoner lifted his pillow to retrieve the water he had left there and found the empty bottle. He shouted in frustration and tossed it across the cell. He was pointing at the others and growling accusations. Alex understood his anger, even if he couldn't understand his language. He snapped at the man who had slept next to him but he just casually shook his head and nodded towards Alex. He gave a sly smile and then turned away. Birthmark took a step in Alex's direction. An older prisoner reached out to stop him but he was set in motion now and easily shook him away. Alex had the briefest of moments to brace himself.

Birthmark hit with tremendous force, lowering his head so it hammered against Alex's chest, and they fell together in a grapple. He began hissing and cursing through gritted teeth and grasped Alex's throat in both hands and began to lever his face down towards the rank cess in the toilet bowl. Alex balked and pushed up from the steel rim, bucking his shoulders and throwing his head backwards. His skull connected with flesh and cartilage and they slipped down together, the Chinese rolling on top for a moment before his momentum carried him over and Alex twisted above him and dug a savage elbow into his throat. He struck the man twice with balled fists and heard his head crack hard on the concrete floor. There was a blow to his face and Alex tasted blood as it began to flow warm and sweet in the back of his throat. He reached his arm back to strike again but was pulled to his feet. He crouched with his back to the wall, waiting for a massed attack, but the others remained still. They stared at him, at the blood trickling over his lip as if it was the manifestation of their worst fears.

Jun saw him as he stepped into the locker room to return his bedding. He squinted at Alex's face as he examined the damage.

'Who did this?' he asked.

'It doesn't concern you.'

'You're lucky your face was already injured. If the warders noticed this, you would be up for more charges.'

'Let's talk about something else.'

Jun shook his head. 'This is serious now,' he said.

'It was a fair fight. It's got nothing to do with you.'

'They were warned. This won't be allowed to go unpunished.'

'Just let me handle it, Jun.'

'It's not that simple, Russia-jin. Everyone has to know who is in charge here.'

He turned and walked back down the corridor, his uneven gait rolling his body awkwardly as he moved. Alex watched him go. He felt drained and tired, powerless to stop whatever course was now set in motion.

The guards formed the men into a line and herded them into the washroom. Alex took his place and followed the others and stood in front of the water trough. Among the scrum of tightly packed prisoners, he saw his Chinese cellmate facing him across the room as he removed his uniform shirt and began washing. He stared at Alex, his face set with purpose as he doused the swellings on his jaw and brow with handfuls of icy water. Alex stared back. A moment of animal intuition passed between them, an understanding of the depths to which people with nothing to lose can sink. Then his gaze softened and he nodded to Alex in respect and began to pull on his shirt.

It was over so quickly that he had no time to react. The prisoners either side seized his arms while they were still trapped by the fabric of his shirt. A young inmate beside them bent down and reached under the sole of his slipper and stood up. He eyes looked vacant, his body so thin that he appeared half-starved. Something glinted in his hand as he turned and flicked it across the Chinese prisoner's face. A spray of bright arterial blood jetted from the wine-coloured stain and he flinched, more in surprise than pain, and struggled to free himself. The trough clattered as the Japanese prisoner tossed away a razor blade half-wrapped in tape, and all three of them turned to run. Alex stood transfixed as his cellmate searched with his fingertips inside the hollow of the socket and found a pulp where his eye-ball had been. Everyone seemed to move as one for the exit as the guards rushed in with batons drawn. The Chinese was staggering now, reaching for the side of the water basin to steady himself, his other hand still groping for his eye, uselessly trying to re-form the bloody remains.

# 18

AFTER TWO DAYS OF LOCK-DOWN, SAITO SENT FOR HIM. THE guards manacled his wrists and strapped a thick leather belt around his waist. They chained the handcuffs tightly to the belt and led him up through the corridors and stairwells of Ushigome. The interview room was untouched since his last visit. The same patches of dirt ground into the walls, the same atmosphere of uncertainty and despair. The escort told him to sit and left the handcuffs fastened while he waited for the inspector to appear. Officer Tomada was trailing behind him as he entered the room.

Saito took a long, scathing look at him before he finally pulled out his chair and sat down. He rested his weathered forearms on the heavy tabletop.

'Your stay here at Ushigome has been most eventful, Malloy-san,' he said, in his deep, steady tone.

'All I've done is keep my head down and wait. You know I had nothing to do with what happened in the washroom. There were many witnesses. Everyone saw I wasn't involved.'

Saito was unmoved. 'We know exactly who is responsible. He has been taken from the holding block and transferred to another facility. We know who forced him to do it. He has confessed to everything, but I need more evidence. I need your co-operation.'

'Whatever his reasons are for the attack, they have nothing to do with me.'

'Is that what you think?'

Alex chose his words carefully. The stakes seemed to be rising every hour. 'It's what I know. Anything else is none of my business.'

Saito reached down and unfastened the locks on his brief-case. He reached in and took out a thick brown Manila envelope and placed it before him.

'Open it,' he said, and pushed the envelope towards Alex.

The steel chain on his wrists rattled on the desktop as he leaned forward and picked it up. The envelope was unsealed. Inside was a thick bundle of ten-thousand-yen bills, the edges sharp and new.

'Is this the *jidan* money?' Alex asked hopefully.

'Yes. It was sent to me personally this morning, for me to send to Ms Yamamoto on your behalf.'

'Then I'm free to go?'

'It would appear that way, Malloy-san.'

Alex felt a rush of relief. He began to smile but his instincts repulsed any premature optimism. He had come to expect only disaster.

'So why am I still here?'

'Because I know where this money came from. I see many foreigners sitting where you are, Malloy-san. And I expect I will see many more in the future. But I doubt I will see anyone in as much danger as you are now.'

'You told me to raise five million yen in order to get out of here. That's exactly what I've done.'

'Do you have any idea who these people are?'

'Yes. They're the only ones who showed any interest in help-ing me.'

'Did you have no one else to turn to?'

'I'm alone down there on the cell block, Inspector. I don't have anyone.'

'What about outside of here?'

Alex shook his head. 'I'm alone out there as well.'

Saito took the envelope and emptied the stack of notes into his hand. He flicked through them like a deck of cards.

'Tell me what happened that night. Tell me the truth and then I can try to help you. We both know Ms Yamamoto's version of events is suspect.'

Alex was determined not to speak against Naoko. He knew that contradicting her statement would only ruin her reputation and that would kill any chance they had of getting back together and putting this behind them. He had made this promise to himself and kept it so far, despite the dangers of being locked up in Ushigome. It made no sense to give Saito what he wanted now.

'I won't say anything against Naoko. I can't.'

'Your loyalty is admirable. But it is misplaced. Do you think she is acting in your interests, or hers?'

'What about you, Inspector? Whose interests are you really concerned with? After everything I've been through, I don't trust anyone.'

The inspector looked down at the money in his hand for a moment, as if it were a sacred object. A sadness had come into his eyes. He slid it back into the envelope and closed the seal.

'Do you want me to pass this money to Ms Yamamoto?'

'I just want to get out of here. If it costs me a year's salary, then so be it.'

'If this is your decision, I will honour it, Malloy-san,' he said. 'But I have a feeling it is going to cost you so much more.'

Officer Tomada accompanied him down to the holding area. She waited outside the locker room as he changed from his blue uniform into his stale, bloodstained clothes. They seemed a size too large after a week of prison rations. His wallet and phone were in a sealed plastic bag. He had no shoes.

'Inspector Saito asked me to give you this,' Tomada said. She handed him a business card printed in Japanese.

'What is it?' Alex asked.

She pointed to the numbers hidden amongst the *kanji* and *hiragana* characters. 'It's Inspector Saito's direct line at Ushigome,' she said. 'His cell phone number is on the other side.'

'Why does he want me to have this?'

Tomada looked up at him with her blank, unquestioning eyes. 'He thinks you are in a very serious situation now. He wants you to be able to get hold of him quickly. I suggest you accept his offer. It's not one I've seen him make before.'

Alex shook his head. 'I don't need it.'

Tomada pushed the business card into his hand. 'I wouldn't be so sure,' she said.

The daylight was blinding when he opened the main doors of Ushigome and stepped out on to the street. It was just after midday and the streets were busy with office workers, walking in groups. The noises of the city, the passing traffic and the snatches of bright, unguarded conversation were disorienting at first. Alex felt dizzy, almost drunk, as his senses were over-loaded. He was walking barefoot, his clothes soiled and stained. A pair of teenage students passed him and stared in unison at his appearance. Alex stared back. He looked like the survivor of some unreported disaster but he was too exhausted to be self-conscious now. He was free, that was all that mattered. He could walk where he pleased without having to follow instructions or be wary of violence. That alone was enough to make him want to cry tears of relief.

At a lunch counter near the station, he ordered a bowl of noodles and a glass of water. The owner looked at his appearance and insisted on payment before he would serve any food. Alex counted the change from his pockets out on to the counter and ate hurriedly, as if fearing someone would snatch the bowl away before he had eaten his fill. The food was quick and cheap but too rich after a week of prison rations. The broth turned over queasily in his stomach. For a moment, he thought he might be sick but he held it down. He walked along the concourse and took the escalator to the western platform and stood at the far end, away from the crowds and waited for the train home.

His room was as he had left it. The blind was rolled up and his laundry was hanging from the drying pole outside his window, the clothes streaked with several days' worth of grime and bleached by the sun. He took them in and tossed them into a pile in the corner of his room. It was only now, alone behind the locked door, that Alex started to feel safe. It was over. What was going to happen in the coming days, he had no idea.

He connected his phone to the charger and switched it on. There were twelve missed calls: ten from the Excelsior School and two from Hiro. No matter how difficult the conversation was going to be, he knew the first call he had to make. He dialled the number for the school and asked to speak to Craig Wyndham.

'You're finally out then?' Craig said.

Alex grimaced at the words. He had hoped the reason for his absence would somehow still be secret.

'How did you find out?' he asked.

'After you hadn't shown up to work for a few days or returned my calls, I contacted the police to report you missing. Imagine my surprise when I found out they had you in custody.'

'It was all a misunderstanding, Craig. I was released without charge.'

'You've been gone for a week.'

'It was a complicated misunderstanding.'

'So what happened?'

'I really don't want to talk about it, to be honest. I just want to come back to work.'

Craig gave a short laugh. 'You really expect me to welcome you back as if nothing's happened?'

'I need my job right now. I can't afford to lose it.'

'All the teachers here know where you've been. Some of them don't want to work with you any more. Some of the female staff are scared of you.'

'That's ridiculous.'

'Is it? What if your students find out? Or their parents? How will that look? I'll be the one in trouble if I take you back, knowing you're a potential threat to others.'

Alex was pacing now, desperately trying to think of anything he could say to make his case. 'Please, Craig. I have to work. I can't lose my income.'

'It's too late, Alex.'

'I really need your help.'

'Now, you expect my help? After all the trouble you've made for me? Well, I'm not inclined to give it. Come and pick up your personal items on Monday. I'll box them up for you.' He hung up.

Alex took a moment to let the gravity of his situation sink in. He knew he should have expected it to turn out this way, but it was still a devastating blow. He felt drained. He lay down on his futon and tried to think. There were footsteps on the landing as the other tenants came and went and greeted each other in friendly voices. They were living lives that seemed unimaginable to him now. Easy and carefree.

His phone buzzed as a text arrived and Alex checked it quickly, hoping it was Craig. He was surprised to see it was from Naoko. He opened it and read the message.

*I have your money. Now it's all over.*

He read it again, saying the words slowly in his head, letting them trickle down like poison. He had protected her from Inspector Saito during his time in prison. He had refused to implicate her in any wrongdoing, hoping that there was a way to salvage their relationship once he was released. But now, as if losing his job wasn't enough, he had to endure this. Had to sit back and have his face rubbed in it as she revelled in her victory.

It was the hardest blow out of the many he had received. He shut his phone off. Fuck this, Alex thought. Fuck Naoko. Fuck Tokyo. Fuck everyone.

# 19

THE EXPRESSWAY HEADING NORTH WAS SHADOWED BY OFFICE buildings and the pale elevations of apartment blocks. Alex slept in the passenger seat. From time to time, he drifted up and looked around but the view was always the same. Slabs of cement and glass and steel, all stacked up like tombstones in the flat grey light of morning. Two hours further and he opened his eyes and there it was outside the window. The real world, lush and green, spreading out across a low, flat plain to a range of dark hills in the distance. Everywhere he looked there were fields of rice ready for harvest and irrigation ditches banked with cinder pathways. Old women stood in rows, bent double, submerged to their knees in the muddy water.

Hiro was driving, tapping the steering wheel along to the radio. 'You should try it,' he said. 'It's good for the soul to get some Japanese soil between your toes.'

Alex shook himself awake and rubbed his face. He felt the raised track of the scar on his cheek. 'It feels good just to get away from Tokyo for a while.'

'I know. But the best thing about leaving the city is going back to it later.'

'Where are we staying?' Alex asked.

'It's a surprise. You'll find out when we get there.'

'I think I've had enough of surprises.'

'Just wait and see, *gaijin*. This is the kind of surprise that's worth waiting for.'

Soon the hills rose up and the trees grew ever bigger and thicker and the hills steepened into mountains. The road twisted and followed the contours and grades up towards Mount Asama. They drove on towards Karuizawa, past the wedding chapels and grand hotels, the air clear and fresh. Beyond the Usui pass, the buildings gave way to clipped golf courses and then forests of larch and birch and the road dipped and rose in tight bends. Hiro took a sharp turn on to a dirt track that led over a stone bridge and pulled up in front of a large Alpine-style house built under the forest canopy. There was a swimming pool to one side and a terraced garden with beds of irises and hydrangeas. Rows of Japanese maples lined the flagstone path leading up to the veranda.

'How did we afford this place?' Alex asked.

Hiro didn't reply. He sounded the car horn and waited. The front door opened and two young women stepped outside into the sunlight. They waved excitedly towards the car. It was Yuko and Kyumi.

'*Okaeri nasai!*' they shouted in unison, their voices high and bright. They sounded excited to have visitors, as if they had waited a long time for their guests' arrival.

'There's your surprise,' Hiro said. 'Two little geisha to spoil us for the weekend and make you forget your troubles. Make you forget your own name if you're not careful.'

Alex had grown suspicious of unexpected company. 'I'm not sure I've got the energy for this,' he said. 'I just need some peace and quiet to get my head together.'

'Don't worry. You can relax here. These girls know how to help you do that.'

'They own this house?'

'It belongs to one of Kyumi's regulars. He's out of the country for a while.'

'And he's given us permission to use the place while he's away?'

Hiro gave a broad, mischievous smile. 'Don't worry. It's just a weekend place. His home is in Saitama. Come on. Let's go and see what's inside.'

The interior was vast. The living room had a cathedral ceiling reaching up to timbered rafters and a huge granite chimney breast with the head of a stag mounted above the mantelpiece. There were certificates and diplomas hanging on the walls from research institutes all over the world and framed letters of gratitude from charitable institutions.

'Who is this guy?' Alex asked. 'Some kind of philanthropist?'

Kyumi shrugged. 'He was a surgeon but he's retired now,' she said. 'He's in Hawaii on a sailing trip until the end of next week. He brings me here all the time in the summer. He won't mind us using the place while he's away.'

There was a note of disbelief in her voice, as if she were trying to convince herself.

'What about his family?' Alex asked. 'What happens if they turn up and find us here?'

Kyumi shook her head. 'There's no chance of that,' she said. 'He never brings them to Karuizawa. Not with the kind of things he likes to do here.'

They walked out on to the sun terrace at the back of the house. Yuko had made a jug of grapefruit sour. She poured drinks for everyone and passed them round.

'*Kanpai*,' she said, and touched her glass to Alex's.

'Cheers,' he replied. 'Thank you for this.'

'How have you been?' she asked. 'It's been a while since I last saw you.'

Alex could tell that she knew the answer already. Hiro must have enjoyed telling her, he thought.

'I've been good,' he lied, not wanting to explain himself. 'How are things with you?'

'So so. My father died.' Her voice was flat and emotionless.

Alex put down his glass. 'I'm sorry to hear that. When did it happen?'

'Ten days ago.'

'You must be very upset.'

'It's okay. He was old and he'd been sick for a long time. Even my mother wasn't too unhappy.'

'You look well, at least.'

'Thank you,' she said. 'I think you've lost weight since I last saw you.'

'I've been fasting.'

Yuko laughed. 'I'll cook dinner soon and fatten you up a little.'

'I'd like that,' Alex said.

Yuko filled his glass and Alex sipped it slowly. The house stood alone, surrounded by pine forest, with no other buildings close by. The manicured lawn was dotted with fallen pine cones dried to husks in the sun. Alex felt the mountain breeze blow over him. The flagstones on the patio were warm beneath his feet. He could feel the tension drifting away. The girls changed into bathing suits and lay out on sunloungers by the pool. Hiro took a seat next to him and poured himself a drink.

'I thought you were still mad at me,' Alex said.

'About Naoko?'

'Yes.'

'I am,' Hiro said. 'But after all you've been through it wouldn't be fair to argue with you now.'

'I should have listened to you. I'm sorry.'

'I've known her a long time. I could have told you it wouldn't end well. But no one could have predicted how crazy you both managed to get.'

Alex felt uncomfortable being chastised after all that had happened. He had changed now, seen a side of life in Japan that Hiro had no idea of. Survived the cell block and the prison yard at Ushigome. It seemed strange to be confronted on the old terms of their friendship, with him always cast as the junior partner but he knew he needed to hold his tongue. There was one more favour he needed to ask from Hiro now.

Alex took a breath before he spoke. 'There's something I haven't told you,' he said. 'I'm in more trouble.'

'What do you mean?'

'I had to borrow money to buy my way out of jail. I need to pay it back quickly.'

'How much?'

'Five million yen.'

Hiro gave a low whistle of surprise. 'Where did you get hold of that much cash at short notice?'

'There were some Japanese guys in there who were eager to lend it to me.'

Hiro looked at Alex from the corner of his eye. 'Yakuza?' he asked.

'I don't know. But I'm wary of owing them money for too long. There was a fight inside the cell block one day – a man had been warned by them to keep away. They took offence when he didn't listen. He was slashed with a razor.'

'This sounds serious, Alex. Why didn't you ask me? I would have lent you the money.'

'I wasn't allowed to make a single phone call all the time I was inside. There were no visitors either. Not even a lawyer. I was lost in there, Hiro. And I did what I had to do to get out. But I need your help now. I want to borrow the money from you and pay these people back. Then I'll be in your debt instead of theirs.'

'Of course,' Hiro said without hesitation. 'I'll get you the money as soon as we go back to Tokyo.'

Alex's face softened with relief. 'You don't want to think it over? It's a lot of money.'

'There's nothing to think over. I'm happy to be able to help.'

'Thanks, Hiro. I'm really grateful.'

'The only thing I ask is that you stay away from Naoko.'

Hiro said the words quickly, as if even he knew his request was too high-handed; the arrogant assumption that he could order people around because he had money. Alex wanted to tell him to forget the whole deal but he stopped himself. There was no other way to find that amount of cash at short notice, and he knew he was in danger as long as he was in debt to Jun and his friends. Naoko's message made it clear that she thought it was over between them anyway. He made a simple calculation.

'Okay,' he said. 'If that's what you want, then I won't contact her again.'

As he said the words, Alex felt hollow inside. Hiro couldn't contain his satisfaction. He beamed with victory.

'Forget about her. That's my advice,' he said. 'Now just do what you should have done in the first place. Get your comfort where it's easy.'

Hiro pointed over to the girls lying in the sun. They were on their backs, with the straps of their bikinis unfastened from their shoulders, their skin slick with sunscreen. Hiro stood and crept up behind them. Scooping up a handful of water from the pool, he edged closer and tossed it over them. The girls shrieked in surprise. Alex watched and leaned back against his chair. The sun was streaking down through the branches above him as they swayed in the breeze. He was starting to feel dizzy from the cocktails. He thought of Naoko and wondered where she was and what she was doing now. There was no point going over it again so he tried to think of nothing. He listened to the sound of the water moving back and forth as it reflected from the tiles at the side of the pool. The sound of water, just like the night in the temple garden, falling from the waterfall into the bamboo pipe. It seemed such a long time ago that a wave of sorrow, almost grief, came over him. He stood and walked to the water's edge and dived in, swimming down to the cool tiles at the bottom of the pool.

*

Yuko cooked *nabe* on a small stove set on the table in the dining room. It was a broth of vegetables and tofu and when they had eaten most of it she added rice and egg to the pot and beat it together. After dinner, they finished the sake and Kyumi found a bottle of vintage *sho-chu*. It was unopened, still sealed in its wooden casket. She twisted off the cork and poured four tall glasses. Kyumi was drunk now and wanted to show off the house. She took Hiro by the arm and dragged him from room to room, proudly describing each piece of furniture as if it were her own. She could see Hiro was soon losing interest.

'Let me show you what the good professor likes to use the house for when we're alone,' she said.

The girls locked themselves inside the master bedroom and when they appeared Kyumi was wearing a full, white wedding gown with a taffeta veil and a long silk train that Yuko carried behind her like a bridesmaid. She paraded up and down the length of the living room in short, unsteady steps.

'It's his daughter's,' Kyumi said. 'Her wedding was in the town last year. It's considered very exclusive to be married in Karuizawa. The Emperor met his wife nearby so it's a sign of good breeding. I'd like to be married here one day, I think.'

Hiro began to laugh and Kyumi sounded hurt.

'What's so funny?' she said. 'I will find a husband one day.'

'I think you might be looking in the wrong places,' he said.

She turned to him and lifted the veil. Her face was grey and pallid and her lips were white, her eyes blackened with make-up to look like a corpse.

'*Honto?*' Hiro said. 'What did you do that for?'

Kyumi shrugged. 'It's what the professor likes. He plays his daughter's wedding video on the cinema screen while I lie there with my arms folded across my chest. He sobs his heart out once he's finished but it's the only thing that gets him going. I've tried everything else, believe me. Maybe it's what happens when you're surrounded by books all day long.'

Hiro looked to Alex. 'This guy sounds a bit crazy to me.'

Kyumi smiled ruefully. 'You're all crazy. Every one of you.'

The smile left her face and tears began to flow over the make-up, leaving black, inky trails down her cheeks. She gathered up the train of the wedding dress and ran from the house and jumped into the pool. The layers of the wedding dress fluttered under the water like the skirts of a jellyfish as she surfaced.

'This isn't fair!' she shouted. 'I'm never going to wear a beautiful dress like this for real. No man wants to marry me. They only want to fuck me.' She was floundering in the pool, lit up in the darkness, her voice coming in sobs.

'Take care of her, Hiro,' Alex said. 'She's too drunk.'

Hiro stood and walked to the poolside and jumped in, laughing. Alex walked around the veranda to the other side of the house. He felt like being alone. He could hear Kyumi's voice, full of tears, crying that she would never be forgiven. She was wrong, he thought. Whoever really cared for her would find nothing to forgive. There was no malice or betrayal in her. She was honest about her motives, even if they were shallow and trivial. That wasn't impossible to forgive. Not like selling out someone who loved you just to save yourself. Not like fabricating your whole life.

He took a seat on a wooden bench in the formal garden, facing out towards the great pinnacles of the mountain range lit up by the stars. An immense night hung above him. A meteor descended, streaking brightly through the dark canopy. An airliner flashed its navigation lights as it passed to the north. There was a chorus of nocturnal calls from the forest and the creaking of timber as it swayed in the wind. He thought about turning and running, going straight to the airport for the next flight back to London, but there was no point. Despite everything that had happened, he still had nothing to go back for.

There were footsteps and Alex looked behind him. Yuko was approaching with two glasses and the bottle of *sho-chu*.

'Do you want me to go?' she asked.

'Come and sit beside me,' Alex said.

She moved in close to him and he placed an arm around her shoulder.

'I don't like Tokyo any more,' Yuko said.

Alex felt her breath against his neck. 'Why not?'

'I don't know really. I don't have any reason to be there now.'

'You have the family business to run.'

'I don't want to be a businesswoman. It's too hard.'

'What will you do?'

'I think I will sell the shop and my mother and I will move away.'

'Where will you go?'

'I don't know. Somewhere quiet.'

They stared out at the night in silence for a while and Alex felt her body rise and fall as she breathed. He could sense her thinking beside him.

'It's hard on your own, isn't it?' she said.

'Yes,' Alex said. 'It is.'

'You must miss your family. Being so far away from home.'

'Not really. I miss my brother, I suppose.'

'I miss him. My father. There's so much I wish I could say to him now.'

'You always miss people when you know you'll never see them again.'

'Shall we talk about something else?' Yuko asked.

'Maybe we should just sit here for a while.'

'Are you comfortable with me?'

'Yes,' Alex said. 'Very comfortable.'

He looked down at her and, soon, she was sleeping. He thought about carrying her back into the house but didn't want to wake her. He took a long drink from the bottle of *sho-chu* and sat in the darkness, watching the passage of the stars.

When he woke, it was dawn and a pale light was rising over the trees. Yuko was beside him, holding his phone to her ear.

'Hello?' she said, and waited. 'Hello? Is anyone there?'

She handed the phone to Alex but the line was dead.

'Who was that?' he asked.

She looked concerned. 'I don't know. I only answered it because it was so early. You were asleep and I thought it might be an emergency. I could hear someone breathing, I think it was a woman. I tried to speak to her but she just hung up.'

# 20

THE MONEY WAS INSIDE HER BAG, STILL SEALED IN THE
envelope Inspector Saito had delivered to her. It had always been
Naoko's intention to hand the whole package back to Alex
unopened. That chance was gone now, she thought.

When she came out of the station into the midday heat, the
boulevard was busy with people walking in the shade of the tall
zelkova trees. The shops near Omotesando station were cheap
and kitsch, not what she wanted at all. She walked in confident
strides, heading towards the signs for Gucci, Louis Vuitton and
Dior in the distance.

It had been 5.51 a.m. when she called his number. Too early
for it to be another tenant in his guesthouse or a teacher at the
school that had answered. It had to be someone intimate at that
hour, someone comfortable answering his phone who had no
expectation of hearing another female voice. At 5.51 it had to
be someone he was sharing a bed with. Naoko couldn't find a
way to figure it otherwise.

She started modestly. In Tsuichi Chimaru she found a selection
of new-season dresses she liked and took them to the fitting
room. She tried them on and chose the two that suited her best
and carried them to the counter. It was as they were being
folded and she took the money from the envelope that Naoko

remembered her goal. She was there to spend it all, not to use restraint. From then on, she was possessed.

She held her head high as she entered the most exclusive boutiques, free of her usual fear of being overawed by the outlandish price tags. YSL, Jil Sander, Ferragamo, Ralph Lauren. She bought a bias-cut skirt from Céline and a blouse with a foliage pattern from Comme des Garçons. She bought underwear sets and formal shoes. Clothes she knew she would never wear, clothes that she wasn't even sure fitted her, anything to get rid of the money. Spending so freely was alien to her nature and by the afternoon it had started to become distasteful. She decided her final purchase would be a gift for Hiro's mother. A scarf from Hermès would be suitable, she thought. In the store, she found a silk square in bright blue, bordered with white and gold and printed with a pattern of cranes in flight. She was tired now and ready to leave, but as she passed the Chanel shop and noticed the window display, she couldn't resist.

The jacket was on a mannequin, softly lit from below. It was vintage, in black with brass buttons, the stitching perfect on the seams and pockets. When she went inside and asked to try it on, the assistant looked dubious at first. But as she saw the armful of branded bags Naoko was carrying and her look of determination, she relented and fetched the jacket from the display. In the fitting room, Naoko remembered the voice she had heard, young and girlish, calling out to her hesitantly down the telephone line. She paid for the jacket with a thick stack of ten-thousand-yen notes and a thrilling sense of satisfaction.

Yukiko closed the door and led Naoko out on to the balcony so they could sit in the shade. Naoko set her shopping at her feet. She noticed how frail Yukiko was looking. She was wearing a thin *yukata* and a sun hat that was too big. She had to keep reaching up to push the brim back from her face. The birdcage hanging from the balcony rafters was empty and the door was open.

'What happened to your songbird?' Naoko asked.

Yukiko shrugged. 'It's gone. It flew away yesterday.'

'Why did you leave the cage open?'

'He was restless. It seemed cruel to leave him in there alone.'

Naoko looked out from the balcony, across the rooftops and rail tracks of Asakusa. 'I wonder where he is now? He's probably out there trying to mate with the local pigeons.'

'If I leave the door open, he'll come back eventually. He looks the type.'

'What type?'

'The type that can't resist putting themselves behind bars.'

Naoko laughed. 'You really think so?'

'Of course. Anyway, it's Hiro fault. He shouldn't have bought such a beautiful one.'

'Where is Hiro?' Naoko asked.

'I haven't seen him for a while now. He said he was going out of town for the weekend.'

'Did he say where?'

'You know he doesn't tell me anything.'

Naoko handed her the package from Hermès and watched as Yukiko unwrapped it and took out the silk scarf. She unfolded it and held it up to examine it closely, her mouth open in amazement.

'It's to thank you for all you've done for me. The cranes are supposed to bring good luck.'

'This looks very expensive,' Yukiko said.

'Of course. I like to buy you nice things. Anyway, look at what I've bought for myself.'

She reached down and handed Yukiko the glossy black bag from Chanel. Yukiko peered inside.

'Take it out and open it.'

Yukiko pulled out the tissue-paper bundle and laid it on her lap and slowly started to unwrap the jacket.

'It's beautiful,' she said.

155

'Try it on.'

'No. It will look silly on me. You try it and let me look at you. I'm sure it's even better when you wear it.'

Naoko took the jacket and slipped into it. The closeness of the fit and the softness of the material felt luxurious to the point of decadence. She turned around to show it from all angles.

'Do you like it?' Naoko asked.

'I think it looks lovely. But it must have cost more than a month's wages. How can you afford it?'

Naoko tried to sound nonchalant. 'I had a windfall,' she said. 'And I think it's important to share good fortune with the people closest to you.'

'A windfall?'

'Quite a big one.'

'So you decided to treat yourself to a whole new wardrobe?'

'Why not?' Naoko said. 'We both know that clothes last longer than men.'

Yukiko looked her in the eye and immediately saw what she was trying to hide. She had known her long enough to see straight through any attempt to disguise her troubles. She glanced down at the shopping bags lying at Naoko's feet.

'I think you'd better tell me what's going on,' she said.

Naoko began to tell the story – about Alex, the gallery, Megumi and Saito – and it all tumbled out of her as if it had been waiting desperately to escape for some time. She could hear herself as she talked and her face began to flush in embarrassment. Her words all sounded so childish.

'Slow down,' Yukiko said. 'Who's Alex?'

'He's Hiro's friend. He was with me the night I brought Hiro here drunk.'

'The *gaijin*?'

'Yes.'

'Why was he arrested at your apartment?'

'He made a big scene and one of the neighbours called the police. You know how stuck-up the people are in my building.

They all think I don't belong there anyway. When the officers arrived, I panicked. I told them the first thing that came into my head. If I told the truth, I knew I could lose my job and my apartment, so I came out with a story to convince them it wasn't my fault. How was I to know Alex was going to come back while the police were still there? Once they had arrested him, I had to stick to my story.'

'And you asked for *jidan*?'

'Yes.'

'Five million yen?'

'That's right.'

'So why not give it back to him?'

'I was going to,' Naoko said. 'That was always my intention. I called him this morning and some girl answered his phone. It didn't take him long to replace me, so now the money is mine. That seems fair to me.'

'Where did the *gaijin* get the money? Is he rich?'

'I have no idea. He lives on a teacher's salary. Maybe he had savings he never spoke about.'

Yukiko sounded concerned. 'And now you've spent all of it on clothes and shoes?'

'Not all of it,' Naoko said, struggling to maintain the moral high ground. 'I spent over half of it but I still have about two million yen left.'

'This isn't like you, Naoko. No good will come of this. It will end up hurting you, not helping. If you want my advice, you should take all of it back. It won't bring you any happiness.'

Naoko knew she was right. 'I don't know how to solve this now,' she said. 'I feel ashamed of spending the money. I was angry and not thinking clearly. But surely I deserve something for all I've suffered?'

Yukiko shook her head slowly. She folded the scarf and handed it back to Naoko. 'The funny thing with suffering,' she said, 'is that, just when you think you've suffered enough, you realize it's only just beginning.'

# 21

THE CAR ARRIVED AT SEVEN THIRTY, AS ARRANGED. NAOKO watched as it pulled up at the entrance to her building and waited at the kerb with the engine running. She fastened the buttons on her new Chanel jacket and sprayed a mist of scent before her, turning through it twice as it hung in the air. She stood for a moment and examined her reflection in the mirror. Tonight was her chance to redeem herself in Mr Kimura's eyes. She would listen and smile sincerely and talk as little as possible. She had been doing this long enough to be able to charm her way through another business meeting at a dinner table of rich, older men. There was no mystery in what they expected of her. She looked at herself one last time and locked the apartment as she left.

The driver held the car door open for her and Naoko thanked him as she climbed inside. She remained silent as he drove through Mejiro and along Showa Dori, towards the heart of Ginza. When they turned east towards the government buildings at the edge of Hibiya Park, Naoko was surprised. She leaned forward to catch the driver's attention.

'I thought I was meeting Mr Kimura at a restaurant in Ginza,' she said.

The driver kept his eyes on the road. 'I'm to take you

to the Imperial Hotel,' he said. 'Those are my instructions.'

'The Imperial? Are you sure?'

He shrugged and glanced back at her in the rear-view mirror. 'Kimura-san said for you to give his name at reception.'

The Imperial Hotel stood in front of the park, its stone façade dotted with squares of yellow light. The car pulled into the forecourt and a doorman helped her out and guided her through the entrance. The cavernous lobby smelled of misery and old money. Naoko approached the desk and smiled politely at the desk manager. When she explained she was meeting Mr Kimura, he told her he was waiting for her in Suite 237. She assumed he would have made a reservation in the restaurant or brasserie at a secluded table where they could conduct business without being overheard. Perhaps the client was more secretive than usual, she thought. The desk manager called over a bellboy, who led her through the lobby and up to the seventh floor in the lift.

Mr Kimura was reclining in a plush suede armchair at the far side of the suite. He raised his head as Naoko entered but he didn't stand to greet her. He was deep in conversation with another man, who was sitting in the chair opposite, only the back of his head visible. Kimura was wearing plaid trousers and his navy club blazer. The negotiations for the *ukiyo-e* sale must have started on the golf course, Naoko thought. They were well under way, it seemed to her. Behind them, a picture window looked out over the nightscape of illuminated buildings, the vast gardens of the Imperial Palace in darkness to one side. The door to the balcony was open and the thin curtains billowed in the breeze. An icicle chandelier glowed gently in the centre of the room, the subdued lighting giving the space a dreamy quality.

'Good evening, Kimura-san,' Naoko said as she approached.

'Good evening, Naoko. Your timing is excellent, as always. You can save us from falling into an interminable discussion of politics.' He indicated his companion. 'I believe you know our new customer already?'

The man raised himself slowly from the deep upholstery of the armchair. His bulk was significant enough to cause him to strain as he pushed himself to his feet and turned around to face her. She faltered as she recognized him.

'So pleased to see you again, Ms Yamamoto. You look delightful.'

He bowed, with his face directed towards her, his gaze bright with a triumphant sheen. It was Togo Nishi, looking as if he had gained even more weight since the evening they had met on the blossom-viewing cruise. His beady eyes sat wide apart on his face, dark and piercing as an owl's. He smiled knowingly, as if fully aware that his presence was unexpected.

Naoko caught herself and took a breath. 'Good evening, Nishi-san,' she said. 'I'm so happy we are finally able to help you find the artwork you were so desperately looking for.'

On a stand in one corner of the room, a traditional Japanese woodblock print stood unscrolled. The print showed a river-bank scene, a medieval courtesan practising the *shamisen* as two herons waded among the reeds before her, their beaks poised above the water as they searched for fish. It was a Kunisada, from the Edo period, and probably a second or third run, a vintage rarely seen outside of a museum. The layers of the courtesan's clothing and the reeds at the water's edge were perfectly etched and the flowing river suggested by subtle brushstrokes of pale blue ink. The delicate paper was rippled slightly at the edges from years of unfurling but the ink was still bright and crisp. It was a rare example of an original, high-quality *ukiyo-e* and Naoko guessed it was supremely valuable, about ten million yen, she thought.

'Would you like a drink while we finalize the sale, Ms Yamamoto? I'm waiting for a call from my accountant to announce the funds have been transferred and the matter is concluded.'

'Whatever you think is best, Nishi-san.'

There was a bottle of vintage Pol Roger in an ice bucket on the cabinet and Nishi poured two glasses and handed one to Naoko. He motioned for her to take a seat. He sat opposite her and ran a hand through his receding hair.

'I hope you like the surroundings,' he said. 'I always find the service at the Imperial first class. It makes for a most conducive atmosphere to celebrate a successful purchase. I've ordered dinner to be served later, once business matters are finished with.'

'That sounds very agreeable.'

'Magnificent, isn't it?' Nishi said, looking admiringly at the print. 'Do you know it?'

She smiled innocently, aware that it was always best to feign ignorance with men like Nishi. 'It's a failing of mine,' she said, 'but I'm afraid I know nothing of traditional art.'

He seemed pleased to be able to show off his basic knowledge. 'It's from a series called *Twenty-two Stations along the Kanda River*. One of the best in circulation. An amazing find.'

'Yes. It's very beautiful. And so well preserved. It looks like it was printed only days ago.'

Nishi basked in the compliment, as if he had painted it himself. 'Tastes were so much more sophisticated in the Edo period. And the craftsmanship is exquisite. I'm going to give it to my wife as a gift for our anniversary.'

'I'm sure she will be overjoyed.'

'I should hope so. A fifteen-million-yen gift is to be appreciated under any circumstances.'

The mention of the price almost made Naoko choke. It was way over even the most optimistic valuation of such a piece. She was unsure why a man like Nishi would be so eager to overpay.

Nishi's phone began to ring. 'This should be confirmation of the transfer,' he said. 'If you don't mind, I'll take this in private.'

He stood up and excused himself and went into one of the adjoining rooms of the suite. Kimura watched him leave with a solemn expression. Once he had left the room, he clapped his hands together with glee.

'Well done, Naoko,' he said. 'You have made some great catches in the past but this is one of the best deals you've brought in.'

She was slightly confused. 'I'm not so sure I deserve your praise, Kimura-san.'

'Nonsense. All day, Nishi has been dropping your name into the conversation. It seems you made a big impression on him when you met back in the spring. I know I can always rely on you to bring new business to the gallery.'

The memory of that evening was still fresh enough for Naoko to picture it clearly. It was surprising to hear their meeting recalled by Kimura in such a positive light. Perhaps Nishi had been too drunk to remember quite how boorish he had been, she thought. She had no way of being sure what his motives were.

'Of course, I expect you to maintain your hospitable manner once I've left you two alone,' Kimura said. 'We both know a sale to a customer is never actually completed. One is only ever the prelude to the next.'

Naoko began to frown but stopped herself. 'You're not staying?' she asked.

Kimura shook his head. 'Nishi has asked that you are left to dine alone together. He very much wants to spend time with you in private.'

'I'm not sure why,' Naoko said.

'Oh, I'm sure you can guess.'

The hair on her arms began to stand up. 'I thought we would all have dinner together and then I would leave with you, as usual?'

'Yes. But our usual customers don't pay such a premium for the pleasure of your company.' Kimura's manner began to take on a harsh, clinical edge. The avuncular warmth he liked to radiate had completely disappeared. 'I would have thought it was instinctual for you by now, Naoko. After all, it's not as if you are a stranger to such circumstances.'

She placed her champagne glass on the table. 'Why don't you tell me exactly what is going on, Kimura-san? Then there's no confusion between us.'

He stood and began to pace before the open window leading out to the balcony, his hands clasped behind his back. The headlights of passing cars silhouetted his figure as he spoke.

'I always believed in you, Naoko. I always thought I knew who you really were. But it appears I have been deceived. I believed you to be shrewd and ambitious but, ultimately, an intelligent and trustworthy employee. Someone who knew which lines were not to be crossed. Then there was that unfortunate business with the *gaijin* at the private view and the involvement of the police in the disturbance at your apartment. My belief in you began to be shaken. Well, now something new has come to light. Something that casts my trust in you as the foolishness of an old man.'

'I'm not sure I understand,' Naoko said.

'I'm afraid Megumi has come to me with certain information regarding your previous life before you came into my employment. Information that she believed she had no choice but to share with me, due to its serious nature.'

'Megumi isn't to be trusted. She's jealous of me and has been trying to discredit me for some time now.'

Kimura stopped pacing. He reached inside his jacket and retrieved something from the pocket.

'I'm not sure I would have believed her without evidence,' he said.

He tossed an envelope down on to the table before her and Naoko picked it up.

It was addressed to him, in Megumi's handwriting. Naoko looked up at Kimura for some sign of what she might find inside but he had turned his back to her and stood haloed by the lights of the city. She reached for the envelope and opened it.

Inside, she was expecting to see a note or letter of some kind but instead there was a business card tucked down in the bottom corner. She reached inside and took it out and instantly understood its meaning.

The name, printed in bold *kanji* on one side of the card, was that of Hisako Ota. The address was on the other side; Naoko hadn't visited for years: *The House of Fallen Leaves, Meidai Dori, Ochanomizu.* She tried to work out how it had come to be in Mr Kimura's possession. Megumi must have overheard their conversation when Hisako had stumbled into the restaurant bathroom. She must have tracked her down somehow and found out all of the details of Naoko's youth. All of the indiscretions that she had tried for so long to outrun. She looked up from the card, her face drained of all vitality.

Kimura slowly turned to face her.

'Megumi was most upset when she came to me with this. She wouldn't tell me how she had discovered the information, but she felt very betrayed.'

'*She* felt betrayed?'

'In the sense that you have pretended to be someone you're not in the time she has known you and that this has continued for so long. It seems that you have taken us all in with your lies.'

'Please, Kimura-san,' Naoko said. 'I've never been anything less than true and faithful. I have given my life to the gallery. Please believe me.'

'I wish I could, Naoko.'

'Does this mean you're firing me?'

'Firing you? No. It means that when people like Nishi make propositions such as the one he has today, I no longer have a reason to turn him down.'

Kimura stood before the Kunisada print to appreciate it one more time. His eyes were full of admiration. As he turned to Naoko, it was replaced with contempt.

'I am going to leave now,' he said. 'If you value your position at the gallery, you will do all that Nishi asks of you.'

When he returned from the side room and quietly closed the door behind him, Nishi seemed surprised to find Naoko in the suite alone. The chandelier cast soft sepia shadows over the tastefully arranged furniture, the redwood cabinet and antique Berber carpet. The night air breezed in through the open window, playing at the edges of the unscrolled print. The courtesan gazing enigmatically from across the centuries. Naoko had managed to compose herself. She was sitting on the edge of the corner sofa, sipping from a freshly poured glass of Pol Roger as if this was the evening she had always envisaged.

'I have to admit I didn't believe Kimura when he said you would obey his instructions. I thought your fiery spirit would overcome your pragmatism. It seems he knows you better than most.'

Naoko smiled to herself. 'Kimura-san has always been a most benevolent and insightful man.'

Nishi picked the business card up from the coffee table and looked it over. 'He said this would be a revelation to you.'

'It is. But not for the reasons he imagines.'

'The House of Fallen Leaves,' Nishi read out loud, his voice full of portent. 'What is this? Some kind of bordello?'

'Something like that.'

'And you worked there?'

'Yes. When I was a student.'

'So I was right about you, after all. You have come a long way.'

Naoko gave a resigned dip of her head. 'It wouldn't appear so,' she said.

Nishi stood above her, savouring his good fortune, turning the card over between his short, grub-like fingers. He read it over one more time, muttering the address under his breath. Then he tossed the card back down on to the table and was on her in a flurry, his body pressing hers down into the soft over-stuffed sofa. She could feel the smooth, damp skin of his face against her neck and the strain of the buttons on her Chanel jacket as he tried to tug them open.

'Wait,' she said, shrugging him off and slipping out from beneath his bulk. 'Let me do it.'

He was flushed and breathless, as if he had just climbed a flight of stairs. 'Yes,' he said. 'Let me watch. I want to enjoy all of you.'

She began to undress.

As each piece of clothing was removed, Naoko began to feel more resigned to her fate. A part of her wanted to turn and run from the room, go up to the roof and throw herself down into the darkened street. She could see that she was losing herself for ever. All she had worked for was gone now and the realization left her numb. She tried to imagine a way that she could salvage some credibility after this was over, to believe somehow that Kimura would still value her. She knew that was impossible now. If he had found out about her past, she would always be a whore in his eyes, no matter what the truth was. She let the thought echo around her mind as she unclipped the fasteners on her skirt and let it fall to the floor. She stood before Nishi in her underwear.

He motioned for her to turn around. His eyes were filled with fascination, fixed on the tattoo emblazoned on her stomach and side.

'Extraordinary,' he said. 'I should have guessed you had some connection to the criminal class.'

She looked down at the lines and patterns running over her flesh and ran a hand across the skin. It was the reaction she had always expected from every Japanese man since it had been done. In a way, she thought, that was the reason she had agreed to be marked so indelibly in the first place. The tattoo meant she would always be scorned by the very people whose values she rejected in return.

She took a step closer to Nishi. A line ran beneath her belly button, covered by the ink patterning, a scar that had been long hidden by the design of the tattoo. Naoko took his hand and traced the tip of his index finger across it.

'At first the tattoo was meant only to cover up this souvenir of my surgery,' she said. 'But once I started, it seemed pointless to stop. Especially as I was paid so much to endure the method of application.'

Now it was Nishi's turn to look puzzled. 'I'm not sure what you mean,' he said.

'You can guess what kind of scar this is, surely, Nishi-san?'

She moved closer to him so he could inspect her more intimately. His eyes were wide with lust.

'So you've had a child,' he said.

'When I was sixteen years old. I had the great distinction of becoming pregnant on the night I lost my virginity.'

'Why are you telling me this?'

'I want you to know all about me.'

'Why?'

'Because it's not important to keep it a secret any more. I've never discussed this with a living soul, not since the night it happened. It was a girl. My parents insisted she was adopted, and she was taken from me in the delivery room. I never saw her again. This business card belongs to a woman who was a nurse on the ward. She recruited the schoolgirls who had the misfortune to meet her there. We were all tainted anyway, so we were easy prey. Some of the girls were happy to sleep with her clients for a few thousand yen, but that wasn't really my style, even then. She had one special customer with a distinctive taste and he was prepared to pay well for someone who would indulge him. None of the other girls could take the pain. He insisted on using a bamboo point, not an electric needle. It was a traditional skill that was dying out, he told me. He began by covering the marks that the birth had left, the ones on the outside, at least. From there I let him unleash his imagination as he saw fit. I used the money to pay my way through college. I saw no reason why I couldn't convert my bad fortune into some favourable knowledge, and then use that knowledge to make a better life. But it seems that there are some crimes that follow you for ever.'

Nishi stood up and grasped both hands around her waist. He seemed maddened by his own appetites. She could smell the sourness of his breath as he spoke. 'I want you,' he said. 'You belong to me now.'

Naoko allowed herself to weaken at the knees, her body falling back into his arms. 'Why don't we have one more glass of champagne, Nishi-san? It's such a shame to let it go to waste.'

He looked around for the bottle and saw it propped up in the ice bucket, outside on the balcony, where Naoko had left it.

'Yes, of course,' he said, and released her. He lifted back the curtain fluttering over the doorway and stepped out on to the balcony to retrieve it.

As soon as he had cleared the frame, Naoko stepped forward and slid the glass door closed and turned the lock. She stood back and watched as Nishi heard the door slam and turned in surprise. He looked for an exterior lock or handle but there was nothing. He tried to slide the door open with the palms of his hands but the huge glass pane refused to move. His face was frozen in a mask of incomprehension.

'Open the door,' he said, his voice only slightly raised, as if he was aware of disturbing the other guests.

Naoko picked up her clothes from the floor and began to dress hurriedly. 'You think I've come this far in my life to be manhandled by you?' she shouted. 'You think I've learned nothing?'

'You fucking bitch,' Nishi hissed from the balcony, straining to pull open the door and get inside. 'Open the door. Think of Kimura. Think of your job.'

She raised a sceptical eyebrow at him and laughed. 'I think that threat has lost its potency now, Nishi-san.'

She picked up her shoes and handbag and turned to leave. Nishi banged a fist on the glass. He was crimson with fury. As she looked around to make sure she had all of her belongings, the Kunisada print caught her eye from the corner of the room.

Naoko stood before it and ran a hand over the surface of the banner, feeling the silken, antique touch of the paper, the slickness of the lacquer used to protect the ink, the mastery and boldness of the draughtsmanship. Nishi seemed to freeze out on the balcony as he began to understand her intention.

'Open the door!' he screamed, in desperation.

She ignored him and opened her bag and found her lipstick and twisted out the point. Holding the scroll in one hand, she wrote 'I DON'T BELONG TO ANYONE' in thick characters the colour of autumn damask down the length of the paper. She turned the display stand towards the window so Nishi could contemplate the wisdom of his investment.

Making sure each footstep was composed and deliberate, she walked out of the suite and closed the door behind her. She pressed for the lift at the end of the corridor. The pile of the carpet was thick beneath her bare feet. In the mirror, she examined herself as she rode down to the lobby, the way her hair was teased out in loose strands and her make-up was smeared. She couldn't help but laugh out loud at her own reflection.

The lobby was empty, except for the cleaner hunched over his polisher, moving the machine back and forth over the black marble floor. Naoko walked to the reception desk, her heels still in her hand.

'I want to pay the bill for Suite 237,' she said.

The night porter checked the computer. 'Mr Nishi usually pays on account . . .'

She set her handbag on the counter and took out the envelope with the remaining *jidan* money. 'Just tell me how much it is,' she said.

Naoko counted out the money in ten-thousand-yen notes and paid the bill. She pushed the envelope back inside her bag and walked towards the revolving exit doors.

'Would you like me to call you a cab?' the night porter called after her.

'No need,' she said, without looking back.

Outside, she felt the moist night air against her face. There was no traffic as she crossed over the wide highway and walked through the gates of Hibiya Park. Old drunks were searching through the waste bins in the shadows beneath the maple trees, trying to find some scraps to eat. Policemen in fluorescent jackets were hunting them in packs, the beams of their torches criss-crossing in the dark. An officer shone a light on Naoko but when he saw she was young and well dressed he apologized and walked on.

Yukiko was right, she thought. The *jidan* payment had brought her nothing but bad luck. She was never going to see Alex again so there was no way of giving it back to him now. But she didn't want it any longer. It felt too dishonest to keep the money, or any of the purchases she had made. The city was full of people who deserved it more. Many of them were in the park with her right now.

There was a rubbish bin near the tennis courts and Naoko stopped and stared down at the old newspapers and lunch cartons rotting inside. She took the envelope from her bag with the remaining money inside and threw it on to the rubbish in the bin. Then she took off the Chanel jacket and bundled it up and stuffed it inside and tossed her new heels on top. When she got home she would give the rest of the shopping away as well.

Naoko found a bench and lit a cigarette and listened as the bums came to sift through the bin. She smiled when she heard their shouts, like some kind of gold rush, and waited there alone until the sun came up and she felt like going home.

# 22

THE *PACHINKO* PARLOUR WAS FULL OF NOISE AND CIGARETTE smoke and staccato flashes of light from the machines. Jun was right where he had said he would be, sitting in the back corner, feeding money into the slots and watching the metal balls drop through the vertical maze behind the glass. He saw Alex approach and smiled warmly, as if they were old friends greeting each other at a reunion. He was wearing an open-necked shirt printed with gingko leaves and his hair was slicked back sharply from his face. The pockmarks on his cheeks looked severe in the stark neon lighting. He had to raise his voice over the din as he shook Alex's hand.

'How are you, Russia-jin?' he asked. 'It's good to see you out of prison uniform.'

'I'm fine,' Alex said. 'It's great to see you too.'

'You found the place okay?'

'I followed the directions you sent me.'

Jun was sitting easily in his chair but his eyes were moving around the crowded room, taking in everything as he talked.

'I told you we would meet in happier times.'

'I've been waiting for you to get in touch. I have good news. A friend has agreed to lend me the money I need to repay my debt.'

Jun waved a hand cautiously and checked no one close was paying them any attention. 'Not here,' he said. 'It's all arranged for us to meet later to discuss it. Don't worry.'

'Meet where?'

'At the *onsen*. It's traditional to meet at the bath house and discuss business there. We can talk without clothes and everyone can see that nothing is hidden.'

'But is that necessary? I can get you the money I owe. Just tell me where to send it.'

'You need to discuss this in person. The arrangements have already been made.'

Alex knew there was little choice but to go along with the plan. 'Whatever you think is best,' he said. 'Are we leaving now?'

'Later. We have enough time to play some *pachinko* first.'

'I don't know how. I've never done it before.'

Jun pointed to the empty seat at the machine beside him. 'Try it. What's the worst that can happen?'

Alex slipped a five-thousand-yen note into the slot and twisted the controls without any idea what he was meant to be achieving. Around him, the old people were hypnotized, chain-smoking and burning up their pensions. The silver balls flowed in great cascades, running down into the cavities of the machine as booming electronic voices urged them on. It was impossible to fathom the fascination amidst the chaos of noise and lights. Jun was losing money fast but Alex seemed to be winning. He poured the bucket of ball bearings into the cash machine and watched as a wad of notes fluttered out on to the tray.

'Beginner's luck,' Jun said. 'It's their way to sucker new players, to get them hooked. They can tell you've never been here before so they let you win.'

'That's fine by me,' Alex said. 'I need the money.'

'You're all crooks!' Jun shouted at the control room, where the uniformed employees skulked to escape the pounding music. They stared back, cowering slightly as he shook his fist at them.

They left the arcade and walked down into the narrow back-streets of Gotanda, where the night market was set up behind the old temple. There were grey-haired women telling fortunes and bookies collecting money in the shadowed doorways. The plastic canopies of the stalls formed an arch over the street, enclosing the people packed beneath. Chicken skewers were cooking over open braziers as men in blood-smeared smocks carved great slabs of roasted pork. Power lines buzzed overhead. Alex stayed close to Jun as they pushed their way through the crowd. He turned into a quiet side alley away from the frenzy and Alex followed. Cats roamed in packs along the darkened street, shying away from their reflections in the rows of empty bottles placed along the kerb. The air was thick with incense burnt for the dead.

The entrance to the *onsen* was unmarked. Only the tall steam vents angling up from the wooden roof gave it away. Jun counted out the entrance fee for them both and laid it on the counter. The owner was hesitant to allow a foreigner inside, muttering under his breath as he looked Alex up and down. He seemed to recognize Jun's face so he didn't protest. He reluctantly took the money and waved them inside, watching warily as they took their *yukata* and towels and walked into the changing room.

The bath house was divided in two by a high wall running down the centre of the building. The place was busy, despite the late hour. Men were directed to one side, women and children to the other. There were two huge wooden tubs set down into the stone floor and banks of showers along one side of the room. Groups of old men were sitting in the bubbling water reading the racing forms and milling naked around the washrooms. From across the wall, women called out shrilly to their husbands, and the room was full of steam and the sound of footsteps falling on the wet floor.

'You have to wash before you can use the bath,' Jun said. 'Those old-timers won't let you in unless they see you scrub all that *gaijin* sweat off you.'

He sat down on a low wooden stool and began to lather his body with black bamboo soap. Alex took the stool opposite and did the same. He could see how Jun's left leg was withered, as if from a childhood disease, the joints gouged and scarred with lesions. Jun filled a bucket with water and tipped it over himself and passed it to Alex across the aisle. Alex filled it again and sluiced it over his head and winced at the unexpected iciness. It was painful but invigorating so he filled it and doused himself once more.

He followed Jun over to the bathtub and the old men made space for them in the foaming water, their wrinkled skin lobster-red.

'The last time I saw you was just before your cellmate lost his eye,' Jun said.

Alex shuddered at the memory. 'I don't like to think about it. It still gives me nightmares.'

'It was the best thing to have happened to him. They had to keep him in hospital so long he missed his deportation date. He's out on licence now. It might take a year or more to process him again. Maybe he'll get to stay in Tokyo permanently, even if he can only see half of it now.'

'I still don't understand why he deserved that. I told you I had taken care of him myself.'

Jun shrugged. 'Those are the rules,' he said. 'Tell me about your girlfriend. How is she?'

'I haven't seen her. I don't think I will again.'

'That's too bad. It seemed like you were unhappy to lose her.'

'I was. But it's over now.'

'Are you planning to leave Japan?'

'I'm not sure. I haven't made a decision yet. If I want to stay, I need to find a new job.'

'You got sacked?'

'Yes. But it's okay. It isn't the first time.'

'You want another teaching job?'

'I think so. I can't really do anything else. Whatever happens, I need to make some money fast.'

An attendant approached and bent down and spoke quietly into Jun's ear. Alex watched the muscles in his face tense as he listened. He nodded his understanding and the attendant stood waiting.

'Okay, Russia-jin,' he said. 'It's time.'

They dressed in their *yukata* and stepped out through a side door into a small, enclosed courtyard. Alex felt the cool night air against his wet skin. They walked through a rock garden, past a long, raised bed of clipped pines with lanterns strung in the branches. The attendant opened the paper door to a private room and stood aside.

The room was dimly lit and full of thick banks of hot, drifting mist. Alex could make out a high-sided wooden tub, slightly smaller than the communal bath in the main *onsen*. Two men were sitting inside, the water up to their necks. They watched Alex silently as he entered. The older man had a square face and a broad chin that had weakened with age. His hair was shaved to stubble, grey and glistening with beads of sweat. He commanded the room, even in repose. Alex recognized him from the prison yard at Ushigome. The younger man had a flattened nose and a web of broken veins across his cheeks. Jun seemed to flinch slightly as the door was closed behind them. He looked nervous and uncomfortable, his shoulders slumped and his hands clasped tightly at his sides. He bowed to the old man and limped unsteadily up the wooden steps at the side of the bathtub and climbed inside. He motioned for Alex to follow him. Floating on the water was a bamboo tray with a ceramic *sake* jug and four small cups. Jun poured the *sake* and handed a cup to each of them.

They leaned forward to touch the rims of the cups and made *kanpai*. Alex saw the men's arms as they raised them from the water. The faded blue ink of their tattoos, sleeves full of dragons and dancing girls and intricate patterns, dug deep into the skin across their shoulders and chests. There was no flesh below the neck left untouched. Alex had seen these kind of gang markings only in newspaper photographs of kidnappings and murders. He had to force himself not to betray any fear.

The old man spoke first. 'Let us talk of the loan that was made,' he said. 'The money was delivered as promised. Five million yen.'

'Yes,' Alex said. 'It was used to pay the *jidan* that was demanded from me.'

'We all know the name of such a woman. One who values money so highly. If this is what she wants, then let's hope that it makes her happy.'

'I don't care what Naoko does now. She's not my concern any more. I have found someone willing to lend me the money so I can pay you back. I can have it for you tomorrow.'

The old man wiped his brow with a towel and fixed his hooded eyes on Alex.

'How much can you pay?'

'All of it,' Alex said. 'I can pay you the whole five million yen.'

He shook his head solemnly. 'That's not enough. The debt now stands at ten million with the interest you owe.'

Alex was stunned at the amount, his nerves howling in the steaming water. 'I didn't agree to this,' he said. 'It's extortion.'

'This isn't a negotiation, Malloy-san. We are not a bank. You now owe ten million yen.'

'I can't afford to pay that much interest. Not on top of the money I already owe you. I won't ever be able to get my hands on that much.'

'You'll need to find a way before the end of the week.'

'That's impossible. Even if I could find the money, I would need a lot more time.'

The old man sipped his *sake*. 'Time is the one thing none of us have enough of,' he said. 'If you haven't paid by then, the debt will increase even further. It will keep on increasing day by day.'

Alex remembered Saito's warning. He'd heard the inspector's words of alarm at the time but had chosen to ignore them. He felt their significance plainly now. The older man maintained a measured calmness but his bodyguard looked desperate to start throwing his weight around, as if the need for action was bred into him. Jun was casting his eyes from one to the other, breathing more deeply than usual, waiting. Alex had always known there was a good chance the night would come to this. His only comfort was that he had never had any other choice.

'Whatever it is you are going to do to me, let's just get it over with,' he said. 'There's no way I can raise ten million yen. Even if I could, I have my pride.'

The old man glowered at him from the far side of the bathtub.

'Pride is an expensive luxury, Malloy-san. Pride may end up costing you much more.'

'I don't care any more. I just want this to be over.'

The old man wiped the sweat from his brow. 'What if there was another way?'

'What do you mean?'

'Instead of paying back the debt, what if there was another way to work it off. Something more lucrative than teaching English?'

Alex felt all eyes turn to him, looking for his reaction. 'What are you suggesting?' he asked.

The old man rubbed the flesh sagging under his chin. He took a hand towel from the edge of the bathtub and soaked it in a bucket of ice water and wrung the towel out over his head.

His eyes on Alex, he said, '*Tada hodo takai mono wanai.*'

Then he lifted his hands and clapped them together quickly and the sound rang out around the room. The steam drifted before him like a haze of smoke. He motioned for Jun to pour more *sake*.

Alex looked at Jun in confusion.

'Nothing is more expensive than that which is free,' Jun translated.

Alex shook his head. 'I don't understand.'

'Well,' Jun said, glancing at the old man sitting rigid and unmoving in the scalding water. 'It means we have a proposition for you.'

# 23

ALEX WAS WAITING IN THE STAIRWELL THAT LED UP TO Yukiko's apartment. He told himself he would give Naoko exactly one hour and leave her alone for ever if she failed to show. That way, she always had a chance, he thought. He had been skulking in the shadows for fifty-four minutes when he saw her turn the corner at the end of the street and stroll towards him. She looked like she was deep in thought, her face clenched, as if some distant memory were still troubling her. When she opened the entry door and began to climb the stairs to the third floor, he called out to her, his voice cracking with nerves as he said her name. Naoko started in surprise as she saw him step forward from the gloom.

'Alex?' she said. 'What are you doing here?'

'I need to talk to you.'

'How did you know I was here?'

'I took a guess.'

She peered up towards Yukiko's door. 'It's not a good idea,' she said. 'Hiro is coming round later.'

'Then let's go somewhere else. Somewhere we can talk.'

Naoko furrowed her brow slightly. 'Why now? I haven't heard from you for weeks. I tried to call you and you wouldn't pick up. I left messages for you and you never called me back.'

'Hiro made me promise to stay away from you.'

'And you agreed?'

'He didn't really give me much choice.'

'It doesn't sound like you needed a lot of persuasion.'

'I was angry with you.'

'Are you angry now?'

'Yes. But I miss you.'

Naoko didn't hesitate. 'I miss you too.'

'Then let's go somewhere we can talk.'

They walked to the all-night restaurant near Senso-ji Temple. The owner remembered them from their last visit and greeted Naoko like a favourite niece. He showed them to the same table in the window where they had eaten before. The place still had the smell of spice and stewed miso ground into the furniture.

'I went to your apartment in Mejiro,' Alex said. 'The concierge said you moved out a few weeks ago. What happened? I thought you loved living there?'

Naoko tried to look casual but her disappointment was obvious. 'I lost my job. I could only live in the apartment as long as I worked at the gallery. That's why I'm staying with Yukiko.'

'Did you lose your job because of me?'

'No. Some other things happened.'

'Like what?'

Naoko gave a resigned smile. 'I don't want to talk about it,' she said. 'You're not the only one who prefers to be silent when it suits you.'

'I lost my job too. After they found out I had been locked up in Ushigome, they didn't want me teaching at the school any more. I can't say I blame them.'

'What was it like in there?'

'Most days were boring and others absolutely terrifying. The worst part was finding out I had to pay you a year's salary to get out of there.'

'The *jidan* payment was suggested by Saito's assistant, Officer Tomada. It was supposed to be a way for you to avoid prosecution.'

'Prosecution for something I hadn't done.'

Naoko looked away guiltily. 'I don't have any excuse for that, Alex. I'm sorry. I didn't plan any of it. I was trying to protect myself, that's all. I never meant to hurt you. It all got way out of hand.'

'I thought you were trying to get back at me for causing you trouble.'

Naoko reached a hand across the table and touched her fingers to his. 'Of course not. I'm sorry for everything, Alex. I really am. I was worried I was never going to see you again.'

'But you said it was over between us. When I received your text just after I was released from Ushigome, you told me that you never wanted to see me again.'

Naoko looked puzzled. 'That's not what I wrote at all.'

Alex took out his phone and showed her the message she had sent.

'"I have your money. Now it's all over,"' he read from the screen. 'I was devastated when I saw that. How else was I supposed to react?'

'I meant that the ordeal was over. I was waiting for you to get in touch. Then I called you and some random woman answered your phone. You must have gone straight from prison to stay with her.'

'It wasn't what you think. She's a friend of Hiro's.'

'I know all about Hiro's friends.'

'I swear to you, Naoko. Nothing happened. All I could think about was losing you, not getting together with anyone else.'

'Honestly?'

'Of course. Look at me. You know I'm telling you the truth.'

Naoko's face softened. 'This has all been like a nightmare. I wish I could erase the last month and start again. I regret every moment of it. I wish we were able to go back to our life as it was before.'

'That's what I want too,' Alex said. 'That's why I came to see you tonight. I think we should go away. Get out of Tokyo for a while so we can think straight. Relax somewhere together and put all of this behind us.'

'Is it really possible to do that?'

'We have to try. Don't we?'

'Where will we go?'

'Where do you want to go?'

Naoko thought for a moment. She looked excited at the range of possibilities. Eventually, she said, 'Somewhere far away. Somewhere no one knows us. Somewhere hot.'

'Okay. Let me make the arrangements.'

'Do you think this will work after all that's happened?'

Alex watched her over the table. 'We've got nothing to lose,' he said.

# 24

ALEX LAID THE TRAY ON THE CORNER OF THE MATTRESS AND pushed back the mosquito net that hung over the bed. He knelt beside her and gently shook her shoulder. Naoko briefly opened her eyes and then turned away from him and curled her body up beneath the white cotton sheet. Alex watched her lying there, her black hair fanned out against the pillow in thick strands.

'I brought you some breakfast,' he said.

'What did you get?'

'Watermelon. I climbed a tree and cut it down myself.'

She turned over and looked at him, her face softened by sleep.

'Watermelons don't grow on trees,' she said.

'Don't they?'

'No. They grow on the ground.'

'I didn't say it was a tall tree.'

'Does it have seeds?' she asked.

'Of course it does.'

'I don't like the seeds.'

'If I have to take all of the seeds out, we will still be eating it for dinner.'

Naoko thought about it for a moment. 'I can spit the seeds out,' she said.

He handed her a slice of watermelon from the tray. 'Come on. We can spit them out into the sea.'

He stood and opened the heavy teak door of the bungalow and a white brightness sliced through at a sharp angle. The warmth of a tropical morning flooded into the shadows and he stepped out on to the veranda and lay back on the hammock suspended from the roof beams.

The bungalow was built on rocks that had fallen from the cliff at the edge of the palm forest and slid down to the sea a thousand years before. It was in a group of huts built in the local Thai style, on tall stilts clustered at the point of the headland. Alex shielded his eyes against the morning sun rising over the cliffs and looked out over the bay. Beyond the headland the water was dark green and rippled by the island current. A horseshoe-shaped reef protected the milky calm of the lagoon and a slope of white sand rose up from the shore to a fringe of curved palms. The forested hillside steepened to the crest of the mountain, outlined against the sky. On the beach a single line of footprints ran the length of the sand to two long-tail boats side by side above the high-tide line. From the hammock, Alex could see the shoals of fish below him, magnified by the deep water, flashing colours as they swam. He felt like he was on a raft, coasting out to the open ocean of the gulf and on towards the South China Sea.

Naoko came out from the darkness of the bungalow. She was wearing a green bathing suit with a sarong tied around her waist. She took a bite of watermelon and walked slowly forward. The sun reflected from the surface of her eyes.

'Does it still hurt?' she asked, and touched a finger to the scar across his cheek.

'Not any more.'

'It looks worse than when we first arrived here.'

'It doesn't tan so it stands out more. That's all.'

She rubbed her fingertips together. 'Every time I look at you I'm going to be reminded of that night.'

'Forget about it. It's in the past now.'

'You mean it?'

'One day you won't even notice it any more.'

'That makes me sad,' she said.

Alex reached out and took her hand. Her palm had healed but there were the remnants of past wounds on her skin, like old, dark bruises.

'You have some scars of your own. Ones you've given to yourself.'

'That's over now,' she said. 'I've promised myself not to do that again. I need to solve my problems more sensibly in the future.'

Alex lay back as the hammock rocked back and forth over the edge of the balcony rail. Two pelicans flew along the edge of the reef, their shadows tracking beneath them on the rolling swell.

'Climb up here with me,' he said.

'Are you sure it's safe?'

'Of course.'

'I don't want to fall in.'

'What makes you think you'd fall in?'

She reached down and placed her hands on the side of the hammock. 'This,' she said.

Alex saw the look in her eyes and he could tell what she was going to do before she moved. She pulled the hammock towards her and then shoved it out over the railing with all of her strength. He felt her hand in the small of his back as the woven fabric slid out from beneath him and he hung, twisting in the air above the clear water. The low sun was on his skin and he heard her laughter as he fell through the surface and felt the fresh saltiness against him. He sank down and flexed his body and breathed out a lungful of air and opened his eyes. The sand on the sea floor felt cold beneath his feet and the fish darted around him in shoals. Through the prism of the surface he could see Naoko looking down from the balcony. He pushed up towards her, bubbles cascading to the surface as he swam.

'Come in,' he said. 'It's good.'

Naoko slipped off her sarong and climbed up on to the railing. She dived forward gracefully and arced over him, hitting the water without a splash.

After breakfast, they took a taxi across the island to the main town at the foot of the mountain. The road that wound up through the pass was a single-lane track and there were small turnouts in places to allow trucks and other cars to pass by. The turnouts were on the cliff edge, barely wide enough for the taxi to stop, and the sheer drop down from the road was dizzying. Naoko tightened her grip on Alex's hand each time the driver edged over to allow someone to pass on the narrow track.

Where the road crested the spine of hills, Alex asked the driver to stop so they could get out and take some pictures of the view. The sky was almost violet where it met the horizon and the green atolls of the nature reserve floated in the distance, disembodied from the expanse of water. The land below them was lush and fertile and terraced with rice paddies on the lower slopes and vast forests of coconut groves on the steep banks of the mountain.

'It's beautiful,' Naoko said. 'I'm so used to seeing endless buildings every day I forget what the real world looks like sometimes.'

'Imagine living in a place like this. Life looks so simple here.'

Naoko pushed her sunglasses up on to her head. 'I'm sure, even here, life gets complicated.'

They drove down the switchbacks that led into the town. Half-built huts and wooden shacks were mixed in among the whitewashed family homes and golden-roofed temples. There were small fires at the roadside where the villagers burned their refuse. Swarms of mopeds choked the streets leading down to the harbour. Alex paid the driver and they walked along the main avenue, where shops and restaurants lined both sides of the street. Stray dogs lay sleeping in the shade of the roadside stalls. They found a café with a covered patio and took a table out of the sun. Across the street, a billboard built on the rooftop of a pharmacy displayed a giant advertisement for a luxury fragrance. A grey-eyed young woman with a snake coiled tightly around her naked body. When Naoko noticed it, she gave a resigned laugh.

'What is it?' Alex asked.

'The photo is one of Masakazu's, the photographer you met at the gallery. It's part of a campaign he shot last year. It feels like, everywhere I go, those people follow me around.'

'I know how much your career meant to you.'

'That's the funny thing,' she said. 'Masakazu is going to defect to a new gallery in Osaka. He's asked me to go with him.'

'And will you?'

'I'm tempted. I've never lived in Osaka before. I don't have a lot of reasons to turn him down now. It's a good opportunity for me.'

'Why didn't you tell me before?'

'I suppose the right moment never came up.'

Alex straightened the linen napkin before him. He cleared his throat. 'I'm happy for you,' he said finally. 'It looks like your life is taking a turn for the better.'

'What about you?'

'I'm not sure. The English-language industry in Tokyo is a small world. It's going to be hard to find a job without a reference.'

The sun had given Naoko's skin a luminous quality. She took a small bite at the side of her lip before she spoke.

'What if you were in Osaka?' she said. 'Would it be easier to find a job there?'

'Are you asking me to go with you?'

'We don't know anyone there and no one knows us. It would be a new start.'

'What's Osaka like? I've never been.'

'It's one of those cities where everything always seems on the way up. You'd like it, I think. To be honest, it's a lot like Tokyo. Except they have an accent in Osaka.'

'Maybe I wouldn't understand anyone.'

'You don't understand anyone in Tokyo.'

'I'm starting to.'

She looked across the table at him, at the dark lenses of the sunglasses shielding his eyes. 'Is that your answer?' she asked.

They were interrupted as a waitress approached their table with menus. Alex smiled at her.

'Is there a payphone here?' he asked. 'I have to make a call.'

She pointed into the back of the café, behind the kitchen. Alex stood up to leave the table.

'Who do you have to call?' Naoko asked.

'I have to check my bank account,' Alex said briskly. 'I have to make sure I still have enough money to pay for us to get home. I'll only be five minutes. Order anything on the menu that you think looks good for me.'

She watched him walk away, weaving between the other tables on the shaded patio. There was an urgency in every step, which was jarring, after the days of drift and slumber. When he was gone, Naoko looked across to his place setting. Propped up against one another, like books on a shelf, were his wallet and his phone.

They ate lunch slowly and then drifted through the market to buy postcards and souvenirs. When the heat became unbearable they paid for a driver to take them back to the beach. They waited for the sun to cool and then swam out from the rocks beneath the bungalow to the middle of the lagoon. They paced each other out to the bank of dead coral that had been piled up by the tide and protected the bay from weather. The water grew steadily colder as it deepened.

'Do you think there are sharks?' Naoko asked.

'Taste the water. That's how you can tell.'

She dipped a finger in and pressed it to her lips.

'It's salty,' she said.

'Then there are sharks.'

She swam towards him quickly, with a panicked look, and placed her arms around his shoulders for protection.

'Do you really think so?'

'Not in the lagoon,' he laughed. 'It's not deep enough. They get scared by sheltered places. But they'll be swimming around out there, beyond the reef.'

'I don't like it,' she said. 'They scare me.'

Alex shrugged. 'They have more right to be here than we do.'

There was a pile of boulders lying at the foot of the cliff and they swam over and Alex climbed out first and hauled Naoko up on to the rocks with both hands. The sun had heated the smooth stone and they lay against it and felt their skin dry.

'Can I ask you a question?' Naoko said.

'Of course.'

'Why are you being so nice to me?'

He look puzzled. 'What do you mean?'

'Why are we here? What's it all for? It's beautiful here – the sea and the palm trees, swimming with you every day and being together. It's wonderful. But what's the reason? Why did you want to come away with me? Why here?'

'Isn't that enough?' Alex said. 'Here, we can talk and work things out and forget about the past.'

'I expected you to be really angry about everything that happened, but you couldn't be more calm about it. I'm not sure why.'

'You can't complain when I'm doing what we agreed. Don't you think that would be unfair?'

Alex stood up and looked around. There was a fissure hewn from the cliff about ten metres above them. It looked jagged and dark. He scrambled up the boulder towards it.

'Where are you going?' she called after him.

'Up there.'

'Why?'

He looked back at her at the water's edge. The surface of the rock she lay on shimmered in the heat.

'To see what's inside the cave,' he called back.

The mouth of the fissure was full of wet sand and pools of seawater where the high tide had flooded in. The entrance was under the overhang of the cliff and Alex felt his skin shrink when he stepped out of the sun and into the shadows. He climbed over the rocks at the cave mouth and walked back into the darkness. It looked like a gouge had been taken out of the headland, a seam that had been gradually worn to a perfect smoothness over thousands of years. For the first few metres, it was possible for Alex to stand tall and reach out his arms at full stretch and still not touch the sides. The rock wall was carved with names and dates, etched there by decades of others who had ventured in to explore. Alex kept going, over rock pools and banks of seaweed, until he was stooping, his head bent to his chest, back into the deep shadows where the sun never reached. He found a crevice in the rock and crouched down, concealed from view.

After a few minutes, he could see Naoko in silhouette at the cave mouth.

'Alex?' she called out. 'Alex?' Her voice echoed in the darkness.

He crouched in silence and waited.

She took a few tentative steps into the cave. 'This isn't funny, Alex. Where are you?'

He watched as she turned around and stepped back into the sunlight and then changed her mind. She climbed over the rocks and came towards him. He was freezing now, the moisture beading on his skin in the cold shadows. He breathed gently and waited.

She was bent low, moving carefully over sharp rocks, finding solid footings before shifting her weight and creeping forward again. She came closer, blinking rapidly to adjust her eyes to the dark and grasping for handholds. There was no sound except her breathing; her almond eyes were wide in the blackness. He could see the skin on her back flex across her ribs, her flesh exposed and her face so close he could feel the warmth of her breath, but she couldn't see him. He remained frozen, watching her.

Naoko moved slowly past.

He lifted his hand out and touched a fingertip to her waist and she screamed a high-pitched full scream that ricocheted from the wet stone.

He laughed and reached out to take her hand and she screamed again. He hugged her close and felt her body tremble against his.

'You bastard,' she said, her voice shaking. 'I thought you'd fallen down a ravine or something and couldn't call out because you were hurt.'

'I thought you were going to wet yourself.'

'It's not funny, Alex,' she said, pushing him away.

'It was just a joke.'

'It's too cold in here.'

'I know. I'm freezing.'

'I want to get out of here,' she said.

Yes, Alex thought. Yes, you do.

Naoko turned around in the darkness and began to make her way back towards the light. Alex followed a few paces behind. He knew he had brought her there to frighten her on purpose, just to see if his lingering anger was able to overpower his affection. The answer wasn't clear and it troubled him. He needed to resent her without question for what was to come.

They swam back through the lagoon to the bungalow. Waves were breaking against the reef, peeling in an emerald line. In the shelter of the bay, the water was glassy and still. Naoko said she was tiring so she held on to Alex's shoulders as he swam. They climbed out under the veranda and took the steps back to their room. The maid had been in to open the curtains and turn down the bed. They went into the long, tiled bathroom at the back of the bungalow and switched on the shower. Naoko rinsed the salt from her hair and Alex watched as the water ran down her spine and across the flesh at the small of her back.

'I really like it here,' she said. 'I can't believe we have to leave tomorrow. I don't have anything important to go back for. Why don't we stay longer?'

Alex shook his head. 'Our flights are booked to Bangkok and the hotel is already paid for. Then we have to get back to Tokyo. It's too late to change the tickets. I like it here too but, trust me, we have to stick to our plans right now.'

He placed his hands on her shoulders and felt her beneath his palms. He smelled the sun on her skin.

Naoko looked up at him. She thought for a moment and then looked away. 'I wish we were never going back,' she said.

# 25

WHEN THE FIRST BOUT ENDED IN A KNOCKOUT, THE CROWD IN the arena rose to its feet. The young fighter in the blue trunks lay prone on the canvas a few feet from the ringside seats. Naoko held on to Alex's arm and he could feel her tensed beside him. The fighter's eyes rolled back in his skull, blood spattered across his face.

'I don't like it,' Naoko said. 'Is he dead?'

'No, he's fine. Give him a few seconds and he'll come round.'

'The other one hit him with his knee. Is that allowed?'

'This is Bangkok,' Alex said. 'Everything is allowed.'

The trainer came into the ring and lifted the fighter's head and placed a towel beneath it. The trainer slapped him hard on the cheek and he started to come to. The boxer in red danced and weaved in victory, his gloves held above him in the air, and the spectators in the ringside seats stood and cheered, with their eyes wide and their teeth bared, caught in the flash of the cameras. The roar from the crowd in the stadium rolled down from the domed roof.

The fighters for the next bout entered the ring wearing ceremonial headpieces and ribbons tied around their biceps. It was a middleweight bout and the boxers were lean and sinewy. The announcer introduced them to the packed arena.

'Which one do you think will win this time?' Alex asked.

'I don't know. I just don't want anyone to get hurt.'

'I'll place a bet for us, but you have to choose, okay?'

Naoko watched the fighters dance and weave. 'I think the one in red is taller and looks stronger,' she said.

'But the other one looks quicker.'

'I don't know how to choose. They both look dangerous.'

She was still holding on to his arm, still tense.

'It's all in the eyes,' Alex said. 'It's won or lost in the eyes. Choose which one has the killer look.'

'I don't see a killer look. They both look scared.'

'Then guess.'

Naoko pointed towards the ring. 'The one in red – I think he's going to win.'

'Okay. Wait here,' Alex said. 'I'll put our money on him.'

He left the ringside and walked back to the gate that separated the seats from the grandstand. The locals stood on the cement steps that climbed up towards the back of the arena. On the higher terraces, the gamblers stood in groups and waved fistfuls of money in the air and shouted the odds. The professionals shouted loudest, holding phones to their ears and calling out in chaotic Thai, their voices high with adrenaline. It was impossible to work out what was going on.

Alex stood up at the back of the arena next to the scoreboard, under the portrait of the king, where he'd been told to stand. He took a roll of dollar bills from his pocket and waved them above his head. The locals ignored him, but he held them at arm's length and waited. In the ring below, the fighters continued their snake dance, twisting and moving and sizing each other up. The crowd was frenzied in the heat.

'No dollar. No dollar.'

A young Thai boy, maybe fifteen, walked along the terrace towards Alex. He smiled and shook a finger at him.

'Only baht,' he said.

'I only have dollars, no baht.'

'No dollar,' the boy repeated.

'I want to put two hundred dollars on the guy in red.' Alex fanned the money in his hand.

The boy looked at Alex through long lashes.

He said, 'You Alex-san?'

Alex nodded. 'Yes.'

The boy clasped his hands in greeting. 'You have everything for me?'

'I have greetings from Tokyo.'

'Very good. You have your hotel address?'

'Yes,' Alex said. 'Chao Phraya Hotel, next to pier fourteen. I've written down the address and the room number.'

Alex took a piece of folded paper from his pocket and handed it to the boy. He looked at it but Alex could tell he couldn't read.

'What time will you come?' Alex asked.

'Midnight. Maybe later. Okay?'

The boy stood with a wide smile and bright white teeth.

'Don't come too late. You understand?'

He made an okay sign with his finger and thumb. 'No problem, no problem.' He turned to leave.

'Hey!' Alex called after him, shouting above the noise of the stadium. 'Place a bet for me. I don't know how to gamble here. This place is fucking nuts.'

The boy laughed and took the money from Alex's hand.

'Fucking nuts,' he laughed. 'Yes, fucking nuts.'

The night boat filled with passengers at the pier next to the arena. It was hot and close and Naoko stood at the railing at the back of the boat with Alex beside her. The ferry weaved a course across the Chao Phraya river, avoiding long-tail boats and the islands of palm fronds that floated slowly out to sea. Naoko held the money in her hand and counted it.

'How much is there?' Alex asked.

'I keep losing count. There are too many numbers.'

'It's only Thai money. We should spend it before we go to the airport tomorrow. It's not worth anything in Tokyo.'

'It's my lucky money. I will keep it as a souvenir.'

'That fighter really came through for you. Maybe you should have given some to him as a tip?'

Naoko furrowed her brow and folded the thick wad of notes and pushed it into her bag. 'I'm Japanese,' she said. 'I don't know how to tip.'

The ferry stopped at the pier in front of their hotel and Alex helped Naoko on to the pontoon. The hotel was a tall, elegant tower surrounded by spidery palms and topped with an illuminated sign that flashed in the night. There was a man-made beach at the river's edge, with fine, white sand imported from the Andaman Islands. The sand was warm underfoot as they crossed the beach and walked up the landscaped pathway leading to the hotel entrance.

Inside the lobby was a lush rainforest of ferns and orchids and a sunken water feature. The Thai staff smiled and clasped their hands in greeting as they walked through the entranceway and waited for the elevator.

Their room was on the twenty-seventh floor, overlooking the Memorial Bridge and the curve of the river where the boats formed a procession as they motored downstream. The room was almost frozen by the air conditioning, the windows were frosted and the marble floor was chilled under foot. Naoko ran a bath in the sunken tub and they sat at either end, facing each other.

'Thank you for bringing me here, Alex,' she said. 'I had a wonderful time in the islands and in Bangkok. I'd heard stories about how great it is here but I feel lucky to have seen it for myself.'

'It was good to relax and talk things through. I knew we just needed some time alone.'

There was a knock. 'Room service!' came the muffled call from the corridor.

Alex climbed out and wrapped a towel around his waist. 'Wait here,' he said.

Naoko lay back in the water and Alex closed the bathroom door behind him.

When he opened the door to the room, he pressed his fingers to his lips so the man, standing there with a blank expression, and the boy, smiling just as he had in the arena, knew not to make a sound.

He showed them into the room and they walked silently over to the bed.

Alex picked up Naoko's suitcase and set it on the mattress. The man unzipped it carefully. He made small breathing noises from his nose as he opened the case and looked through Naoko's clothes folded neatly inside. She had packed lightly, just as Alex had told her. At the top were the sarongs she had bought to give as gifts when she returned home and the man pulled these out gently, trying to keep them in the same order they had been packed. Alex noticed he was wearing blue latex gloves, the kind surgeons wore. He stood dripping water on to the tiled floor, the towel tied tightly around his waist.

The man slipped a backpack from the boy's shoulders. He opened it and took out a package of thick plastic, securely wrapped in layers of silver insulation tape. He leaned over Naoko's open suitcase and lowered the package carefully inside. When the stack of clothes and sarongs was replaced, he smoothed them down and zipped the case shut again and looked at Alex as he peeled off the latex gloves and pushed them into the side pocket of his creased jacket. The boy smiled and made the okay sign again with his finger and thumb.

Then they turned and quietly walked out, closing the door behind them.

Alex stood alone in the empty hotel room, the water pooling around his feet. He couldn't remember what the man looked like.

As he walked back into the bathroom, Alex noticed how fast

his heart was beating. He had known this moment was approaching ever since they had arrived in Thailand but he still felt in shock. The magnitude of the situation was overwhelming. The potential danger waiting in the future impossible to comprehend. He opened the door and looked down at Naoko reclining in the bath, the hot, soapy water up to her neck. She had placed a wet cloth across her eyes.

'What did room service bring us?' she asked.

Alex climbed slowly into the bath and leaned back against the tiles.

'Nothing,' he said. 'They got the wrong room.'

# 26

'YOU DON'T OWE HER A THING, ALEX. NOT ANY MORE.' JUN'S *voice was trembling as he spoke. Alex could hardly see him in the steam of the bath house. He could feel drops of cold sweat run down his temples and drip into the swirling water. The two Japanese men quietly sipped their sake, watching for a reaction.*

*'What are you saying, Jun? I don't understand.' Alex's voice rang around the wood-and-paper room.*

*'Right now, you are in debt for five million yen plus interest and it is growing by the day. You have no job and no way to pay back the money. We're giving you a way to wipe the debt clean – more than clean. We will arrange everything – the flights, the hotel, everything – and we will pay you extra for your trouble.'*

*'How much extra?'*

*'Another two million yen. All you have to do is collect a package for us. It will be brought to you. There's no effort required on your part.'*

*'What's in the package, Jun?'*

*'You don't need to know. It makes no difference. Think of it as a box of oranges or a sashimi bento. Think of it as a load of dirty laundry. Whatever you want. You'll never touch it. It*

won't be you that carries it – Naoko can do that for you, in return for all the trouble she's caused.'

'And what happens if she gets caught? I couldn't do that to her. No matter what she might have done.'

Jun was emphatic. 'She won't get caught. She's a Japanese woman – all crime in Japan is caused by foreigners, you know this. You've experienced it first-hand. Naoko will walk on to Japanese soil with no one raising an eyelid.'

Alex shook his head. 'This all sounds too much for me.'

'Think, Alex.' Jun pointed at his temple. 'What did you do to deserve this? This way you will wipe the debt out and earn some extra money of your own. Then you can do whatever you want – go back to London, stay in Tokyo, go and spend it gambling in Macau, for all I care. Do you remember sitting in that police cell night after night? Naoko didn't care about you then, only herself. You don't owe her a thing – she owes you, and this is her way to repay.'

Alex swallowed a mouthful of sake and thought for a moment. He looked at the older man, watching him calmly, the brawler sitting back in the tub staring arrogantly, impatient to hand out a beating. Alex remembered Jun's face when he had first approached him in the yard at Ushigome. The furtive glances he had taken from the corner of his eye as he'd sized him up. Then it clicked and he realized he had been set up from the beginning.

He turned to Jun with a crazed expression. 'You always knew we would end up here. You knew it from the minute you laid eyes on me. Didn't you?' he shouted. 'You saw the trouble I was in and you knew you could manipulate all of this to your advantage. Then you'd have me by the balls. I bet this isn't the first time you've done it. This has been a stitch-up from the moment we met.'

Alex stood up from the tub and climbed out. He took his yukata and slipped it on. The young bodyguard stepped out of the water and blocked the door with a tattooed arm. They all looked at the old man, calm and unmoved in the bathtub.

'I don't think you understand the situation here,' Jun said. 'They aren't asking you. They're telling you. They don't care about the money now. If you don't go through with this, it will end badly for everyone.'

He looked down at Jun, sitting in the murky water. 'I can't do it,' he said. 'I'm sorry.'

Before he could turn there was a blow to the back of his head and Alex fell forward on to the wooden banking around the bath. A knee struck his back and pinned him there, his chest crushing under the weight. Two hands shoved at his head and his face plunged down into the water before he could take a breath. He gagged as the hands pushed him deeper into the bath, his nose and throat filling and the heat burning the back of his sinuses as his arms flailed helplessly in the air above him. When the hands pulled him clear, he inhaled the slew of water in his mouth, choking again as he was pushed back under. Soon he was lying on the floor of the bath house, gasping for breath, staring up at the tattooed body standing over him. He saw Jun's face as he crouched down, and wiped the hair away from his eyes. His expression was almost pitiful.

'Remember what I told you,' Jun said. 'Uchi soto. From now on, you're either inside or outside.'

# 27

SHE WRAPPED HER LEGS AROUND HIS WAIST AND PULLED HIM into her and he ran a hand through the sheen of her blue-black hair, so thick he could see every strand shining. Her eyes half closed, breathing unknown words in whispers beyond his ear, the ceiling fan flickering above them, rippling over the bed sheets; he looked over at the blue suitcase sitting alone on the cold, tiled floor.

Naoko reached up and turned his face towards hers. She peered deep into his eyes, searching for the thought that was hidden there, and ran a hand along his back, over the uneven, scarred skin, and began to move faster. He tried to keep his gaze in constant motion, over the ink lines of her tattoo rising and falling on the swell of her flank, the bamboo forest, a peacock eye staring straight up from her hip. She was moving beneath him, the fan eddying chilled air over them in gusts, her sweat-soaked hair stuck to her shoulders in knots. He took a handful and gripped close to her scalp, his other arm leveraged against the carved mahogany headboard, angled to block his view. The suitcase was still there in the corner of his eye and he was staring at it now, over his shoulder, twisting more hair in his fist, as if she weren't there. Naoko saw the look on his face, the isolation, and she called out to him. He looked down at her as if he had just come back into the room after a reverie.

'I don't like it,' she said. 'What's up with you?'

Alex lay back on the bed, breathing hard. 'Nothing,' he said. 'I'm sorry.'

Naoko touched a hand to his chest and he pushed it away. Sweat was running from him. They lay together for a while in silence, their bodies not touching, his flesh separated from hers, and then he sat up on the edge of the bed. He tried to keep his eyes moving around the room, taking in the generic furniture, the patterned wallpaper, the creased bedlinen, anything except the place that his gaze kept returning to: the suitcase lying on the floor, the shadow of the ceiling fan turning steadily over it.

'Tell me what's wrong, Alex,' she said.

He felt dizzy for a moment and stood up to find his balance. 'Nothing's wrong,' he said. 'I'm going to take a shower.'

She was at the table on the balcony when he came out of the bathroom and began to towel himself dry. He pulled on a pair of shorts and a T-shirt and stepped outside into the closeness of the night. The porch lights were on and mosquitoes swarmed the glowing bulbs, rattling against the glass as they burned their wings. Traffic sounded shrill horns from far below. Naoko carefully tapped the ash from her cigarette. She kept her eyes turned down as she spoke.

'You are angry at me, aren't you? Even though you're trying so hard to hold it inside.'

He tried to deny it but the hesitation betrayed him. 'I always knew you were trouble. From the first moment I saw you, it was obvious.'

Naoko looked up at him with her dark, wide eyes. The lights of the city were sparkling in them, ferocious oranges and vivid greens.

'You mean like *jaja uma*?' she said.

'Yes. Like a horse. A crazy, untameable horse.'

'But I don't always want to be this way.'

'What do you want?'

'I want some peace. I want to belong somewhere.'

He glanced away, over the edge of the balcony, down into the dark channel of the river. The surface of the water was thick with tangled palm fronds.

Naoko stubbed out her cigarette. 'Have you thought any more about my offer?'

'Which offer?'

'Of moving to Osaka with me.'

'A fresh start?'

'Why not? We both need to make a change.'

Alex gave an ironic smile. 'Moving to Tokyo was supposed to be my fresh start. That didn't work out so well. Maybe I'm not suited to new beginnings.'

'You have a good heart. Surely that's what counts?'

There were tiny lizards zigzagging up the white walls of the building, their dark, beady eyes flicking wildly as they moved.

'Can I ask you something?' Alex said. 'When you said you were scared you weren't going to see me again, did you mean it?'

'Of course I did.'

'Do you really believe we can make a life together?'

She looked up at him. 'Yes, I do.'

'What if you regret it later?'

'I already have too much regret. It's the worst feeling there is. I want to make it work between us. I don't want to spend my life waking up and wishing I had done things differently. Wishing I had found a way to solve our problems. I know you feel the same.'

Alex breathed in deeply. The night air tasted hot and moist in the back of his throat. Over the city, clouds gathered in the night, brimming with a pressure that hummed in the darkness. He pictured Naoko waking in the morning and rushing to be ready for the early flight. The two of them sitting together on the plane, her head resting on his shoulder. The magazine she would flick through as the in-flight meal was served. Her face as she waited in line at passport control. He pictured every moment of it and himself next to her, alive to the danger she was unaware of.

'So do you have an answer?'

'About Osaka?'

'Yes.'

He had hoped he would be able to resent her enough to go through with it. But he wasn't that cynical. He knew there was no other choice.

'There's something I want you to do first.'

'What?' she asked.

'I want you to go and look inside your bag.'

He watched through the glass balcony door as Naoko picked up her suitcase and unzipped it and tipped the contents out on to the unmade bed. Her clothes and shoes and underwear came spilling out and the plastic package followed. She picked it up and turned it over in her hands, looking at him from inside the brightly lit room, her face slackened in confusion. Alex stood up from the table and opened the door and went inside.

'What's this?' she asked.

'Honestly, I don't know.'

'What's it doing in my bag?'

'Five million yen.'

Naoko frowned. The delicate lines on her forehead creased. 'What are you talking about?'

'That's the reason it's in your bag,' Alex said. 'Five million yen.'

'I don't understand.'

'Where do you think I got the money, Naoko? I was locked up, with nowhere to turn. I had to borrow the *jidan* money and this is how they want me to pay them back.'

'You put this in my suitcase?'

He shook his head.

'Then how did it get there?'

'It was put there while you were in the bath.'

'The room-service people?'

'Yes.'

'And you let them do this?'

'It doesn't matter. I was always going to tell you it was in there.'

'You still haven't told me what's inside.'

'I think it's drugs.'

Naoko held the package up to the light, trying to find any indication of the contents hidden beneath the layers of silver tape. She turned it over in her hands but it was wrapped too tightly to make anything out.

'What kind of drugs?' she asked.

Alex tried to smile but the tension showed on his face. 'The illegal kind.'

She picked up her toiletries bag from the bed and opened it and took out a small nail file. Holding the package in one hand, she slit open a corner and peered inside. She turned the parcel over and held one hand below the opening. A handful of small white crystals, like shards of pure quartz, spilled out into her palm. She held them up to the light to examine them closer.

Alex said, 'It looks like crystal meth.'

'What's that?'

'*Shabu*. Speed. At least, that's what I think it is.'

She looked at him in disbelief. 'You think?'

'I'm not an expert. We can take some and find out if you want?'

Naoko turned the crystals over in the palm of her hand, as if she were looking for clues. 'The plan was to let me carry this through customs at the airport? Walk through without any idea what was inside my bag?' Her voice was low and gentle, directed inwards, as if she were talking to herself.

Alex wanted to take a step towards her but his feet were rooted to the spot. 'I would never have gone through with it,' he said.

'But you considered it.'

'I had to make it look that way. I had no choice. The people I'm dealing with are serious, Naoko. We're both in too much danger to refuse.'

He could see that she wasn't listening any more. The anger was mounting on her face and her eyes were vacant, as if she were watching an image come into focus in her mind.

'All the time we were in the islands you knew this was going to happen. You took me there as a smokescreen to make sure I was relaxed and off-guard, just so I wouldn't be suspicious when you got me to this hotel room. You've been lying to me the whole time, haven't you?'

He took a step forward and she took an equal step back as he did so. Her face displayed the true depth of her feelings about his betrayal. She dropped the parcel on the bed and turned on her heels, opening and then slamming the door behind her as she ran out into the corridor. Alex ran after her. He followed her along the pale, carpeted corridor, past the rows of numbered doors and through the emergency exit on to the fire stairs. He was barefoot and the steel treads tore at his soles as he sprinted down the levels, trying to catch her before she reached the lobby. He grabbed her on the thirteenth-floor landing and Naoko fell against him and they both tumbled into the whitewashed corner. There were tears in her eyes and she refused to look at him.

'I didn't do it,' he kept saying, trying to position himself in her eyeline. 'I didn't go through with it. I could have just kept quiet but I knew I had to tell you. I wanted to keep you out of danger. You've got to grant me that.'

'I'm not granting you anything,' she shouted. 'You fucking liar.'

He was trying to use a calm tone to soothe her but his voice kept shaking. 'I know this looks bad but I never would have let you do it. I promise. I always knew I was going to tell you eventually.'

'What difference does that make?'

'I know how to solve this without you being in any danger.'

'How?'

'I've thought this through. There's another way.'

'What other way?'

'I'll do it. I'll carry it in my bag. That way I take the risk, not you.'

She began to come together behind her tears. She wiped her wet eyes with the back of her hand. 'But what if you get caught? What happens then?'

Alex tried to shrug casually. 'Then I go back to jail.'

'That's insane,' she said, drawing out the words for emphasis.

He looked into her eyes, kneeling before her, his face almost touching hers. 'What choice do I have?' he said.

A door opened below them and they could hear voices and footsteps descending the stairwell. Alex checked over the metal bannister to make sure they hadn't been seen.

He turned to Naoko. 'Let's go back to the room and talk there. We can't stay out here or someone will get suspicious. Then we're both in trouble.'

She looked at her knees as she thought it over and then reached out a hand for him to help her up. 'Okay. Let's go,' she said softly.

# 28

THE PARCEL WAS STILL ON THE BED WHEN THEY RETURNED TO their room, lying there openly, almost brazenly, like some totem of disaster. Alex picked it up and opened the wardrobe and placed it inside to hide it from sight. He felt better as soon as it was gone. Naoko lit a cigarette and smoked in deep, nervous gasps.

'I'm having trouble processing all of this,' she said. 'My head is spinning.'

'I know this must be a shock to you. If there was any way I could have avoided this happening, I would have. It's the only way.'

'You have some history with drugs, don't you?' she said. 'If I'd known that when I met you, I might have made a different choice.'

He sat on the foot of the bed with his elbows resting on his knees. 'I don't take drugs,' he said. 'I've never done anything worse than smoke a joint. That's the truth.'

'What about all the trouble you had in London?'

He held his chin in his hands and looked at her from beneath his brow.

'You listen to Hiro too much.'

'Who am I supposed to listen to, Alex? You won't tell me anything.'

He paused for a moment. 'I promised myself when I left London that I would forget about it, that's all. I don't want to drag my past around with me everywhere I go.'

'It seems to me that's exactly what you're doing.'

'Everything Hiro told you was completely back to front. I wasn't involved with drugs and I didn't have a habit. It was my brother, Patrick. I just took the blame for him. My parents were so devastated when he died that I couldn't face making it worse for them. They always thought I was a disappointment and wanted someone to be at fault for the death of their perfect son. Why not me?'

'So you let everyone think you were to blame?'

'It seemed the right thing to do. I had to protect Patrick's reputation and my parents drew their conclusions quickly anyway.'

Naoko took a long drag and let the smoke trickle from her mouth. 'You probably think that's heroic, don't you? A noble self-sacrifice? You probably think you saved your family from heartache by letting them believe that version of events? What a futile, empty gesture. Why wouldn't you tell them the truth?'

'Because they didn't want to hear it.'

She looked at him with clear, sharp eyes. 'No,' she said. 'It's what *you* want. *You* want to play the martyr. *You* prefer failure so you can escape the responsibility of having to succeed.'

'That's ridiculous,' Alex said. He shook his head dismissively but Naoko continued. She had the look of someone who had stumbled on a long-hidden truth.

'You made the same choice with us as well,' she said. 'I wanted to keep our relationship secret to protect us both. But you came to the gallery on the night of the private view because you wanted to test my loyalty. Not everyone can afford to take such risks. Some of us have to live in the real world and carry on the best we can. You always think you're so generous when, actually, you're thinking of yourself. You know why? Because it always has to be about you, doesn't it?'

210

Alex could feel his cheeks flush, the skin stinging hot across his bones. He let the words hang between them for a moment, then he stood and faced her directly.

'Who were you thinking of when you denounced me to the police? How was that an unselfish act?'

'I'm sorry. I made a mistake. But that was why I asked you to stay away from the gallery that night. If you had done as I asked, none of this would ever have happened.'

'I came there on impulse. I just wanted you to know that the stories Hiro had been telling you were wrong.'

'But why do it then? On that particular night? It's like a sixth sense you have, Alex. You're always drawn to danger. Look at where we are now.'

'I certainly didn't get here on my own.'

Naoko stepped towards him and placed her hands on his shoulders. 'I know. It's my fault. I made this happen. But why don't we just flush this stuff down the toilet and get rid of it? Then we can go home and forget this madness.'

'I can't, Naoko. There's too much at stake now.'

'If it's just about the *jidan* money, I can find a way to borrow it to pay these people back.'

'It's not that simple any more. I've offered to repay it and they just kept increasing the debt to make it impossible. There must be two kilos of meth in that bag. That's got to be worth four or five times the money I borrowed. That's a serious amount. If I carry this stuff back to Tokyo and deliver it as arranged, then it's all over. We can forget everything that's gone wrong between us and start again. If I don't do it, then I am just making more trouble. I've got a good chance of making it back if I try. The bag is wrapped to fool the X-ray machine at the airport. They're looking for weapons and explosives at the boarding gate, not drugs. There's got to be a fifty–fifty chance of success. Maybe better than that. Everything considered, I'm going to take those odds.'

Naoko looked into his eyes. 'You really believe that?'

Alex felt the room grow smaller. He knew this was the worst time to start looking for alternatives. He had to keep his resolve for both their sakes.

'It's just a question of nerve,' he said.

# 29

HE WOKE WITH A HEADACHE IN THE STALE ROOM. NAOKO was taking a shower in the bathroom and he sat up to look at the clock on the nightstand. It was 6.15 a.m. and their flight was at nine thirty. He rubbed his eyes and slowly climbed from the bed. His limbs were heavy and his joints ached. From the window, he could see the first commuters of the day start to emerge from the metro station twenty-seven floors below. The streets were full of gridlocked buses fighting their way slowly forwards while tuktuks weaved nimbly around them, racing through the narrow gaps. Life was continuing, Alex thought, despite his problems. No matter how desperate the situation seemed, he knew he had to carry on.

He slid open the wardrobe door and took out the heavily bound package from the shelf. His holdall was at the foot of the bed and he emptied the contents out and spread his clothes across the sheets. The bag was too small to contain everything so he began to select clothing that could be discarded to make room. There wasn't any time to be sentimental so he gathered up some T-shirts and underwear at random and tossed them into a pile on the floor. Spreading out a thick beach towel, he picked up the package and laid it in the middle. The corner was torn so he peeled back a strip of the silver tape and tucked it over the gap to seal it. He wrapped the package inside the towel so it was tightly covered and then stowed it at the bottom of the empty holdall. He began to stuff his clothing into the spaces around it to make sure it was hidden, leaving a layer of neatly folded shirts on the top. He zipped the bag closed and tested the weight. It was heavier than before but not noticeably so and he appeared natural as he moved with it in his hand.

'Naoko?' he called. 'We need to hurry now to get to the airport on time.'

He tried to sound positive, conscious of not giving her any excuse to get upset again. When there was no answer he walked to the bathroom door and opened it gently.

'Naoko?' he called out again.

The shower was running inside the glass cubicle, the water pounding on the screen and steam billowing out into the bathroom. There was no one inside.

He checked each way, peering around the frame of the door into the corners of the room. The bathroom was empty. His fatigue instantly disappeared as his adrenaline surged.

To make sure he wasn't deceiving himself, he walked over to the balcony and slid the door open and checked outside on the patio. The morning sun seared into his eyes as he scanned the balcony. Content that Naoko wasn't there, he closed the door and looked around the room. He opened the wardrobe again and checked inside. Nothing. Knowing how foolish he looked, he knelt down and checked under the bed, but there were no clues there either.

Now he was starting to panic. Where the hell was she? Maybe she'd gone for breakfast without him. But why would she leave the shower running? Why wouldn't she wake him and ask him to join her? He started to worry she had done something really stupid.

He walked back out to the balcony and stood at the railing and looked directly down into the street. Smartly dressed office workers meandered down the wide pavements and hawkers carried baskets of fruit and soft drinks along the lines of cars stopped at the traffic lights. There was no sign of any commotion, no shouts or crowds gathering, as if someone had leaped from twenty-seven floors above. He stepped back inside the room and closed the door.

It was when he returned to the bathroom, reaching inside the shower cubicle to shut off the water, that he noticed the piece of folded paper on the glass shelf above the sink. He took it and unfolded it carefully, almost fearful of what he might find. There was a note in Naoko's neat handwriting. He began to read.

*Alex,*

*I'm truly sorry. I really am. But there's no way I can go through with this. I know if I try to talk you out of it, you will just do your best to convince me and eventually you will make us both go to the airport and fly back to Japan together. I think that will be a big mistake for both of us. I've got a chance now at a new life and I can't risk it because you're too stubborn to see sense.*

*I'm going to find another hotel and stay in Bangkok for a few days. I need some time to think. I'm sorry to leave you but I can't see any other way.*

*Naoko*

He was reading at speed and when he reached the end he went back and read the message again. He couldn't believe it. Now who was being left behind? he thought.

He found his phone and rang her number and listened to her voice inviting him to leave a message. He hung up without speaking and tried again. There was no way to tell what time she had left. She must have crept out like a thief while he was sleeping. It was all so well orchestrated she must have spent half the night planning it.

Alex knew there was no time to try to think her actions

through. Before him lay the task at hand, cold and implacable like the face of a mountain. He dressed in a hurry and took one last look around the room and closed the door behind him. The corridor was busy with housekeeping staff pushing their laundry carts along the hallway. They all smiled and wished him a good morning as he passed and Alex tried to smile and return their greetings. He realized he needed to stay calm. From now on, he was out in public and any sign of anxiety was the surest way to get caught. He was going to prove Naoko wrong, just to show that her wild theories about him were off the mark. He pressed for the lift and rode down to the lobby.

'How was your stay?' the receptionist asked as he returned his room key.

'Very good, thank you,' Alex said, and keeping his tone as casual as possible added, 'Have you seen Ms Yamamoto this morning?'

'Yes, I have,' the receptionist said. 'She came down and asked for a taxi to take her into the city a little earlier.' Her teeth were straight and white, with a gap at the front that showed when she spoke.

'Into the city?'

'Yes. She said she was going downtown alone this morning. She said you would be down to check out later.'

'What time was that exactly?'

She glanced at the clock behind her. 'About half an hour ago. Just after 6 a.m.'

'Oh. I see.'

'Is everything all right?'

Alex waved away the suggestion that it could be otherwise. 'Of course,' he said. 'Everything's fine.'

He settled the bill and the desk clerk called for a porter to assist him. The porter insisted on carrying the holdall out to the taxi rank and Alex released it from his grip reluctantly. He followed him outside and watched as the bag was placed in the boot of the cab at the head of the rank. In a strange way, he felt relieved at being parted from it, if only for a few seconds.

The driver headed beneath the monorail tracks and followed the downtown traffic towards the expressway. Alex tried to call Naoko again but there was no answer, just the same invitation to leave a message in her bright, cheerful voice. He hung up again, without speaking. The city outside the window passed in a haze of dust thrown up by passing cars, the old colonial-style buildings crumbling gradually beside the new office blocks and department stores. Soon the airport came into view and the deep turbine roar of passenger jets filled the cloudless sky. The pavement was full of travellers unloading their baggage and wheeling trolleys along the transit area and in through the automatic doors. The driver pulled up between two coaches and stopped the engine. He stepped out on to the kerb and opened the boot. Alex paid the fare and tipped the driver as he accepted his bag, clenching his hand around the worn leather handles. From the corner of his eye, he could see uniformed Thai policemen as they patrolled along the line of vehicles. He turned quickly and followed the crowds into the terminal.

He found the desk for his flight and joined the queue to check in. There were posters mounted on every wall detailing the punishments meted out for customs violations and Alex tried not to read them. When he reached the head of the line he presented his passport at the desk.

'Are you travelling alone today, Mr Malloy?' the young attendant asked. She was wearing heavy foundation and dark lipstick that made her look much older than she probably was.

'Yes. I am.'

'Do you have any bags to check in?'

He needed to be certain about his decision. If he checked the bag into the hold, he knew it would be screened in his absence. That way, he would never know if there was a problem until he felt a hand on his shoulder as he boarded the plane. If he kept the bag with him, at least he would be aware of prying officials and could do his best to avoid them. He knew he was taking a risk either way.

Finally, he said, 'I don't have any bags to check in, only carry-on luggage.'

She looked down at the holdall. Satisfied it was within the size restriction, she asked, 'Did you pack this bag yourself?'

Alex nodded. 'Yes, I did.'

'Have you left your bag unattended anywhere today?'

'No,' he said.

'Are you carrying any of these prohibited items?'

She indicated a sign on the counter with symbols of various types of contraband. Her movements were cursory and robotic.

'No, I'm not,' Alex lied.

The attendant barely listened to his answer. She reached down quickly and wrapped a cabin tag around the handles of his holdall and held out his passport and boarding pass.

'Enjoy your flight,' she said without conviction, already looking to the next passenger in line.

As he approached the security gate, the holdall seemed to grow heavier in his hand. He tried to focus on Jun's words from the night in the bath house, his insistence that the package would be insulated so that the contents wouldn't show up on the screening equipment. Do you think the authorities care about people smuggling drugs out of the country? Jun had said. They're only looking for explosives and weapons – anything that can endanger the plane or the passengers. It's at the other end that you need to be wary. Just keep calm in Bangkok and there won't be any problems.

He lifted the bag on to the conveyor belt and watched as it disappeared into the heart of the machine. He placed his phone in a plastic tray, along with the coins from his pockets and waited to be called forward through the metal detector. When he was summoned, Alex stepped confidently through the archway and handed his passport and boarding card to the official.

The young officer staring at the X-ray screen looked bored and weary. His chin was propped up on his hand, as if he was nearing the end of a long night shift and the items moving across the monitor before him had long ago merged into one another. Alex took his documents as they were returned and waited at the end of the conveyor belt. He watched as the holdall rolled along the channel, followed by the plastic tray containing his other possessions. He calmly fastened his belt and walked into the busy departure area.

He found a quiet corner in a café and sat at a table with his bag beneath his chair, watching the cup of coffee before him. People were milling in and out of fast-food restaurants and discount cosmetics shops, trying to kill time before their flights were ready to board. Every face seemed to watch him with furtive glances. The skin on the back of his hands grew tight and cold. He waited patiently, braced for disaster.

When his flight was announced, Alex gathered himself and followed the signs to the gate. The white hull of the Boeing gleamed in the sunshine beyond the window. The flight attendants called the passengers forward by rows, filling the plane from the rear. When his row number was called, he presented his boarding pass and walked along the gangway towards the open hatch. He resisted the temptation to check back over his shoulder as the stewardess welcomed him on board.

He shuffled along the aisle and found a space in the luggage container above his seat. He stowed the holdall and slipped along the row and buckled himself in. The plane was filling steadily with young western backpackers and distracted Japanese parents attending to their children. Alex waited as the last remaining seconds slipped by, still refusing himself the luxury of believing he was safe.

Then the cabin door was sealed and the plane began to back away from the gate and taxi to the end of the runway for take-off. He felt his tension dissipate as the engines started to whine and the plane gathered energy. The fuselage began to vibrate as the engines powered up and then the plane began to accelerate down the tarmac. There was a surge and a moment of weightlessness and then they were airborne. The ground slipped away and Alex looked down at Bangkok as the pilot banked hard above it. Naoko was down there somewhere, he thought. He pictured her face as she'd lain sleeping in the bungalow, the sound of the water moving across the rocks below their room. He wondered if he would see her again.

Turbulence over the East China Sea. The cabin lights were dimmed as the plane pitched and bucked, the steel skeleton groaning as it struggled through the buffeting cross wind. Babies cried and passengers gasped aloud as they were pummelled in their seats, drinks spilling in the aisles. Alex felt himself relax internally as the ordeal worsened, the sound of freight shaking in the hold beneath his feet like handfuls of dropped cutlery. He took Naoko's letter from his pocket and read it again.

How had he ended up here, he thought, shuttling narcotics across international borders? Was this really how low he had sunk? What a waste of everything he could have achieved. Naoko was right about that, at least. It was little wonder she had deserted him.

The weather cleared as they approached the southern tip of Japan and the flight eased down smoothly from the storm at high altitude, beginning the long descent to Narita. The thick white deck of clouds had broken up to the south and rays of sunlight formed flares on the glass.

Alex stood up from his seat and walked along the aisle to the toilet at the rear of the cabin. He locked himself in and ran some cold water into the bowl and splashed it on his face and neck. Hunched slightly in the cramped cubicle, he stood before the small mirror and watched his reflection.

This is how it's going to happen, he thought. You're going to remember that luck is on your side. You're going to take your bag and carry it from the plane like it's some kind of trophy. You're going to look every customs officer and border official in the eye and answer every question without hesitation. You're going to walk through the airport like it was a day at the park and out through the exit gates and on to the express train back into Tokyo. Then you're going to call Hiro and you're going to go out and get drunk.

He kept his resolve as the passengers left the plane and he followed the pack into the terminal. Electronic announcements in Japanese marked their progress as they funnelled through the gleaming corridors and endless doorways of Narita. It was at the passport desk that he sensed the period of high danger had begun. There was no other choice but to travel through the cogs of the machine now, all ability to control his fate beyond his grasp. Alex knew his only choice was to surrender.

He selected a customs desk and headed towards it.

# 30

As the dog began to bark and snarl, Alex felt all eyes in the terminal turn to him. The handler paid out the leash and the German shepherd reared up at the end of the line, using all of its strength to close in on the scent. The other passengers froze around him, fearful of moving in the presence of such controlled fury. Alex stood and waited. No one was in any confusion about its target.

The handler reined the dog back and gave it the command to rest, and it sat quickly, its long tail sweeping excitedly over the floor. Two young officers left their station at the nearest customs desk and approached cautiously. They looked at each other, unsure of the correct procedure. They both had adolescent complexions and cheap blue uniforms that were too large for their youthful frames.

One of the officers motioned for Alex to follow. He obeyed without thought, walking between them, moving automatically through a series of security doors down into the hidden recesses of the airport. He had no time to think ahead or plan what he should say, he just marched alongside mutely, his footsteps sounding time with theirs. They turned down a steep stairwell and through an open door into a windowless room.

A senior officer was talking on a telephone mounted on the

wall at the far side of the room. He broke off his conversation as they entered and turned to face them. He was older, his bearing authoritative and upright, as if preparing for a parade. There was a desk and a chair under a strip light so powerful that Alex had to squint when the officer told him to sit. He placed the holdall on the inspection table and emptied his pockets as instructed. First his wallet, phone and change. Then his passport and Naoko's letter. The officer opened the passport and held it up to check the photograph for authenticity.

'Do you have anything you want to tell me?' he asked. 'You seem unsettled.' He spoke with a severity that was disconcerting, his voice too loud in the confinement of the room.

'I'm fine,' Alex said. 'I had a rough flight. That's all.'

'You are coming to Japan as a tourist?'

'No. I work here.'

The officer flicked to the visa page of the passport. 'You live in Tokyo?'

'Yes. In Koenji.'

'You have your *gaijin* card?'

Alex reached to the table for his wallet. He searched inside the compartments and found his resident's card tucked away with some old receipts and scraps of paper. As he pulled it out something else caught his eye. He handed the ID card across the desk.

The officer examined it carefully. Satisfied, he tossed it on to the table.

'What was your point of departure today?' he asked.

Alex could sense the implication in the word before he said it. 'Bangkok.'

The official stepped into the light. He pointed at the holdall on the table. His lips and teeth were wet with anticipation. 'Is there anything in your luggage that would alert the detection dog, Mr Malloy?'

Alex looked at the holdall, the brown leather worn and cracked under the stark lighting. The maker's emblem was embossed on one side: St James's of London. It occurred to him that the bag had belonged to his father. Thank God he wasn't here to see this now, Alex thought. His instinct was to buy as much time as possible, even if it was futile. He could sense time pouring away fast.

'No,' he said.

The officer looked to his subordinates and spoke quickly in Japanese. The nearest one stepped forward and began to unfasten the zipper. He was young, with a crew cut and a nervous expression that made him look guilty. He was wearing pristine white cotton gloves with buttons at the wrist. He lifted out the layer of folded shirts from the top of the bag and placed them one by one on the table. The second officer began to unfold the clothes and carefully feel along the seams and check inside the pockets. He took out a pair of flip-flops and held them up to the light, squeezing the soles between his fingers. He flicked through the pages of a book, standing over the desk to catch anything that might fall out. Alex thought of the stories Jun had told him about the foreigner's prison at Fuchu. Tales of hard labour and punishment cells. Tales that made his time at Ushigome seem easy. He felt like a swimmer far from shore.

As they searched, the officers placed all the checked items into plastic storage boxes and stacked them at the side of the table. Soon Alex knew there was nothing inside the bag except the object they were searching for. The last grains of hope were tumbling down. The room grew smaller.

Reaching down into the bottom of the holdall, the young officer gently retrieved the folded beach towel and lifted it out of the bag. It was obvious from his movements that he could sense the bundle had a weight and bulk that was out of proportion to its size. He placed it on the table and started to unfold the material slowly, as if he were removing a bandage from a wound. The package was inside, where Alex had wrapped it. The officers all moved forward to look closer, their faces widening with excitement at their discovery. Alex felt his jaw tighten.

'Were you aware this was in your luggage?' the senior official asked.

Alex nodded, his mouth too dry to speak.

'Do you know what's inside?'

He nodded again.

'You are aware that any form of narcotics is illegal in Japan?'

'Yes,' he said.

The officer looked at one of his juniors. He stepped forward and took a sharp knife from a pouch on his belt. He picked up the parcel and held the point against one side, applying minimal pressure, as if trying to protect the contents from damage. He began to pull the knife gently across the seam.

'Wait,' Alex said.

The officer paused, startled at the interruption. The blade had barely pierced the protective insulation tape.

'What is it?'

'Before you open it,' Alex said, 'there's something I need to show you.'

He reached down and took his wallet from the tabletop. He took out the business card he had found earlier and held it out across the desk. The officer read it, turning the card over in his hand.

'What is this?' he asked hesitantly.

'This is the direct number for Inspector Saito at Ushigome police station,' Alex said. 'Call him and tell him to come here. I won't say anything else until he arrives.'

He remembered the solemn face of Officer Tomada, forcing him to accept the card as he was released from custody. He was grateful now that she had been so insistent. Saito's name felt like a solitary lifeline.

'Why should I call him?' the customs officer asked. 'The police have no jurisdiction here.'

Alex looked up through the harsh light pouring down from the ceiling. He hardened his face for effect. 'Inspector Saito is a

225

senior officer in the Ushigome crime division,' he said. 'If you open that package without him present, you'll be disrupting a major investigation.'

# 31

IT WAS LATE IN THE EVENING WHEN THE INSPECTOR ARRIVED. He wordlessly assumed authority as he entered the room and hung his raincoat on the rack by the door. Both of the young customs officers bowed to him in deference and he stood upright, waiting patiently for the supervisor to follow. Finally, grudgingly, he did so and Saito accepted his concession of command with a curt dip of his small, grey head.

Alex was unsure whether to feel relief or apprehension at his presence. He remained still as Saito took a seat, staring coldly at the silver-bound package on the table. It lay in the glare of the spotlight like a secret exposed.

'I see my warning to you went unheeded, Malloy-san,' he said.

Alex kept his voice clear and level. He knew that Saito wasn't going to respond to pleading. 'I had no choice, Inspector. You know who I'm dealing with.'

'What did you tell the customs officials?'

'I just made up a story to buy some time. It was all I could think of.'

Saito touched a finger to the slit cut in the corner of the plastic wrapping, peeling back the tape around the edges. 'I knew you were headed for some kind of trouble, but it looks like you've outdone yourself.'

'It wasn't my idea, believe me.'

'So you were pressured into this scheme to pay off your debt?'

'Exactly.'

'So why am I here?'

'You said you would help me before, Inspector. Now I want to take you up on the offer.'

Saito adjusted his glasses. His eyes were calm and unreadable behind the lenses. 'Why now? Why didn't you call me when this proposal was first made to you?'

'I had no idea how you would react. I didn't know if you would believe me or not. I could have just created more trouble for myself.'

'Don't treat me like a fool, Malloy-san. You took your chances to see if you could get away with it. If the customs officers hadn't stopped you, I'm sure you wouldn't have felt the need to contact me.'

'I'm not doing this for personal gain,' Alex said. 'You know how dangerous these people are. I was hoping you could help me out of this somehow.'

Saito leaned back in his chair, his chin raised slightly and his head tilted as if trying to gain a better vantage point of the scene before him. 'And what service do you think I can perform for you?'

'You can explain my situation to the customs authorities. Let them know how I ended up here.'

'What do I get out of this?' he asked. 'What can you do for me?'

Alex sensed a flicker of hope. 'What do you want?' he asked.

Without hesitation, Saito said, 'Who organized this?'

'It was one of the prisoners I was locked up with at Ushigome. One of the older men who looked like they ran the place.'

'Just one man? That's all?'

'There was another man with him. Kind of a bodyguard. And also one other.'

'Who was that?'

'A go-between who set everything up. He was at Ushigome with me as well.'

'This isn't exactly prime information,' Saito said with a resigned shrug. 'I need more. I need names.'

Alex paused for a moment. 'I can't do that, Inspector.'

'Why not? These people aren't exactly your friends.'

'I'm not trying to protect anyone. I'm just looking out for myself. As soon as I give you a name, I won't have anything left to trade.'

'Well, there's one name that I have already. You can confirm that for me, at least.'

'Who?'

Saito reached down and lifted the piece of folded paper from the tabletop. He carefully smoothed out the creases and spread Naoko's letter out on the desk.

'This is practically a confession,' he said. 'It's even signed.'

'But it says that she wanted no part of this.'

'She didn't try to stop you, though, did she? She didn't alert the authorities. That makes her complicit under the law.'

Alex shook his head slowly but deliberately. 'No, Inspector. She has nothing to do with any of this.'

'Of course she does. It's all written here.'

'I can give you all the details you want of everyone involved. I can give you the name that I know and descriptions of everyone I met. I can give you phone numbers. But I won't say anything against Naoko.'

'Why not? What has she done for you?'

'She's innocent of any involvement in this.'

'Even if you tell me about these others, it means nothing. What offences have they actually committed? What can you prove? Give me Naoko and I will try to work something out for you. Maybe you will even be able to go home without prosecution.'

Alex remained steadfast. There was no part of him that wanted to accept the offer. 'No,' he said.

'Why not?'

'Because it's not right.'

Saito got up from the chair and walked over to the coat rack. He pulled his overcoat on and fastened the buttons. He opened the door to leave.

'So you won't help me?' Alex asked.

'I don't have any reason to.'

'That's it?'

Saito turned and gave Alex a sharp stare. 'You don't have anything I want,' he said. He called the young customs officer forward and asked for his knife. The officer nodded dutifully and handed it to him.

The inspector walked towards Alex, into the light, and picked up the package from the desktop. He ran the blade of the knife along the open corner and sliced through the thick layers of plastic wrapping. He tipped the widened opening down towards the table and the contents shifted inside. With a rush, a stream of dry, pale sand ran out in a thick flow and settled in a perfect mound on the table.

Alex watched the inspector fold the blade of the knife away. The senior customs officer came forward and raked his fingers through the pile, as if trying to find some traces of contraband hidden inside. Saito opened his briefcase and placed the empty packaging inside.

'Is that what I think it is?' Alex asked, looking down at the fine sand spread across the table. It was the white Andaman Island sand from the hotel's river-front beach.

'Whatever it is, it's not illegal,' Saito said. 'It was unlucky for you the residue on the wrapping alerted the security dog. Fortunately, you can't be arrested for residue.'

'How did you know about this?'

He wiped some stray grains of sand from his coat and looked at Alex with a weary air. 'Because Ms Yamamoto has been wise enough to telephone me already.'

'From Thailand?'

'No. She's in Tokyo. She flew back a few hours ago.'

'I don't understand.'

'She has what you were expecting to find inside this package. She's already told me everything.'

'So what happens now?'

'Now she wants to make a deal.'

# 32

It was rush hour in Shinjuku station. The platforms and concourses were jammed with passengers, secretaries and salesmen marching shoulder to shoulder as they forced a passage through the crowds, fighting to catch the packed commuter trains home. The beat of train carriages shunting over the rails and the scream of hydraulic brakes echoed around the vast hall. Naoko walked steadily against the flow.

Near the Chuo line platform, she took the steps down to a long passage lined with coin lockers. Row after row of grey-fronted cabinets, each identical to the next. There must be thousands of them in every station in the city, she thought. Who knew what secrets they contained? She selected an empty locker and opened the door. Checking no one was watching, she opened her suitcase and took out a plastic 7–11 shopping bag. She placed it inside and stood for a moment, looking at it lying there, the handles twisted and knotted together. All that effort and heartache for a few pounds of chemical poison. So much trouble over so little.

It had taken most of the night for her to make up her mind. Lying there, watching the ceiling fan spin above her, listening to Alex toss and turn, the cold chills of anxiety dreams forming in beads of sweat on his back. She knew he was reckless enough to go through with it, to storm through the airport like he was storming a barricade, but he was also reckless enough to get caught. Naoko could see that.

She had felt bad about deceiving him, but she was positive it was the only way. If she had tried to discuss it, Alex would have been too stubborn to change his mind. He would have tried to stick to his plan, just to satisfy his sense of honour. Naoko knew this wasn't the right time for abstract notions like honour. Practical solutions were her only concern. She had been through the security checks at Narita many times and had never been stopped or questioned before. Surely if she kept her mind clear and acted as usual she would have a good chance. It was true that the airport officials had been trained to focus their attention on foreign travellers entering Japan. Alex seemed to stand out more than most. A Japanese woman was the lowest of their priorities. The more she had considered the options available, the more this had seemed the best chance of success. Like Alex had said, it was all just a question of nerve.

She paid the five-hundred-yen fee and closed the locker. There was a plastic key with a round number tag attached and Naoko memorized it, then ripped the tag from the fob and threw it in a bin. She locked the door and placed the key in her bag. She climbed back up the steps to the main hall and followed the signs for the exit that led to Yasakuni Dori. It was dusk and the neon hoardings were switching on, beaming down from buildings overhead. The streets were scattered with bright-eyed touts handing out flyers for topless bars. Silent monks standing on the corners held out their begging bowls, their eyes cast down. There was the sharp scent of Korean barbecue from hidden kitchens and the bright fluorescent lights of the video arcades. Tokyo, always alive, she thought. It was good to be back on home ground.

Naoko smiled to herself as she pushed her way through the crowds and started walking down to Golden Gai, to the all-night café where she had told Inspector Saito to meet her.

*

She saw Alex at a table in the window. His face was drawn, almost hollowed out, and he was sitting back in his chair with his arms closed tightly around him. Saito was sitting opposite, upright and calm, as always, blowing hard on his black coffee, the steam spiralling up from the paper cup. They both saw her as she entered.

She touched her fingers to Alex's hand under the table as she took a seat. 'We're even now,' she said. 'I think that makes up for everything I did to get you into trouble in the first place.'

He turned to her and smiled slowly, almost reluctantly. 'You really are crazy,' he said.

'Believe me, you haven't seen anything yet.'

Saito sipped his coffee. 'This is very touching,' he said, 'but this isn't the time for heartfelt reconciliations. You are both in serious trouble.'

'I called you voluntarily, Inspector,' Naoko said. 'I could have just gone through with the delivery as instructed but I thought the best course of action was to speak to you and come clean. I don't want the supply of drugs on my conscience.' She took the key from her bag and dropped it on to the table. 'What you want is in a locker and this is the key. You can have it. Just tell me that both Alex and I are safe, then I'll tell you where it is.'

'And you think that will be the end of it?'

'You'll never find it on your own. There are thousands just like it all over the city. I know you aren't really interested in us. We aren't behind any of this, really. You want the people who set this whole business up.'

Saito shook his head. 'I'm afraid it's not going to be that simple. You both have only limited options now, so I propose you listen to me and make a decision fast. Firstly, you could throw that key away and we can all go our separate ways. I can't prosecute you without evidence, so you will have no problem with the police. But you will have a big problem with a man called Ichiro Tanaka. I wouldn't recommend crossing him, but then I'm sure you've already considered this or you wouldn't have called me. Secondly, you could go ahead and deliver the narcotics to him, as arranged. That way, you keep him happy, but then I will have cause to pursue you. Distributing illegal substances in this country is a serious offence and I will devote as much energy to prosecuting you as I will to Tanaka. Thirdly, you can show me that you believe in the rule of law and help me catch the real criminals. You can guess which choice I prefer. You're a smart young woman, Ms Yamamoto. I think you've always known that this is your only true option or you wouldn't have contacted me once you were safely in the country.'

'How do you know Tanaka is behind this?'

'Because I know where your *jidan* payment came from. Tanaka is not the kind of man to lend such a large sum without expecting a substantial return on his investment.'

'Who is he?'

'Ichiro Tanaka sits at the top of a very big and powerful tree. A very old tree. His influence infects everything it touches, often fatally. He's a very dangerous human being. The less you know about him, the better.'

'And if we help you, then we're free to go?' Naoko asked.

'If I wanted to, I could take you both into custody now and let you spend the next twenty-one days in Ushigome. Malloy-san will tell you that it's not a pleasant experience. But you're right about one thing – I don't really want you. I want Tanaka and as many of his gang as I can take down with him. Removing him from society would make all of Tokyo safer. After that, I no longer have any use for you. Go your own way and put this behind you.'

'How do we know we can trust you?' Naoko asked.

'Right now, the only people you can trust are at this table. You've both proved your loyalty to each other by not taking the easy option to save yourselves when it was offered to you. As for me, you will have to take my word for it. If I was going to arrest you, I would have done so by now. Beyond that, trust no one. I know that I don't trust too many people where Tanaka is concerned. His people have managed to destroy everything and everyone they have touched. Lawyers, judges, policemen. Anywhere people value money above all else. As far as he is concerned, everyone is suspect and everyone is corrupt.'

'So what do we do next?' Alex asked. 'The clock is ticking. They're expecting me to call them to confirm we made it through.'

Saito looked around the coffee shop at the bored-looking dropouts and solitary night owls. No one seemed to give him any cause for concern. He glanced from Naoko to Alex and back again and pursed his lips in a gesture of resigned acceptance.

'This isn't going to be easy,' he said, 'but you've managed to stick together after all you've been through. At least that's a good start.'

# 33

THE FAIRGROUND WHEEL WAS VISIBLE ABOVE THE YOKOHAMA skyline for miles around. It was set on a boardwalk at the edge of the harbour, turning gently against the night sky and towering over the amusement park at its base. Thick steel spokes radiated from the centre of the wheel, with viewing capsules connected at intervals along the circumference. Tourists pressed their faces against the capsule windows as they took in the view from the revolving structure. An electronic clock at the centre shone brightly, colouring the thin clouds that had rolled in over the bay.

Jun was waiting at the ticket office, as arranged. He was alone, standing to one side, away from the crowds, scraps of paper and empty food cartons blowing on the wind around his feet. He looked disconcerted, searching the crowds around him with quick glances from beneath his brow. He stubbed out a half-smoked cigarette as he saw Alex approach.

'I don't like this, Russia-jin,' he said. 'I don't like this at all.'

Alex tried to radiate calm. 'Relax. I'm here now. Let's just get this over with.'

'I still don't know why you wanted me to come all the way out here. What was wrong with the original meeting place?'

'I couldn't meet you in a bar I'd never been to before, Jun. Look at it from my point of view. I had no idea who was going to be there with you. I thought we should meet somewhere neutral. That's all.'

Jun looked around suspiciously at the rides and attractions covering the boardwalk. The soaring roller coaster, the carousel, the Ferris wheel slowly turning above him.

'Why does it have to be here? I hate fairgrounds.'

'Naoko and I came here on the night we met. Maybe it was sentimental but I thought it would be fitting. Coming full circle, or something like that.'

'It makes me nervous to do this in a place that's so public.'

Alex nodded. 'I know,' he said. 'That's what makes me feel safe.'

'You have it with you?'

'It's close by.'

Jun cocked his chin quickly in surprise. 'What do you mean, "close by"?'

'It's safe. I want to give it to you on the Ferris wheel. We can have some privacy there.'

'But where is it, if you don't have it with you now?'

'A friend is looking after it. They are going to join us.'

'You're kidding me? This is all becoming alarming, Russia-jin.'

Alex reached out and touched a reassuring hand to Jun's shoulder. 'It's your turn to trust me now.'

He handed Jun a ticket and they both joined the snaking queue leading up the ramp to the entrance platform where new passengers were waiting to board. Shrieks, thrilled and terrified, rang out from the roller-coaster tracks high above. Jun smoked constantly, lighting one cigarette from the butt of the first. He moved with his familiar rolling shuffle, his head down and his eyes scanning the crowds for any sign of danger. Alex watched the capsules descend on the turning wheel and pause at the docking station. Soon they were near the head of the line, each gondola quickly emptying and then moving into position to take the next party.

When they reached the barrier, Naoko pushed her way forward to join them. Jun turned to watch her as she approached.

'Is that who I think it is?' he said.

'She's knows everything, Jun.'

He turned to Alex. 'Everything?'

'I couldn't go through with it as planned. I had to tell her.'

'She carried the stuff through customs knowing it was in her luggage?'

Alex nodded.

Jun gave a low whistle of respect. 'This night is becoming very strange indeed,' he said.

Naoko stood beside Alex and took his arm. She gave Jun a stony look but said nothing. Jun seemed to decide that having Naoko's complicity made her trustworthy. He bowed to her with a flourish.

'My congratulations,' he said. 'It's quite something the first time, isn't it?'

'Thrilling,' she said with disdain.

'Alex never told me how striking you are. I'm not sure I would have recommended you for the job if I'd known.'

Naoko waved his compliment away. 'Shall we just get this over with?' she said.

The barrier lifted and they walked across to the boarding platform and stepped inside the next available gondola. As the doors began to close, Alex heard the sound of surprised voices and scuffling feet. He turned to see two Japanese men, thick-necked and thuggish, push their way through the queue of waiting tourists. He recognized one of them as the scar-faced bodyguard who had been with Tanaka the night he had met him in the bath house. The other was burly, with a bald head that shone in the lights of the fairground. The little fingers on each of his hands were missing below the knuckle. Jun stood in the doorway and motioned for the men to board and they slipped through as the doors were closing. Now the five of them were alone. Cranks and gears turned as the capsule began to climb.

'You want to feel safe, Russia-jin? Well, so do I. My associates are going to make sure nothing bad happens to me. I hope you don't mind.'

Jun's companions stood behind him, crush-nosed and razor-lipped.

'Not at all,' Alex said. 'I would have bought them tickets if you'd warned me.'

'Our friend is very upset about this. He thinks you're trying to cross him.'

'Our friend from the bath house?'

'That's right.'

'You mean Tanaka-san?'

Jun narrowed his eyes at the mention of the name. His bodyguards stood and glowered. The gondola rose steadily as the wheel turned.

'How do you know that name?' Jun asked.

'It wasn't difficult to find out.'

'Then it should be easy to forget. Take my advice and never mention him again. Especially as you are already in deep trouble. Changing our meeting place was a bad idea.'

'Think about it,' Alex said. 'What would you have done in my place?'

'I would have done as I was told. You're acting like this is some kind of game where you can make up the rules. This is serious. People get hurt for less.'

Alex nodded towards the brawler standing behind Jun. 'You mean like that night in the bath house? The night when your friend tried to see how long I could breathe underwater?'

Jun bristled at Alex's tone. 'That was just business, Russia-jin. Nothing personal.'

'You set me up from the beginning. I was in trouble and you knew I had no one to turn to. I trusted you and all you saw was easy prey.'

Jun looked him straight in the eye, the beginning of a self-satisfied smile starting to form on his lips. 'There is no trust,' he said. 'Trust is just betrayal waiting to happen.'

The capsule moved higher, up towards the apex of the wheel. The lights from the buildings along the horizon created a distorting effect through the criss-cross pattern of the wheel's structure.

'I want the package,' Jun said.

'I want the money you promised me.'

'You go first.'

Alex shook his head. 'After everything you've put me through, I think you can pay what you owe me before I do anything else.'

Jun reached inside his jacket pocket and took out an envelope and handed it to Alex. He opened it and riffled through the thick wad of notes inside. It looked like the correct amount but there was no time to stand and count it.

'This is for you,' Alex said, and passed the envelope to Naoko.

She opened her bag, tucked it inside, then lifted out the silver-wrapped package. She handed it to Jun.

'It's all there?

Alex nodded.

'What's this?' Jun asked, and pointed to the corner that had been opened.

'We sampled it,' Naoko said. 'In Bangkok. There's only a little missing.'

Jun turned the package over, weighing it in his hand. He tore the opening wider at the corner and peered inside. He shrugged when he saw the contents to be as expected.

'I don't see a problem with you taking a gram or two for your personal use. I hope you both had fun. You know where to come if you want more.'

The capsule began the long descent towards the docking station. Jun seemed happier now that business was concluded.

He took out a pack of Lucky Strikes and lit one. Wisps of blue-grey smoke filled the capsule.

'I've been told to ask if you would consider doing another trip. It's always easier the second time.'

'How much will you pay if we do this again?' Naoko asked.

'Another two million yen. More if you can make deliveries that are higher value. We like to start beginners with small-time stuff, then you can progress to the lucrative goods if you can be trusted.' He smiled lecherously at Naoko. 'Of course, you'll earn more money if you make the trip on your own. Is it really worth sharing the proceeds when you do all the work?'

Naoko looked at Alex. 'We work best as a team,' she said.

The two young brawlers were peering out at the view, their body language showing they had decided the need for vigilance was over. Jun took a long, deep drag on his cigarette, waiting for the wheel to complete its turn. Everything in the capsule was calm.

The silence was broken by a muffled ring tone. Jun reached into his jacket and removed his phone. He looked at the screen and answered.

He gave no greeting, just stood and listened to whoever was at the end of the line, nodding his understanding as the conversation progressed.

Quickly, his expression changed. His cocksure demeanour was replaced by a rat-like survival instinct. He hung up the phone and leaped towards Alex. The two heavies saw his movements and followed. The atmosphere inside the capsule sparked with adrenaline.

He ripped open the front of Alex's shirt, popping buttons on to the floor. The microphone, connected to the hidden recorder, was taped to the skin of Alex's chest. There was a bald patch where the police technician had shaved him to help the adhesive stick.

Jun was breathless with fear. 'You're a fucking dead man!' he shouted, spittle flying from his lips. 'You set me up.'

Alex pushed him away. 'Now you know what it feels like.'

'We were almost home and dry. Why fuck it up now?'

Alex reached and grabbed Jun by the throat with one hand and swung for him with the other. His fist connected with the side of Jun's skull with a crack and Jun stumbled back against the window of the gondola.

'Because I can't stand to see you win,' he said.

The two yakuza were on him quickly, pressing Alex's body into the corner of the capsule, where it was impossible for him to fight back. One of the men held him while the other began to pummel his chest and abdomen. Jun was swiping at him, trying to rip the microphone away, while Alex covered up and protected himself as best he could. The bald-headed thug stepped back and pulled a long-handled butterfly knife from inside his coat. Turning his wrist in a swift motion, he flicked out the blade and stepped forward and began to raise it up.

Suddenly, the figures in the capsule seemed to freeze in a bright flash of illumination. Jun and his henchmen instinctively reached up their hands to shield their faces from the painful glare streaming from the capsule following behind. Naoko turned to peek through her fingers at the source of the light.

There were four uniformed police officers inside, along with Inspector Saito, standing at the window, looking directly towards the commotion. One of the officers had a long-lens camera to his eye and was hurriedly snapping pictures; beside him, another officer shone a searchlight towards them. Saito stared ominously at the scene before him, his stillness a warning.

Jun looked at his friends. He was heaving from exertion, the veins standing out angrily on his temples. He nodded to them and they stood down. The knife clattered to the floor as it was dropped. The wheel finished its turn.

# 34

THEY WAITED AT THE BOARDWALK RAIL, LOOKING INTO THE cold, dark water of the harbour. The fairground was closing and the rides were shutting down for the night. Above them, the illuminated wheel was plunged into darkness section by section. Naoko touched a tender hand to the bruises on Alex's ribs.

'How does it feel?' she asked. 'Is anything broken?'

He was inhaling in small lungfuls, patting himself gingerly on the chest to feel for damage. 'I'm fine. I think.'

'Is it painful?'

'Only when I breathe,' he said, and winced. 'I should be getting used to it by now.'

'I'm sorry you got hurt. I wouldn't have involved the police if I'd known that would be more dangerous.'

'Don't worry,' Alex said. 'We did the right thing.'

There hadn't been any dramatic showdown at the end. It seemed that even arrests in Japan followed an organized structure where everyone involved tried not to lose face. Jun had stepped from the capsule defiantly, his hands held up in a show of surrender to the officers waiting on the platform. His henchmen had followed suit. Jun had turned to Alex with a look of burning contempt as they led him away and Alex had glared back in return, keen to show his satisfaction in revenge.

He watched as Jun was escorted across the boardwalk to one of the waiting patrol cars and manhandled into the rear seat. The late-night visitors who remained in the fairground stood aside as the police officers passed, huddling close to each other and whispering with subdued excitement. It was by far the biggest thrill of the night.

Saito waited until the police vehicles had pulled away in a close convoy, ferrying the suspects back to the city. He walked tall over to the boardwalk railing, his usually dour expression replaced by the trace of a smile.

'Well done,' Saito said. 'I've listened to the tape and we have everything we need. There's enough evidence to build a strong case.'

'What about the phone call?' Alex asked. 'Someone must have tipped them off.'

'Are you sure it was the call that made them suspicious? It could have been a coincidence.'

'No way. Jun went straight for the microphone as soon as he hung up. Someone had told him exactly where to look. How could anyone have found out about the surveillance so quickly? Only the police officers under your command were aware of it.'

The inspector seemed unconcerned. 'It wasn't one of my men,' he said. 'We traced the call to a public phone booth in Kabukicho. I've given orders for the local CCTV to be checked to see if that shows anything. Until then, I don't want to speculate. We have all we need on the voice recording. That's the main thing.'

'So now you're going to prosecute Jun and the others?' Alex asked.

'I want Tanaka, not them. They know that. Tonight's evidence is only useful to convince them to accept a deal. It solves little to lock them up and leave the boss free.'

'But you'll keep Jun in custody?'

'Only until I interview him and explain his options. If I

hold him too long, Tanaka will know the exchange was compromised. Anyway, it's best that he tastes freedom while he thinks his choices through. It will give him focus. Prison time tends to dull the senses.'

'But what about Naoko and me? I thought we would be safe, otherwise I would never have agreed to this. If they are out walking the streets . . .'

Saito interrupted him with a reassuring wave of his hand. 'I will make sure that my officers monitor them day and night. You have nothing to fear. Just go back and live your lives as normal. Take the usual precautions and, if you see or hear anything suspicious, call me. Only me, just to be sure.'

He gave each of them a respectful nod of his clipped grey head and turned and walked away, leaving them alone on the deserted boardwalk. Alex looked around at the shuttered attractions, the torn tickets and scraps of paper blowing around on the wind. There was a melancholy, end-of-season feeling about being left alone there.

'Do you remember the last time we were here?' he said. 'It seems so long ago. Imagine if someone had told you back then all that would happen to us?'

Naoko laughed. 'It would have been a very short first date.'

'And now this is over, what do you think we should do next?'

She turned to face him. 'My offer still stands . . . ?'

'Which offer?'

'Of going to Osaka. Of you joining me out there and the two of us starting again.'

'You mean it?'

'Of course. It's what I want.'

He looked out at the dark water. 'With so many people holding grudges against us now, maybe it's the best option we have.'

'Is that the only reason you would come with me?' she asked.

He stood up and took her face in his hands. 'Of course not,' he said. 'I can't think of anything I want more.'

They walked from the fairground and caught the last train back to Shinagawa station. They were both exhausted and sat close together, propping one another up and trying to stay awake in the moving carriage. There was a couple opposite with a young daughter, about five years old, Alex guessed, clutching a stuffed pink rabbit she had won at the fair. She stared at him, transfixed, as the train zoomed through tunnels and over bridges, back into the heart of Tokyo. Her mother tried to quietly divert the child's attention but without success. When they reached their station, the train slowed and Alex and Naoko stood to leave. The mother spoke nervously and the child looked up from her seat with wonder as the doors closed.

'What was that about?' Alex asked as they walked along the platform.

'The girl's mother wanted to apologize to you. She said her daughter was being rude.'

'Why? Because she was staring at me?'

'She thought you weren't real. She said you looked like a mannequin. She'd never seen blond hair and blue eyes on a real person before.'

'You're kidding?'

'She kept asking if she could touch you to see if you were really human.'

Alex held a hand up in front of his face and examined it.

'One hundred per cent flesh and blood,' he said.

'How long do you need to collect your things from Koenji?'

'Not long. A few hours at most. I'll be ready by the morning.'

'Why don't we just get the train to Osaka tomorrow and get out of here? Why hang around?'

Alex shrugged. 'We can leave on the early train if you want to?'

'There's an evening service. Let's wait and get that one.'

'Are you sure?'

'Meet me at Tokyo station,' Naoko said. 'At the Shin–Osaka bullet-train platform at 6 p.m. There's something I have to do before we go.'

# 35

It was late when Alex returned to his guesthouse. The communal living room and kitchen were silent and empty, the sink piled high with unwashed dishes. He walked quietly up the five flights of wooden stairs to the attic floor. Light crept gently from beneath a few door frames as he passed but, mostly, all was dark. The house was sleeping. He searched through his bag and found his keys and unlocked the door to his room. He closed the door behind him and switched on the bare bulb. There was a letter lying on the tatami floor that someone had slipped under the door. He picked it up and looked at the envelope. It was stamped and postmarked London. He opened the envelope carefully and took out the letter. After he had read it twice, he left his room and went back downstairs. In the hallway, he dialled the number on the house telephone.

After three rings, someone picked up. Alex took a breath.

'Hello?' the voice said.

He hesitated. He could feel emotion begin to fill him from the soles of his feet until his face grew warm and flushed. He realized it was shame.

'It's Alex,' he said, and paused. 'How are you?'

His mother gave a soft exhalation into the receiver. He could hear the creak down the line as she slowly took a seat.

'Alexander,' she said. 'Are you still in Tokyo?'

'Yes.'

'Are you well?'

'I'm fine. And you?'

'I'm not too bad.' A pause. 'Did you get my letter?'

'Yes.'

'Your father. Well, he's not very well. I wanted you to know.'

'Your letter said he's had a stroke. Is it serious?'

'It was terrifying at the time, but he's recovering.'

'Is he in hospital?'

'He was. He's at home now.'

'Can I speak to him?'

'He's just gone to sleep. He'll be terribly upset he missed you. He's been asking for you ever since it happened.'

'Will he get better?'

'The doctors say he should recover most of the function he's lost in his arm. His speech may be impaired but we think it's not too bad.'

'Your letter said it happened in June. Why didn't you let me know sooner?'

'I wanted to wait until I knew what to tell you. It's been so long since you've contacted anyone, I wasn't sure if you would be concerned.'

'I'm always concerned about Dad.'

His mother's tone became sharper suddenly, more defensive. 'But not if it was me. Is that what you mean?'

'He never wanted to turn his back on me.'

There was a long pause. 'That's another reason why I wanted to get in touch with you. I saw Monica.'

'Patrick's ex?'

'I bumped into her on the tube. I hadn't seen or heard from her since Patrick died. Anyway, I told her what had happened . . . with you. She looked shocked when I said you'd lost your job and moved away. She said she'd had no idea that you had been implicated at all. Then she told me why she and Patrick had split up. About his problems. She said she'd been too upset to come to the funeral and she'd decided that a clean break was best. A fresh start, so to speak. She said if she'd known about you she would have told me sooner.'

Alex listened, the receiver pressed to his ear. The house creaked and groaned around him, only the pale blue light from the telephone display breaking through the darkness.

'Alex? Are you still there?'

'Yes. I'm here.'

'Aren't you going to answer?'

'What do you want me to say?' he asked.

'Why didn't you tell me any of this at the time?'

'I tried to. You wouldn't listen.'

'Then you didn't try hard enough. How else am I supposed to know the truth?'

'There are some things you either know or you don't.'

'Oh, Alex. You and your impossible standards. You've always been like that.'

'Like what?'

'Stubborn and wilful. Ever since you were a child.'

'It's always my fault, isn't it? Never yours. You wouldn't have let me explain the truth to you about Patrick. You wanted to cling to your illusions. Nothing I said would have made any difference anyway.'

She swallowed hard and adjusted the handset. Alex could hear her breathing. She sounded almost tearful. 'I'm sorry. I truly am,' she said.

'So is that why you wrote to me now? You want to make amends now you've found out the truth?'

'I wanted to speak to you as soon as your father was sick, but you were very difficult to track down.'

'How did you find me?'

'With difficulty. No one here knew where to get hold of you. Your friends, or the people you used to work with. They said

251

you'd disappeared without a word. In the end, I spoke to someone at the embassy in Tokyo who contacted the police to see if they could trace you. Apparently, you have to register as a foreign resident in Japan. It took a while but they found you. They said you'd been in some trouble again.'

'What do you mean, "again"?' Alex said.

'Is it drugs, Alexander?'

'No, of course not. That was Patrick's problem, not mine.'

'What is it, then? I'm worried about you.'

He thought of everything that had happened in the past weeks. There seemed no way to explain it. 'It's nothing. A misunderstanding, but it's blown over now.'

'Are you sure?'

'Yes.'

'Will you be able to come back to London? Even if it's just for a short visit. Your father would be so happy to see you.'

Alex smiled at the thought. 'There are a couple of things I need to take care of first. Then I'll see if I can fly home for a week or two.'

She gave a short sob but caught herself. 'We all miss you here.'

Alex felt his chest grow heavy. 'I'd better go. It's getting late.'

'Do you want me to pass a message on to your father?'

'Tell him to get well and I will see him soon. Tell him you spoke to me and I'm fine.'

'Goodnight, Alex.'

'Goodnight.'

# 36

THEIR TABLE WAS RESERVED FOR ONE THIRTY BUT NAOKO arrived twenty minutes early and took a seat at the bar. She wanted to be settled and poised when Megumi came in to meet her for lunch. The bartender placed a coaster before her and asked what she'd like and she thought for a moment and said that a mineral water would be fine. She took out a compact from her handbag and discreetly checked her reflection. Her new shoulder-length hair was going to take some getting used to, but she was pleased. She could tell instantly that it suited her.

She had woken that morning with a sense of relief that life had reached a new chapter. What better way to celebrate that than with a new look? she had thought. Also, there was something deeply personal at stake about the meeting she had arranged with Megumi and she wanted to make sure that everything was to her advantage. She had matched her new hair with a patterned skirt and a tailored jacket that gave her an air of authority and composure. She didn't want Megumi thinking her scheming had caused a loss of standards on her part.

The restaurant was in Iidabashi, on the southern bank of the large lake that was fed by canals running alongside the palace gardens. There was a floating pontoon terrace in front of the restaurant's picture window, with white-clothed tables that overlooked the water. The cluster of tall buildings that stood in the Ichigaya district reflected sharply on the lake's surface. The restaurant had a reputation as a place for grand lunches and high-level business meetings. Naoko had chosen it to appeal to Megumi's vanity. She knew that an invitation to be seen dining here would be hard for her to turn down.

She had felt nervous about meeting Megumi ever since she had called the gallery. She'd had no contact with anyone since the incident with Togo Nishi at the Imperial Hotel. Although she was sure that Megumi was ignorant of the exact details of that night, Naoko guessed she would have her suspicions that something significant had taken place. As soon as she saw her face, Naoko knew her instincts were correct.

Sweeping past the doorman without thanks or acknowledgement, Megumi's arrogant bearing betrayed instantly how her new-found seniority had gone straight to her head. Naoko had questioned the integrity of what she was about to do, but when she saw Megumi smile so falsely in greeting as she approached the bar, she knew it was the right course of action.

'Naoko. How are you? You look so well. I love your new look. I hardly recognized you.'

Naoko gave a modest smile. 'Thank you. You look good also. Thank you so much for agreeing to see me.'

'Please, Naoko. We're friends. Having lunch together is a pleasure, not an obligation.'

'I know how busy you must be at the gallery now. The Shanghai Expo is coming up soon.'

'We fly out tomorrow. Kimura-san has arranged two days of sales meetings before the actual exhibition starts.'

'I'm sure you don't need my goodwill but I hope you have a successful trip.'

Megumi smiled but the insincerity was evident in her eyes. 'I'm really looking forward to it. Of course, all the arrangements you made before you quit certainly gave me a head start.'

She looked down at the small suitcase beside Naoko's bar stool. 'It looks like you're going on a trip somewhere as well?'

Naoko nodded. 'I'm going to Osaka. Maybe permanently. My train is in a few hours.'

'Oh, how wonderful,' Megumi said patronizingly. 'I hope you won't miss Tokyo too much.'

Their table was ready and a waiter escorted them out to the patio and showed them to their seats. The sky was clear and crisp. Couples were rowing in wooden boats on the lake. Megumi ordered a green salad and oolong tea and Naoko said she would have the same.

'It's a pity I have to go to dinner with clients tonight,' Megumi said. 'I hear the menu here is fantastic but I don't want to ruin my appetite.'

'I'm just happy to have your company. It's been a while since we were able to talk.'

Megumi looked out wistfully across the lake. 'I love October. It's my favourite month in the city.'

'Thank God the summer is over.'

'I know. The last few weeks have been especially hard. It was all I could do to . . .' Megumi theatrically lifted a hand to her mouth. 'I'm so sorry, Naoko. How insensitive of me to talk of trivial things when you've had so many troubles.'

Naoko heard the note of spite half hidden behind the false concern. 'Life has taken some unexpected twists recently,' she said. 'I never would have suspected I could lose everything so quickly.'

'You're very resourceful, Naoko. I'm sure you'll make something good from a bad situation.'

'In a funny way, I'm thankful. I realize I was so caught up in my own world that I was neglectful of the real rewards I'd been given.'

Megumi pushed the salad around her plate. 'It's good that you can be so positive. It sounds like a valuable life lesson.'

'Of course, you played your part in everything that happened,' Naoko said.

Megumi placed her fork down gently on her plate. 'That's ridiculous, Naoko. I did all I could to help you.'

'Really? How did Mr Kimura find out about my private life? And the night with Alex? Was that you helping me?'

'I don't know what you're talking about,' she said, turning her chin up slightly, as if she had taken offence.

'You have to admit that it all played out perfectly for you. You got what you always wanted.'

Megumi took a moment, as if deciding whether to continue with her denials or tell the truth. Just as Naoko had predicted, she couldn't resist a chance to revel in her victory.

'Don't be a bad loser, Naoko,' she said. 'It's not attractive. I saw my chance and took it. You would have done the same. I never heard you complain about the rules when you were winning.'

Naoko leaned forward slightly in her chair. 'I never saw the need to stab anyone in the back to get ahead.'

Megumi licked her lips as she savoured her triumph. 'And you have such a beautiful back, Naoko. I couldn't believe how easy it was. And the best thing was, I didn't really have to do very much. You did all the hard work yourself. Especially after you took up with that *gaijin*.' She lifted the napkin from her lap and set it on the table. 'Now, if you'll excuse me, I'm going to the bathroom.'

When she had walked from the terrace and into the restaurant, Naoko bent down and took Megumi's handbag from the floor by her chair. She looked around to check no one was watching and opened the bag. She found a seam at the edge of an inside pocket and picked at the stitching until it came loose and then pulled out a long strand of thread. Without tearing the material of the lining, she made a small opening in the seam and worked the split with her nail until it was wide enough to push her little finger inside. She reached into her pocket and found the handful of amphetamine crystals she had taken from the package in Bangkok. There were about ten of them altogether, each jagged and opaque like small, uncut diamonds. Naoko pushed them one by one into the torn seam until they were all hidden in the lining. Megumi's bag was from Hermès, a gift from her family, and Naoko knew it was her pride and joy. She would certainly take it with her on the trip to China. Of course, there was no guarantee that she would be stopped entering the country: that would depend on the level of security the airport had deployed that day, the vigilance of the staff, the other travellers. In short, it would depend on fate. Naoko had no idea what the penalty for carrying illegal drugs into the country was but she knew it was substantial enough to alter the course of a life. Now Megumi would have exactly the same chance she had given her.

When she had pushed the last rock of meth into the lining, Naoko bent down and replaced the bag where she had found it. She eased herself upright without haste and gave a glance around to make sure she hadn't been seen. Then she quietly sipped her oolong tea and waited for Megumi to return from the bathroom.

# 37

Alex took one last look around. The tatami floor was swept clean and his room was bare now, except for the old postcards tacked to the wall. The ragged map of the Japanese islands still hung by the window, dotted with markers showing the places numerous people had visited during their time in the country. Alex took a pin and pushed it into the blue bay of Yokohama and locked the door behind him.

He paid the outstanding rent and gave the landlady the key. She bowed formally to him and wished him luck for the future as she tucked the money into her housecoat. He thought about saying goodbye to the other tenants he had come to know but decided against it. It was always wisest to move on as quietly as possible. He picked up the leather holdall and let himself out. It had begun to rain, a drifting autumn mist so fine it seemed to fall upwards. He began to walk towards the highway, where he could hail a passing taxi.

A dog padded out from the shadows behind the tall apartment block and watched warily as it circled him. It looked hungry, the honey-coloured fur along its spine bristling as it came closer. Alex reached out a hand, palm up to show he was friendly, and the dog sniffed it curiously and tilted its head. The world's a mystery to you, isn't it? he thought. You and me both.

The dog edged closer but something caught its eye over Alex's shoulder and it took fright, running off into the safety of a side alley.

Without warning, a voice called out behind him in a high, angry tone. For a moment, Alex froze. He realized how exposed and alone he was. How vulnerable. He turned to look back with a fearful expectation of who he might find.

'I knew you would run away again, *gaijin*!' the voice shouted.

Alex breathed out audibly. It was Hiro, his face and clothes soaked by rain but still looking as if he was burning with a righteous anger.

'What are you doing here?' Alex asked. 'You scared the shit out of me.'

Hiro came close enough so he could lower his voice to a whisper. 'Naoko told me everything, Alex. How could you be so reckless after all I've done to protect her?'

There was an authority behind his words that made them seem more damning. Alex tried to guess exactly how truthful Naoko had been.

'I . . . I don't know what to say, Hiro. Everything got out of hand. I did all I could to make sure she was safe. It was a bad situation but it's over.'

'So now you're leaving Tokyo and taking Naoko with you. Why? Just so you can ruin her life as well as yours?'

'She's an adult, Hiro. She can make her own decisions. She doesn't need you making them for her.'

'This is your second new beginning in a year. How many more will you need before you finally destroy her?'

'I only want what's best for Naoko. You know that.'

Hiro reached into the pocket of his overcoat and pulled out a brown envelope. It was stuffed to bursting. He held it out for Alex, who took it and pulled open the seal. Inside was a thick stack of new ten-thousand-yen notes.

'What's this?' Alex asked.

'The money you asked to borrow from me. I've had it ready for you for weeks.'

'Five million yen?'

'It's the amount you need to pay back Tanaka.'

Alex bristled when he heard Hiro use that name. 'So Naoko told you who lent me the *jidan* money?'

'This man is dangerous, Alex. I've come across him before. He's yakuza. I can't believe you got her involved in this.'

Alex was startled. 'What do you mean, you've come across him? Where?'

Hiro gave a solemn shake of his head. 'I can't tell you,' he said.

'I need to know. You might be in danger if Tanaka can connect you to me.'

Hiro took a moment to consider his options. 'He's an investor in one of our portfolios at the bank. A major investor.'

'You mean you take care of the financial interests of a gangster? Surely that's illegal?'

'This isn't London. We have our own ways of doing business here. Tanaka's custom is very profitable. He doesn't interfere with our work and we don't ask where his money comes from. It's the Tokyo way.'

Alex looked at his friend in disbelief. 'You used to be so different, Hiro. You used to be honest. All your success has ruined you as a person.'

'What about you, Alex? You're a danger to everyone who knows you here. Why don't you just take the money and leave? You know it makes sense.'

'I don't need you to lend me money any more, Hiro.'

'I don't want to lend it to you, *gaijin*. I want you to take it and keep it. In return, I want you to leave Naoko alone.'

Alex let his friend's words sink in. 'You're not serious? You really think you can bribe me?'

'You were willing to stop seeing her the last time I offered it to you.'

'I was never going to go through with it. You left me no choice but to agree with you. It wasn't as if you were prepared to debate the subject. I was wrong to ever let you think I would do it. But you were wrong to ask me in the first place. You can't buy everything you want.'

Hiro took a step closer. 'So you lied to me?' he said.

Alex stood his ground. 'Look around, Hiro. Everything in this city is money and lies. That's all Tokyo is.'

'You'll never be good enough for her, *gaijin*.'

'You know what I think,' Alex said. 'I think you're jealous.'

Hiro sneered at the suggestion. 'She's like a sister to me.'

'That's what hurts you. She's all you've got. You can chase all the women you want to but, really, there's nothing good in your life. You love it when others fail because it makes you feel like a success. Deep down, you're lonely, Hiro. Whatever else happens, I've no intention of ending up like you.'

He tossed the envelope back and Hiro caught it reluctantly. Alex began to look for a taxi in the passing traffic on the highway. The rain was falling more heavily now. The passing headlights seemed blinding in the spray. In the distance, the towering office buildings of downtown Tokyo were enveloped in cloud. A taxi drove past and Alex waved a hand to hail it. The driver pulled up at the kerb and opened the rear door. He turned to watch his friend stand motionless in the rain.

Hiro looked defeated. 'So that's it? You're leaving?' he said.

'I'm meeting Naoko at Tokyo station. We're taking the evening bullet-train service.'

'To where?'

He was about to answer but Alex stopped himself. 'I'll call you when we get there,' he said.

Hiro held out the envelope again. 'I'm giving you a chance, Alex,' he said sternly. 'Take the money.'

Alex shook his head in pity. 'Look after yourself, Hiro,' he said. 'I'll take care of Naoko for you.'

He climbed into the taxi and told the driver to go and the cab pulled out into the evening traffic. Through the rear window, he watched his friend recede into the distance, alone, standing forlornly in the downpour.

The driver followed the signs for Tokyo station, moving sluggishly with the congested evening traffic on the Shuto expressway. The windscreen wipers beat against the flood, leaving oily smears on the glass. Alex tried to keep calm throughout the journey but his chest was still tight with adrenaline. Hiro had gone too far. They had been friends for a long time but Hiro still had no right to treat anyone like that. To assume that his commands took precedence over the wishes of others. No matter how much he cared for Naoko, he was wrong to try to control her life. But Alex knew that the best course of action was to prove him wrong – to go with Naoko and start a new life and make a success of it. After everything they had been through, it was time for them to have some luck.

The traffic was snarled on the ramp leading down to the Kanda tunnel and Alex began to check his watch anxiously. This was a train departure he didn't want to miss. Finally, the driver reached the exit and dropped him outside the entrance to Tokyo station. Alex paid the fare and fought through the evening crowds to buy a ticket and make his way to the *shinkansen* platform, following the signs along the subterranean passageway leading from the main hall. He moved with the flow of bodies along the walkway and on to the rising escalator. A southbound train had arrived and the passengers were funnelling on to the opposite side. Alex watched the stream of people descending, idly looking at the passing faces, some heavy with the fatigue of travel, struggling to manoeuvre their luggage on the narrow gangway. A flash of recognition sharpened his focus suddenly. A moment of instinct awakening senses honed by weeks of danger. The hair on the back of Alex's neck stood on end.

His eye was snared by the gaze of another, a face hidden in

the crowd, watching him. His brain instantly registered the details. A Japanese man, mid-thirties, athletic, with a sharp, lean face. Staring. Alex looked away instinctively but then looked back. The face had gone now and no eyes met his as he searched, but something about that gaze had given him an unmistakable sense of peril.

He twisted cautiously and glanced back over his shoulder. Below, in the crush of travellers following behind, another pair of dark eyes was watching. At least he hadn't been paranoid, Alex thought. He moved to his left and started to walk up the rising escalator, trying to look as nonchalant as possible, mounting the steps briskly, squeezing past luggage and outstretched limbs. From below, he heard heavy footsteps following on the metal stairs.

The pitch of the escalator levelled and Alex stepped on to the concourse leading to the ticket gates. The passengers leaving the eastbound service were crowded together, cutting across his path as they streamed towards the exit. He gripped the holdall close and narrowed his shoulders and tried to force a way through.

On the far side of the barrier, standing on the platform beside the slick white hull of the Shin–Osaka bullet train, Naoko was waiting. She had changed her hair but he still recognized her. She saw him and gave a broad smile full of possibilities and raised her hand as if to wave but changed her mind when she registered the concern on his face. He was conscious of moving normally, unhurried among the herd of passengers. He gave a half-turn to look back over his shoulder and there was the same man, moving towards him, striding up the escalator two steps at a time. As he began to quicken his stride towards Naoko, Alex realized there were more faces glowering at him as he approached, blocking his way through the barrier. For a moment, he saw himself as if from above, a head taller than the people around him, blond-haired and blue-eyed, strange enough to be mistaken for a mannequin. Distinct enough to stand out like a beacon.

The two strangers began to move in his direction, heading him off from the gate. He knew Naoko was safer without him. It was easy for her to blend in. She had passed them by unseen and was now among the crowd beyond the ticket gate, waiting at the open doors of the train, its sharp nose and silvered windows gleaming under the station lights. To his right, Alex saw there was a foot tunnel connecting the concourse to another platform.

He kept his eyes away from hers as he moved but Naoko was smart enough to sense danger. She glanced to her left and saw the two Japanese men with their focus trained on Alex, moving quickly towards him as a pair.

He looked towards the waiting *shinkansen*, willing her to get on board. Naoko understood his meaning instantly.

Alex watched as she picked up her small suitcase and gracefully mounted the steps. She waited in the doorway for a moment, her chin held high in her usual defiant manner. The determination on her face reminded him of the night in the Thai boxing arena in Bangkok. The measure of the born fighter. The killer look. Who would ever bet against her? Alex thought. He had the impression they were looking at each other through glass.

Then she was gone, disappearing into the safety of the carriage, and he turned towards the tunnel and began to run.

He heard the clatter of footsteps and the howl of angry voices behind him, echoing down the empty tunnel.

He kept his body low, his head and shoulders leaning forward to create momentum, his legs pumping beneath him, the soles of his shoes pounding hard on the cement slab underfoot. Advertising posters blurred by. The passageway curved steadily until it reached another escalator and Alex bounded on to the moving stairway and sprinted upwards. Gasping for air, his mouth dry, he forced himself to keep moving, eyes forward, no time to slow himself and take a look backwards. The other passengers moved to the side to allow him to pass, their faces full of alarm. There were voices crying out behind him, calling out in Japanese, the shouts devoid of meaning in the squall of motion.

At the head of the escalator was another tunnel and Alex spun on his toes and sprinted down it to a short stairway leading to a junction. He took the stairs in a single lurching step. At the foot, he could see the right-hand passage leading off to a platform with a guarded ticket barrier, passengers lining up in orderly fashion to pass through and board the waiting trains. The left-hand tunnel led off into the unknown. He was unsure if his *shinkansen* ticket would allow him through the barrier to other platforms. A millisecond of hesitation and the decision made itself. He gathered his remaining energy and went left.

Running, veins bursting with raw adrenaline, the tunnel curved on and on, almost doubling back on itself. Alex moved at full speed, his lungs beginning to burn from the exertion. Long banks of bright white lights lined the spiralling ceiling, the vanishing point always receding before him. Then he came to a full, crashing halt, his shoes slipping slightly with the momentum.

The tunnel finished in a dead end.

There were two doors at either side of the sealed passageway: a blue door marked with the symbol for a female bathroom; a red door marked male. There was no way to go back and retrace his footsteps. He could never make it back to the stairway without running into his pursuers. Alex knew that. He was cornered. He had to make a split-second choice.

He chose the blue door and pushed his way inside, gambling that this might buy him a few precious seconds. A row of white basins hung beneath a long mirror and four toilet stalls stood opposite, their doors ajar and unoccupied. Alex chose the toilet stall furthest from the entrance and closed the door behind him.

The lock was broken so he pushed the door back into the frame and sat up on the cistern, his feet resting on the toilet seat and his holdall clutched to his chest. He cursed himself silently, trying to ignore the sense of disbelief that this was actually happening. He listened for any sound and heard the dripping of a tap, pipes creaking, the sounds of moving trains far away working through the structure of the station. There were no human noises except for Alex's breathing.

He needed to call Naoko to make sure she was unharmed but he couldn't risk any noise. He quietly took out his phone and set it to silent and tapped out a message as quickly as possible.

*I'm fine*, he wrote. *Take the train. I will follow you to Osaka somehow. Don't worry about me and don't turn around.*

He pressed send and slipped the phone back inside his jacket pocket. He began to wonder if the coast was clear.

The door from the corridor swung open and he could hear urgent voices, followed by a single pair of footsteps as someone entered the bathroom and walked along the line of stalls. He tried to suspend all functions that could betray him. No breathing, no blinking, no thoughts.

The hinges of the first door squealed as it was pushed open. Then the next. There was no one in either stall and the footsteps grew louder as they neared. Alex looked around him in a futile attempt to see if there was a final, unseen escape route but it was hopeless. He willed himself invisible. When the third stall had been searched, Alex knew he was next. He braced his body and crouched forward, ready to protect himself when necessary.

He looked down. Two black Nike running shoes topped by a pair of blue denim jeans stood in the gap beneath the stall. The grey, graffiti-covered door began to open, swinging slowly on its hinges. Alex tasted raw, metallic fear in the back of his throat.

The door banged against the wall of the toilet stall as it was opened.

Alex fought the instinct to leap forward, his breath caught in his lungs. A female face locked eyes with his, her expression blank. He recognized her immediately. It was Officer Tomada,

Saito's deputy from Ushigome. She stepped inside, as if the cubicle were empty, as if she hadn't seen Alex waiting inside, and shut the door. Outside in the corridor, the voices receded as they ran off to continue the search.

Tomada smiled at Alex with familiar calm, one corner of her mouth curling upwards; she seemed almost amused at his obvious relief.

'Come with me, Malloy-san,' she whispered. 'We need to move fast.'

# 38

Tomada unlocked the car and motioned for Alex to climb inside as she hurried around to the driver's door. She checked no one had followed them before she started the engine and pulled away quickly. The interior was protected by clear plastic, as if it had come straight from the factory. She drove out of the station car park and merged with the flow of traffic on the highway, making no conspicuous manoeuvres that could draw attention.

Alex was still breathless. 'I have no idea what the fuck is going on,' he said. 'Who were they? Why were they waiting for me?'

Tomada's tone was quick and efficient. 'Tanaka sent them. He knows the delivery at Yokohama was compromised and knows you can identify him from your meeting at the bath house. I don't know how he found out about you coming to the station today. You were lucky I was there. Saito asked me to follow you to make sure you were safe.'

'I was sure I was finished back there. I couldn't hide any-where, despite the crowd. This city is full of people who want me dead.'

Tomada reached out a comforting hand. 'Relax. No one

knows where you are now. Only me. Just do as I say and you'll be fine. There is an old saying in Japan: the nail that stands out gets hammered down.'

'That's why I had to leave Naoko. I stand out everywhere in Tokyo but she's able to blend in.'

Tomada turned to him in surprise. 'Naoko was with you? I didn't see her there.'

'She was ahead of me. We were going to meet on the bullet-train platform.'

'Is she still waiting for you?'

'No. She could see what was happening and boarded without me. Then I ran. It was the only way to draw their attention away from her.'

Tomada looked flustered for a moment. 'You needed to tell me this sooner, Malloy-san. Now I have no idea if she is safe. We have to go back.'

Alex looked at the clock on the dashboard. 'It's too late. The train will have left by now. I don't think they want her, anyway. I'm the only one who can identify Tanaka. It's only me that's dealt with him directly. Naoko has no connection to anything that could incriminate him.'

'Tanaka doesn't care about details like that. He will eliminate anyone who can harm him in any way. Didn't Saito explain how dangerous these people are? While you were at Ushigome, Tanaka was there, awaiting trial on extortion charges. There were three main witnesses in the case. We found them in the Sumida river last week, with their hands and feet missing. These people are serious.'

'Saito promised me we would be safe. I never would have agreed to this if I'd known how much danger we would be in.'

Tomada thought for a moment. 'Let me call the inspector and tell him about Naoko. I need to find out what he thinks we should do now.' She took out her phone and dialled it quickly.

She held the phone to her ear and spoke calmly, following the flow of traffic as she talked. Alex realized he had never paid

Tomada any attention. She had always been in the inspector's shadow, silently fulfilling his commands. Her face was wide and unblemished and her manner coolly professional. It was striking how youthful she looked.

She left the expressway and took the exit heading west towards Kawasaki, the road twisting through the vast network of factories and industrial plants. A haze of pollution drifted down from the towering chimneys, lit up by the passing traffic against the grey evening sky. Tomada was silent for the last minute of the call, occasionally muttering her agreement into the handset as she drove. Finally, she hung up and looked over at Alex in the passenger seat.

'Saito has a plan. He says there is a station nearby. He says that all the *shinkansen* lines from Tokyo pass through it on their way out of the city. He thinks you should join Naoko and get out of Tokyo for a while. At least until he can make sure you are both safe. He is going to arrange for her train to be stopped so you can board it.'

'Saito can do that?'

'He will contact the rail control centre and tell them it's an emergency.'

Tomada pulled the car on to a deserted side street. There were pale streetlights standing in crooked rows, illuminating the lines of empty, shabby-looking warehouses, the rain collecting in puddles on the cracked pavements. At the end of the street was the entrance to a suburban train station. It was old and dilapidated, the corrugated roof suspended over the rail tracks by rows of rusted steel pillars. A flock of crows hovered in the gloom above. Alex looked at the flaking paint on the façade and the shadowy stairs leading into the dark building.

'Is it even open?' he asked. 'It looks derelict.'

Tomada looked at him with steady authority. 'It hasn't been used in years,' she said, 'but the rail tracks still run straight through. Saito says we are to go up to the westbound platform and wait for him there.'

270

They stepped from the car and Alex felt the rain on his face as they crossed the street. Tomada pulled her overcoat around her tightly as she walked. The stock of the pistol holstered at her waist bulged through the wet fabric. Alex followed her up the steps to the elevated landing. The rusted iron turnstiles were unlocked and they pushed their way through and went out on to the deserted platform. Weeds were growing in thickets at the sides of the rail embankment and the trackbed was choked with rubbish. Wind gusted at the torn edges of advertising posters tacked to the forlorn station buildings.

Tomada stopped at the edge of the rain-swept platform. She seemed to have grown more substantial now, imposing in the surroundings, despite her small stature. Alex noticed she wore a thin gold wedding band and toyed with it nervously as she stood and faced him. It was the only outward sign she gave of any tension.

'Now you need to tell me where Naoko is going,' she said briskly.

Alex heard the urgency in her voice. There was something surprising in the change of tone.

'You're sure I can trust you?' he asked.

Tomada pointed to the badge hanging on a chain around her neck. 'I'm a police officer, Malloy-san. Who can you trust if not me?'

His hands were pressed deep inside his pockets for warmth and he suddenly felt the silent vibration of his phone as a call came through. He guessed it must be Naoko. Without removing his mobile or making any movements that could alert Tomada, he pressed to connect the call. He gripped the phone firmly inside his pocket.

'Inspector Saito told me to speak only to him,' Alex said. 'He was clear that I wasn't to trust anyone else. Even you, Officer Tomada.'

'But I'm his assistant, Malloy-san. You've seen me with him at Ushigome many times. Trusting me is as safe as trusting him. Why would you need to be wary of a police officer?'

Alex made sure the phone in his pocket was free of any obstruction before he replied. He raised his voice and spoke clearly.

'It was you that made the call to Jun, wasn't it, Officer Tomada? You tipped him off when we were in Yokohama. You told him I was recording our conversation on the fairground wheel. You almost got us killed.'

'I don't know what you're talking about,' she said.

'And this?' he said, pointing around at the run-down station. 'This is all bullshit, isn't it? Saito didn't tell you to come here. It wasn't him you were talking to on the phone. It was Tanaka. This is all a set-up, isn't it?'

Her expression became suspicious. 'What's in your pocket, Malloy-san?' she said. 'Show me.'

Alex released the phone from his grip and started to remove his hands from his jacket. He wanted to show Tomada something, anything to allay her fears. There were some scraps of paper balled up at the bottom of his pocket and he grabbed them and pulled them out inside his fist.

Tomada looked wary. She reached one hand to the stock of the pistol at her waist. 'What is that?' she asked.

Alex opened his hand and showed her. They were torn pieces of thick white paper. He remembered they were the *omikuji*, the blessings he had ripped from the camphor tree the night he and Naoko had gone to the temple gardens together. It seemed so long ago now. He held the scraps of paper up in the faint light.

'It's my good fortune,' he said.

Tomada shook her head. 'I don't have time for your games, Malloy-san. I need to know where Naoko is going. Tell me now.'

'Only if you answer one question first. How did Tanaka know I was there?'

She looked at him with sympathy. 'One of your friends called Tanaka about an hour ago. He told us where to find you.'

'Which friend?' Alex asked.

'You already know,' she said.

'Tell me.'

A gust of wind came up as Tomada replied. Alex strained to hear her over the howl. He was sure none of her words could be heard down the telephone line.

'Hiro Ozawa. He called and told us everything.'

Alex felt the devastation of his friend's betrayal. His head pulsed with disbelief. 'You're lying,' he said. 'He wouldn't do that.'

Tomada looked triumphant at his distress. 'It's the truth.'

'But that meant putting Naoko in danger as well. He might betray me, but not her.'

'His one condition was that she wouldn't be harmed. We have no intention of honouring that promise, of course. Now tell me where her train is going.'

Alex thought of all the possible answers he could give and their myriad consequences. He watched Tomada click open the strap of her holster and begin to grip the butt of her pistol. Her face had assumed a fearsome composure. He knew what was coming and wanted to laugh at its inevitability. There was only one last action he was able to perform. One final lie in the endless series that had led to this point. He spoke before it was obvious that he had hesitated too long.

'Niigata,' he said. 'Naoko is on the fast train to Niigata.'

Alex was braced for the danger from Tomada but a quick movement came from the shadows behind him. Footsteps, sudden and unexpected, in a broken stutter step. Alex took a breath and waited. He was still looking at the torn scraps of paper in his hand when he felt the blade of the knife pierce the flesh below his shoulder blade and cut through his ribs. There was a wave of nausea and his knees began to buckle. With the second thrust he felt a burning and his mouth began to fill with blood. He staggered slightly, turning on his heels, to see Jun's face as he fell. He hit the cold stone of the platform hard and rolled on to his side. The paper scraps fluttered from his hand, twisting in the wind. For a moment, he knew he had seen them somewhere before. Then he remembered, the night in the snow. The bitter flakes falling. The cold. Hiro had got what he wanted, after all. He had made sure there were no new beginnings or fresh starts. No blessings stronger than fate. On the tracks below him, he could hear the eerie hum of distant trains travelling over the rails.

# 39

AFTER SHE HAD PULLED THE EMERGENCY CORD AND THE *shinkansen* had ground to a halt, the air brakes squealing as the train decelerated rapidly on the rails, Naoko opened the door and climbed down on to the tracks. She still had the phone pressed to her ear as she ran back along the length of the train, the gravel crunching under her feet. Passengers stood and watched her through the carriage windows, their faces full of confusion as she passed. She was screaming into her phone as she stumbled over the sleepers.

'Alex. Tell me where you are! I can't hear you!' she shouted.

Nothing. Just the static hum of a phone tumbling inside clothing.

'Alex. What's happening? You're scaring me. Why can't I hear you any more?'

Naoko had listened to fragments of the heated conversation, broken up by the roar of the wind and the confusion of voices. From the pieces of information, she could build a picture that was almost coherent. At first, she was unsure how to process what she was hearing – Alex's voice, the muffled female arguing with him. But she knew he had been in danger when he ran from the ticket gate at Tokyo station. If he was making a point of taking her call, she knew it was for a reason. When she heard

Officer Tomada's name, she started to put the pieces of the puzzle into place. She could trace Tomada's involvement all the way back to the first meeting at Ushigome. Naoko could see now how she had manoeuvred everyone into position to take advantage right from that point. She wondered exactly how far Tomada's web had been spun.

She reached the rear of the train and stopped and looked out at the rain-drenched city from the vantage of the high embankment. He could be anywhere out there, Naoko thought, lost among the endless grey buildings and empty parks and dark, naked trees. She pushed the phone against her ear to try to listen closer and looked about her in the twilight.

Suddenly, the interference cleared at the end of the line as the handset was lifted free from obstruction.

'Alex?' she said.

A soft gasp and a voice muted, as if through foam.

'Naoko.'

'Yes, it's me. Where are you? Look around and tell me what you see. I will be able to find you if you tell me the landmarks you can see close by.'

He made a sound halfway between a groan and a knowing laugh, his voice harsh and strangled. Every syllable seemed to take an effort to sound on his lips. He tried to say something but it was ill-formed and she struggled to understand him.

'Say it again. I can't hear you.'

'Tomada.'

'Tomada? I know, Alex. I heard her speaking. I know she was there. But you've got to tell me where you are. What's happening to you? I will come and find you if I know where you are. Tell me.'

'*Soto*.'

'Outside? What do you mean? What is outside?'

'*Soto*,' he said again, his voice growing weaker.

She began to cry at her own powerlessness. 'You're scaring me, Alex. Tell me what I need to do? Please . . .'

There was a gentle gasp of submission and then nothing. The line was still connected and she continued to call his name into the handset, repeating it again and again until it began to lose meaning.

Passengers started to step down from the open doors of the *shinkansen* and gather at the side of the tracks, talking in hushed tones as they speculated about the cause of the emergency. Parents gathered their children together for safety at the edge of the embankment, where the knotweed grew in dense thickets. They looked back at Naoko, who stood out there alone. The train conductor approached, his cap held in his hands before him. He began to ask if she was hurt or needed help but Naoko waved him away. She pressed the phone to her ear in case she heard Alex move or speak again. She knew it was impossible now. Emergency lights flashed in the distance. Soon she would hear sirens approaching and then she would have to explain all. She would ask to be taken to Ushigome, to unburden herself, and then the search would begin. Naoko promised herself she would hang up the phone only when they had found him.

# Acknowledgements

Thanks to Jonathan Caplan, Steven Buckler, Jane Lord, Richard Lonsdale and Sean Kirkegaard, for their invaluable feedback and encouragement. Thank you also to M. J. Hyland and Trevor Byrne at www.hylandbyrne.com, who edited and advised on an early draft of this novel.

Special thanks to my agent, Jane Finigan, and all at Lutyens & Rubinstein for their dedication and hard work. Also to my insightful editor, Frankie Gray, and the team at Transworld.

Finally, my wife, Isabel, without whose patience and belief this novel would never have happened.

**James Buckler** grew up in the south-west of England and currently lives in London, though he has lived in America and Japan, where he worked as an English teacher. He studied Film at the University of Westminster and worked in film and TV for many years, most notably as a post-production specialist for MTV and BBC Films. *Last Stop Tokyo* is his debut novel.